AN
IMMORTAL
SPY
NOVEL

THE
SHACKLED SPY

K. A. KRANTZ

Dad
For all the things up with which you will not put.

CHAPTER 1

S now flurries flirted with tourists bundled up against the biting winds rolling off the Potomac River. Frosty gusts skipped along the Tidal Basin and mixed with sprays from the World War II Memorial fountains at the foot of the National Mall, Washington, DC, Primary Mid World. Bronze streetlamps sputtered on with hums and flickers, limning the manicured grounds leading from the Lincoln Memorial to the Capitol. The crush of rush hour traffic cutting through the tributes to human history sent up the stench of exhaust fumes. The din of stereo systems clashed with speakerphones and frustrated engines. White lights slung in barren trees lured pedestrians along the side streets toward Metro stations and idling busses while food trucks and tchotchke vendors packed up for the evening. Traffic signals rotated through their cycles of green, yellow, and red, only to be interrupted by the blue flashes from emergency vehicles.

Bix reveled in the chaotic routine of mortals blundering through their finite lives, determined in their constant struggle of dreams versus responsibilities as she strolled along the Reflecting Pool. The null spaces created by humans, who grounded magic, balanced the swirls of dichotomous magics belonging to the myriad races of Chwedlonol glamoured to blend in among neighbors who weren't allowed to know of their existence. An ogre in a park service uniform looked every bit the weary middle-aged human woman, shuffling along the sidewalk and picking up trash with a grabby stick. A trio of vivacious fae scampered along a crosswalk in the form and attire typical of Congressional aides, bright eyes fixed on the massive Christmas tree nearer the Capitol. The common day slid into a normal evening for folks utterly unaware of the armies of anti-gods encroaching on this bastion of safety.

Bix wasn't entirely sure whether their ignorance was a good or bad thing. Nearly a hundred Mid Worlds had been infested with the anti-gods known as Devourers, who, true to their name, were intent on devouring every last wisp of native magic until nothing remained of the Mids but fumes. Because she considered this collective of Worlds home, as did her dearest friends, she'd given more aid than she ought to its wholly corrupt representative government scrambling to devise a defense a thousand years late. Thus, when summoned to attend the Consortium in their sprawling headquarters located beneath this capital human city, she'd reluctantly followed her four-legged escort.

Stuffing her hands deeper into the pockets of her hunter-green wool coat, Bix smiled at the humans fawning over the sleek, hip-high hound leashed to her wrist with an illusion the dog controlled. The District had leash laws that even the steadfast companion of a war god respected. Humans attributing the hound's red pupils to the reflection of headlights rather than the dog being an Other World entity was an assumption she was disinclined to correct.

Crosswalk lights flipped to grant pedestrians right of way. Bix and her companion melded into the gathering at 17th Street heading for the Washington Monument. Frozen soil kept her Santas-impaled-on-candy-canes booties from sinking into the grass as the hound led her away from the sidewalks and across monument grounds. Each step closer to the infamous phallic monument tickled her flesh as wards unlocked, triggering masking illusions. The terrain sloped steeply downward, and green grass yielded to jewel-toned ground-cover plants. Iridescent blooming trees doubled as vigilant sentries throughout a sprawling courtyard. The instant she cleared the ramp, the access to the realm of humans closed as soundlessly as it had opened, leaving Bix in the fantastical domain of the Consortium's headquarters.

Birds and small mammals bore little resemblance to their kith aboveground: scales instead of feathers, armored plates instead of fur. Consortium guards. Shapeshifters. To a one, they studied Bix with flagrant hostility, which simply added extra sway to her swagger as she followed her escort across the beautifully deadly courtyard. Inky streams gurgled, and bright fish swam under crystalline footbridges. Paired fountains lined the entrance path. Armed guards beneath a skim coat of gray stone lay in wait atop bubbling basins. Chiseled eyes tracked Bix under the ornate silver archways leading to double-wide iron doors intricately engraved with protection spells.

The intense scrutiny by Consortium staffers and security lasted along every overwide hallway, through every ostentatious lounge, and down every sweeping stairway. The Consortium's headquarters had never met a minimalist decorator. Then again, most of the décor would spring to life if ever there was a need. The last time there'd been a need was when they'd dragged Bix, heavily chained and badly beaten, through here as part of the pomp and circumstance leading up to her trial. It'd been a bit over a decade since that debacle, and many things had changed, to include the Consortium's leadership and Bix's status as most abominable felon.

Her smirk grew into a full smile as the hound led her into a large barrel-ceilinged chamber of rich loamy browns and crimsons. Two men stood over a tall iron table, their voices little more than rumbling undercurrents. A half dozen holograms of animated maps danced between them. The men's shared builds of great height and greater brawn ended there. One was dark, one was light. One was bald, one was hirsute. One wore a long white tunic and matching trousers, the other dark denim and a snug

Henley. One had both his beefy arms, the other had a prosthesis filling out a sleeve.

Bix's gaze lingered on the rear view of the one in denim. She couldn't help herself, not that she was trying. A pair of vibrant blue eyes peered over a broad shoulder, mischief shimmering within their depths before her big blond Berserker straightened and faced her fully.

"Sweetheart." Tobek leaned a hip against the table.

"Bix," greeted his coconspirator, arms opening wide as he waved her into his office. "It has been too long since I've seen you. Come in, come in, come in."

"I assume the parade route your companion forced me to walk served a purpose, Ogun?" Bix asked as the leash faded from her wrist and the hound bounded to his master's side. "Or do you prefer I address you as Chairman now?"

"Let us save the titles for public interactions, eh? In private, we know each other too well, I think, but not as well as you two know each other." The god of war held her by the shoulders and kissed the air beside her cheeks before taking her coat from her and draping it over a low table covered in assorted weapons. "And yes, the long march was necessary, so thank you for playing along. The time of the Consortium and the Chimera being at odds is over. Our innate arrogance has no place in this time of crisis. It is a lesson to be driven home throughout our membership, and there is no louder proclamation than actions."

"I have to admit, I'm beyond surprised the Consortium voted you—a greater god and a god of war, no less—into the position of Chair. Gods of your standing have been banned for so long and for arguably good reason." Bix followed her host to a cluster of tufted red leather chairs sized to accommodate extra-large men. A flick of Ogun's wrist, and one chair reshaped to suit her proportions.

"Of the extensive stable of war gods, I suppose I am seen as a lesser evil." Ogun laughed, and wise wickedness tinged the tone. "Though, I was able to be politic on the grounds of having beaten back the old foes before. Add that to the knowledge you've permitted me to glean from your adventures of the past year, and how could I not be a shoo-in?"

Bix closed her hand over the second of two pendants she wore, this one a metal gargoyle Ogun had given her as a thank-you gift for rescuing his hound from a Mid World prison. Of course, any gift from a god allowed that god access to the bearer. She might not have realized that gotcha at the time of the pendant's bequeathing, but after she'd figured it out, she hadn't begrudged Ogun the privilege. She'd needed allies, and he'd volunteered. As far as she knew, he hadn't abused the connection.

"The current evolution of Mids' magic is allowing the greater gods to exist here without them being a detriment to the collective," Tobek explained, settling into one of the larger chairs. "It's the dawning of a new era."

Bix refrained from openly questioning the long-term wisdom of inviting greater gods into the collective. Sure, short-term, using them and their powers to battle the anti-gods was a strategic win. Long-term though, postwar? Pretty sure that would lead to all kinds of complications.

"In this new era of Consortium cooperation, what does your organization want from me?" Bix scratched the hound behind his ear as he sat beside her, ever so regal in his bearing.

"My chief of the new Resen Immigration and Defense Division warned me you'd be down to business." Ogun passed a tumbler of tawny elixir to Tobek, the head of said division.

"I'm guessing, since he's here, whatever you need has something to do with Resen's launch?" Bix waved off the tumbler Ogun offered her. She didn't drink the libations of mortals nor the nectar of gods; she consumed divinity. God and anti-god, each with their benefits and detriments. "Are we finally ready to stand up an actual defense against the Devourers? Have human colonies settled around the Resen data centers to ground the magic the system will generate?"

Ogun pointed to one of the holographic maps, and it

expanded to cover the wall. Tiny white lights glittered on the faces of scattered globes. "Humans, being extremely territorial while being simultaneously cruel, have supplied us with plenty of starter colonies. They are being introduced to their new homes as we speak."

"Alien abductions?" she joked. Sort of. Humans, by Consortium law, had been kept ignorant of the existence of the other races and the myriad Worlds that were part of the Mids. Bix had a hard time imagining the mass migrations being voluntary.

"Refugees, mostly, be it from war or weather," Tobek answered. "Ships that sink. Caravans that disappear. Tent cities ravaged by storms. Those who left families behind are given the option of being reunited in the new towns. We also have recruiters on the streets talking to the homeless. It's not quite the numbers we need to be comfortably within the estimated grounding demands, but we're scaling."

Bix snorted. "Climate change and the rise of tyrants. Really? Could you maybe not turn the Primary Mid World into an armpit while you're shifting populations?"

"We're planning birth booms but are trying to keep those organic to minimize panic among the settlers and to placate the indigenous races already rebelling against the arrival of humans." Ogun made a pattern in the air with two fingers. Symbols shimmered for a beat before an iridescent scroll appeared.

The document plopped in Bix's lap. Magics mixed and potent skittered up her thighs all the way to her eyelashes. Of greatest interest was her own magical resonance echoing among those oozing from the scroll.

She stopped petting the dog and eyed the scroll. "What's this?"

"A copy of the contract between you and the Consortium that authorized the existence of the ether." Ogun spread his arms along his chair. "You'll be interested in the fine print, but what is of current relevance is the clause detailing the removal of said ether."

Bix stifled a shiver as reluctance and resistance wound together.

She'd been expecting this moment ever since she and her team had obtained the build specs of the defense system. The ether was a moat of sorts surrounding the Mids and slithering between the Worlds. It was highly destructive unless one happened to be a god, an anti-god, or a greater cosmic entity. Resen could not coexist with it. Since the army of Devourers was staging in the ether, it no longer served its defensive purpose. Resen had to launch, come hell or high water. Unfortunately, the ether embodied some of the worst moments of Bix's immortal life. Some she remembered vividly enough to awake in a cold sweat, others she wished she could recall. This mission promised to be less than fun.

"I'd imagined this request happening with your predecessor." She struggled to keep her voice even and her fight-or-flight response in check. "I'd planned such a different rejoinder that I find myself at a loss right now."

"Not going to tell me to kiss your ass, eh?" Ogun guffawed. "Too bad. I invited your consort to do the honors."

Tobek choked on his drink, which made Ogun laugh harder.

"Since you've been eavesdropping on my life lately, you know my memory isn't all it ought to be. I don't recall the creation of the ether, much less how to take it down." Bix unrolled a few inches of the scroll and was pleasantly surprised that the lines and squiggles were a language she recognized. Most of it at least. Fortunately, linguistics was a hobby of Tobek's, so he could help her translate. But not here, not in front of a god she liked but didn't fully trust— spying pendant, case in point.

"It's a shame the previous administration chose to exploit your amnesia rather than help you heal. It played no small part in how we ended up as deep in this mire of Devourers as we have." Ogun placed his fist to his lips and whispered into it. When he opened his hand, the whisper fled across the room and out the chamber door. "Though, I doubt you would have been as dogged in your pursuits to save the Mids had you been fully yourself."

"It wasn't my job, Ogun. It never should've been. Fates, angels, dragons, and gods were appointed the caretakers of these

Worlds. They chose personal gratification over the greater good." Bix slapped the tightened scroll against her palm. "I will figure out how to remove the ether as this contract demands, but I will not lift a finger in the actual battle against the Devourers. The Consortium's dependency on me must end with the launch of Resen. I hope I make myself perfectly clear."

Mulish ruthlessness flashed across the Chairman's features for two beats before being replaced by a sly regard of the Berserker sitting next to him. "Cooperation should always be on the table, I would argue, for the benefit of all who call the Mids home. One never knows when allies will be useful. To wit…"

The clank and rattle of chains echoed down the hall. Long shadows and slow shuffling brought Tobek and Ogun to their feet. The hound's ears perked and twitched. Darkness writhed along Bix's spine as a trace of Devourer magic prickled her skin. Tobek must have felt it too, judging by the change in his posture from neutral to wary.

Consortium guards in their black uniforms and matte-black logos dragged a fettered and disheveled woman into Ogun's office. Her black hair hung in loose thick braids, obscuring her face. Her simple red sheath was clean, as were her bare feet. Deeply etched shackles clamped her wrists, waist, and ankles. The chain links in the shapes of magical symbols fluctuated in color and hum.

Tobek cursed under his breath, and his stance relaxed. Any stranger could tell he knew the prisoner and that he bore a certain affection for her. Interesting.

Bix met Ogun's openly assessing regard.

"You don't recognize her." The Chairman grunted, dismissing the guards with a flip of his chin. "Then her value to you is more than my predecessor assumed. May I introduce to you the knowledge goddess Sophia."

At the mention of her name, the goddess raised her head. Her attention fell first on Tobek. A flare of panic, a flush of shame, then Sophia's gaze skipped to Ogun and his hound before settling on Bix. Pale eyes widened, and her lips parted in a soft "Oh" before she hung her head once more.

Incomplete memories of Sophia flitted through Bix's mind. Fragments of conversations and settings. Indifference was the emotional constant. Bix didn't think too hard on the recollections, lest her mind craft assumptions to fill in the blanks. Lying to herself was the greatest danger of having reclaimed most but not all her arcane knowledge. Sadly, until she assimilated the final two segments of her missing memories, she was better off relying on third parties to educate her.

"Why are you bringing me your prisoner, Ogun?" Bix prompted.

"She was arrested by my predecessor after you returned to the Mids as an amnesiac. She's been locked in the Chairperson's private dungeons ever since." Ogun walked a slow circle around Sophia, his tone sympathetic. "Apparently, she's a spy."

"For whom?" Tobek grumbled.

"For the Chimera." Ogun smirked as Bix scowled. "Oh yes. Made the mistake of coming to the Consortium to warn us about the Devourers finding a way into the Mids. No good deed, and whatnot."

Bix unfolded from her seat. "Probably has something to do with the Devourer taint I sense coming from her."

"I was the anti-gods' prisoner first," Sophia whispered, her voice rough and ragged as though disused. Frequent swallowing broke up her cadence. "I escaped and came here. Only I…"

"You ran afoul of their allies within our ranks." Ogun patted Sophia on the shoulder and drew forward a hologram. "Security footage from her cell. It's graphic."

Bix ambled to Tobek's side as the hologram showed Sophia bedraggled and whimpering in a corner of a white crystalline cell. Sophia's whimpers escalated to soft cries of "No, no, no." Her filthy skin split, exposing her veins as she screamed in agony. Ichor brightened and bubbled, weeping from her body. A blinding flash obscured the view. Eerie silence held the room and the recording.

The light ebbed, revealing ichor dripping from the cell walls while fleshy particles the size of quail eggs lay scattered over the floor. Seconds turned to minutes watching the particles shiver, moving in barely perceptible increments toward each other.

"She exploded?" Bix breathed in horror.

"It takes a week or so before she can rebuild herself." Ogun closed the hologram. "A few days' reprieve, then the cycle starts again."

"Are you cursed, Sophia?" Tobek asked.

There was a long silence in which they waited for the goddess to speak. Eventually, Sophia tapped her throat yet gave neither a nod nor a shake to answer Tobek's question.

"By the old foes," Ogun responded in the goddess's stead, hooking a finger in Sophia's chains. "These shackles, although crude, limit the effects. Removing the curse is beyond the pantheons' abilities. She is your spy, Bix. Her cure, your burden. Her knowledge, your boon. I return her to you in hopes she can help you bring down the ether and that you will grant her peace one way or another."

Bix stepped toward the goddess. Sophia dropped to her knees, stretched her clasped hands above her head, and kept her gaze on her lap. The goddess's supplication unnerved Bix enough that she backed into Tobek, seeking his reassurance. Being revered was not a thing to which Bix was accustomed. Being the target of hostility? Very comfortable with it. Being the bogeyman feared by the masses? Old hat. Idolatry from a *god*? Totally suspicious.

Tobek rested his prosthetic hand on Bix's hip. His gentle touch silently conveyed encouragement, however the squeeze and nudge were less subtle.

"Rise, Sophia. I need you to feed me intel. I don't need you to feed my ego." Bix offered the goddess a hand.

Sophia stood with the effortless grace of divinity and nodded, notably refusing Bix's offer of help. Bix didn't take offense. Not wanting to be touched? Not uncommon for prisoners subjected to horrific torture.

"Very well, Ogun. I will take my contract and my spy and see what I can do about the ether." Bix collected her coat from the table. "Resen better be ready to go the instant your current defense system is gone. I do mean instant, not a bureaucratic 'we'll get around to it.'"

"That's for you and Chief to negotiate." Ogun moved to the tall iron table, hound at his side. "I've got a representative government to whip into wartime readiness and humans to rehome. Good luck, all of you. Alert me before the deed is done. It is important for the Consortium to witness the end of this lackadaisical era."

Bix looked to Tobek. "Whenever you're available, *Chief*."

"I believe I was just dismissed." Tobek held out an arm to her. "May I attend Sophia's debriefing?"

"Might as well. You two clearly know each other. Could prove useful." Looping her arm around Tobek's, Bix leveraged her gatekeeper magic to relocate herself, her Berserker, and her shackled spy far from the Consortium.

CHAPTER 2

In space beyond the Mids, between the collectives of the overbright Upper Worlds and the moody Under Worlds, sprawled a divine suburbia of Worlds belonging to midlevel gods. The colorful array of customized biomes shimmered against the blue-black of a curious universe. Through the seemingly disorganized community, a wide swath of Worlds had gone missing. Consumed by Devourers. The path led to the infamous ether.

This place between places offered no sound, no movement, no scents, no opportunities for unwanted observers in the debriefing of an agent Bix had purportedly recruited while still the original Chimera.

"If you cannot use your voice to speak, Sophia, then I suggest you broadcast your thoughts," Bix advised without preamble as the knowledge goddess took in their location with a slack jaw. A passing thought opened small gates to the uninhabited World in which Bix stored her things, allowing her to dispose of her coat and the contract. Perusing the fine print would take time and concentration, neither of which Bix could afford in her agitated state. She didn't mean to come across as a raging bitch, but after countless millennia having Tobek filter her emotions, she'd recently found herself dealing with their full brunt alone. She wasn't handling it well.

I would not presume to intrude on your mind without invitation, mighty Chimera, Sophia said, employing the typically annoying but occasionally useful method of telepathy all gods possessed.

"Sophia in chains? There are those who would pay handsomely to see her brought this low," drawled the newcomer to their group. His voice carried an erudite yet sinister undertone that was part of his calling as the Greek god of fear. Phobos was the spymaster for his pantheon and their allies, and he was an experienced campaigner against the Devourers. He'd been with Bix every step of her recovery, though it hadn't been intentional on either of their parts. She'd been starving, and he'd been in need of intel. What had begun as an operative's commendable effort to hook an asset had resulted in their roles being swapped as he helped her rediscover who and what she was. He was now her operative inside the pantheons and as dedicated to the eradication of the Devourers from the Mids as she.

You would bring a Greek into this, Chimera? Despite her bedraggled state, Sophia raked Phobos with the haughty disdain expected of a knowledge goddess from an opposing pantheon.

"News flash, Sophia, none of us are who we once were." Bix let go of Tobek, allowing him to drift as he pleased in the space between places. Unsurprisingly, he homed in on the ether, a seemingly black cosmic tar pit swallowing the Mid Worlds.

This is apparent by the magics radiating from the original Berserker that are a far cry from the magics he once possessed, Sophia remarked, her brows knitting as she failed to hide her less than surreptitious study of Tobek, while he remained more interested in the ether than discussing himself.

Although born a demigod, Tobek had spent epochs evolving on a track different from his divine peers. He wasn't a god or a titan, but something Other and undefined. He was still growing and changing, ever rising to new challenges that would hopefully result in him being a new class of cosmic entity that brought him closer to being Bix's peer and partner. Intimate relationships were complicated enough before dumping a gross power disparity into the mix. It was a good thing Bix and Tobek had been blessed with immortality's abundance of time to hash things out.

"Why did the Devourers curse you and what does it have to do with bringing down the ether?" Bix prodded Sophia, not allowing the goddess to derail the debriefing.

"Bringing down the ether?" Phobos echoed, drawing abreast of Bix, one dark brow arched to a sharp point.

They cannot husk me, not even their generals, for you protected my essence, my mind, and my knowledge when you recruited me to be one of seven divine watchers tasked to monitor the ether on the day it was created. Sophia bowed and extended her arms to Bix, palms up in deference. *After they stole my shard, this curse was the worst they could do.*

"Go back to the beginning and explain the formation of the ether, the watchers, and this shard as though I remember nothing." Bix regretted her acerbic tone, but her quixotic feelings plunged straight into the defensive and hostile.

No one understood the emotional entanglement Bix had with the ether. It'd been her haven and her prison during her weakest moments. She'd been brutalized and cosseted within its endless expanse. She wanted to understand its deepest secrets while simultaneously, she dreaded its truths. Alas, of the memories she'd reclaimed, none dealt with the creation of the ether or the events leading up to her ruin. She had to rely on rumor and hearsay, the most distressing of which was the rumor she'd given up everything—including her mind and her magics—to reinforce the ether. To protect the Mids a little longer, to allow the Consortium more time to prepare for an outside invasion. Yet she couldn't trust a damn thing anyone said, because most folks had a bone to pick with her, an old score to settle, or a burn of revenge to satisfy. Her original job had been one of imposing cosmic balance with a sidecar of justice. That job didn't foster friends; it amassed enemies.

You had a contract with the Consortium to delay the arrival of the

Devourers for fourteen hundred years in the time of the Mids. Sophia shambled toward Tobek and his view of the ether, the rattle of her chains brutishly loud. *They were furious you refused to eradicate the Devourers, but they were on the cusp of the cyclical war amongst themselves and were incapable of setting aside their traditions to address the outside threat. They had to take what grace you gave them.*

"Fourteen hundred years? The ether has only been around for fourteen hundred years?" Bix looked to Tobek, then Phobos. "The way everybody talks about the ether, it seemed it's what killed the dinosaurs."

"Been around a bit more than seventeen hundred years." Tobek hooked a thumb in the front pocket of his jeans. "The overage is the three hundred years you drifted unconscious in the ether, plus the last few decades of your reawakening."

"The Dark Ages of the Primary Mid World are known as such for a rather literal reason." Phobos pulled the filigreed fob of a still-beating heart from his vest pocket. "Up to that point, it was possible to glimpse the Worlds of the gods beyond the protective atmospheres of the Mids."

When you returned to the ether twelve years early, the other watchers and I had hoped it was to begin preparation for its final days. Instead, you divested yourself of your magics and reduced yourself to a husk. We were flummoxed by your… choice.

"You were there when I tried to reinforce it? Do you know what happened to me in the ether?" Bix blurted, hope overriding common sense.

Reinforce it? Sophia tipped her head, blinking rapidly. *Chimera, there have never been changes to the ether, not from the day it was created until the day I escaped the Devourers. I've been gone from their camp mere decades.*

"What?" Bix whispered as her heart stopped, her brain spun, and her knees buckled. It couldn't be. She had been told repeatedly and from different sources that she'd given up all her memories as a preventative measure because she had to reinforce the ether. And yet, the timing…there was something about the details of the timing that poked the pustule of painful memories she refused to examine.

A strong arm around her waist caught Bix before her tumult sacrificed her corporeal form. She looked up to see her confusion mirrored in Tobek's expression. He tucked her against his body and held her close as she trembled. Darkness unwound from Bix's spine; thorny tentacles snapped around her in response to her hurt and rage. They passed harmlessly over Tobek, her rock throughout time.

"If she didn't try to reinforce it, what the hell happened to her?" Tobek snarled, holding Bix tighter.

I did not witness the moment of the Chimera's sacrifice. Sophia swept her braids from her face, revealing a wealth of pity that spoke volumes about all Sophia had witnessed after Bix had gutted herself to exist as nothing more than a powerless, comatose amnesiac.

A frisson of defiance shot through Bix. Lots of bad things had happened to her inside the ether, things she really didn't want others to know, but it all had been seen by formidable entities, including gods and Devourers. Her enemies had gotten their kicks, literal and figurative, from it. She hadn't known she'd had allies, much less that they too had been watching. Shame had ridden her hard for years. Even now it lingered.

"After her sacrifice, what happened to her?" Tobek challenged.

Bix opened her mouth to prevent an accounting, but Sophia spoke first.

Best for us to focus on the ether itself, I think. It is a contained and continuous explosion. The currents, concussive waves. Sophia redirected the conversation to the actual subject of the debriefing and gestured to the silent sentry surrounding the Mids. *The disorientation and illusion of limitlessness are due to vortexes drawing in everything, then dispersing pieces to random locations within its confines. Nothing remains fixed in the ether by design, not even time.*

"Time is not fixed within its boundaries?" Phobos asked, aghast.

One minute in the Mids can be as swift as a nanosecond or as interminable as a century. It varies by location.

"And location is also a perpetual variable." Phobos grunted.

"Possibly a little too clever with its construction, Chimera."

"We know you were the architect but not the builder of the ether, sweetheart." Tobek loosened his hold on Bix as her darkness slithered around him like pets craving attention. "Explosions, even those made by gods, dissipate eventually, which means you likely employed titans to create the ether. Their destruction, their warping of space, their barriers."

"Titans creating the ether would explain how it lasted despite the Chimera being out of commission." Phobos eyed Bix with a gaze too perceptive. "It would also explain why the Consortium was eager to keep her name affixed to it. Rather than an apparatus of defense, the ether would've been classified as an act of aggression had the titans' involvement become known. All about perception that."

"If multiple titans established the perimeter, it would also explain why my gates have no effect on the ether," Bix conceded, compelling her darkness to cease its fawning and return to her. "It's akin to the World collectives like the Unders or Uppers. Sure, I can destabilize individual Worlds, but not the collectives as a whole. At least not as far as I currently know."

"Does this mean we're hunting titans now?" Tobek asked with a hopeful chuckle.

Phobos gave him a flat stare. "We're struggling with Devourers. How do you think we'd fare against titans?"

It would be unwise to involve titans at this point in the Chimera's… recovery, it is also unnecessary. Sophia flinched and shot away from their little gathering with a whimper.

Phobos gave chase.

"What is this?" Phobos seized Sophia's arm. The goddess's veins brightened and strained their confines.

"She's been cursed by the Devourers," Tobek explained hastily. "The shackles mute the effects."

Phobos's laugh was full of malevolence. "It's a gathering curse. They want her to fetch things for them. The longer she takes, the worse it gets. What is it they want, Sophia?"

The containment prism. Sophia twisted free of Phobos's hold. *The artifact that will capture and condense the ether, allowing the bearer to wield it as a weapon of cosmic destruction.*

Tobek and Phobos muttered nothing good under their breaths. Bix, however, perked up.

"It's an actual thing? The means of removing the ether? Not a super spell or a convergence of cosmic powers, but a doodad?" Bix slapped a hand over her mouth as her emotional pendulum swung into the manic. She didn't have to recruit her family, some of whom she remembered and who would help her without eradicating the entire galaxy. Some of whom she didn't remember but were definitely responsible for the no good and very bad memories she couldn't afford to examine until Resen was launched and her friends able to protect themselves from the Devourers.

"Anything capable of containing the ether is itself a weapon," Tobek cautioned. "You mentioned a shard earlier, Sophia. Was it part of the containment prism?"

Sophia nodded, wincing and clenching her fists. It took long moments before her veins dimmed and receded. She sighed loudly with relief. *The Chimera divided the prism among seven races with the most to lose by the invasion of the anti-gods. Gods were one of the races. The watchers she assigned to the ether were also keepers of the gods' pieces. I don't know who else has them nor in what proportion.*

"Of course it'd be seven races." Bix massaged her temple. Seven was her sacred number, born of her being the seventh child of the origins of all existence. To say she was old was a gross understatement. "The races most affected by the demise of the Mids would be the four superpowers and the races they rule: the Chweds and the humans. But that's only six. Tobek, any ideas for the seventh?"

Tobek had been her closest companion back then. Presumably, she'd consulted him. Then again, he'd seemed surprised by Sophia's revelations, so maybe the original Chimera hadn't let him in on the details…which was odd no matter how she looked at it.

Her Berserker shook his head. "If we can figure out who

among those six races received the segments, then whatever the individuals have in common might lead us to the seventh."

I must warn you, Chimera, the Devourers captured all the watchers. They have the gods' shards, and those shards are not inert. They carry significant power. If the Devourers amass enough pieces of the containment device, they will have a weapon. It might not be as devastating as the ether itself, but it will bring large-scale destruction.

"So, we have competition for the shards." Bix smoothed her dress and shook her hair from her face. "Alrighty, then, it's a race to completion. I'll start with the Angelic Host. Hopefully, they still have their segment."

"I'll see if my resources have any leads about the gods' shards or the captured keepers." Phobos tucked his fob into his vest pocket. "We'll need to steal back what the Devourers took to complete the prism."

Sophia made a series of steeples with her fingers, weaving a long sheaf of gossamer parchment. *You'll need this. It's a list of the keepers. The enemy camps aren't fixed in location. The nature of the ether doesn't allow it. Their camps exist because the components and the occupants are physically linked together.*

"If we capture the right foot soldiers, they'll lead us up their hierarchy to the camps." Phobos examined Sophia's list, scowling. "That means we will not be subtle in our raids on Devourer enclaves within the Mids, Berserker. Might want to alert the relevant Mid World armies."

"Pot stirring, got it." Tobek scratched his beard. "Since we need Resen to launch the moment the prism is complete, I'll do my job of making sure we're ready. Sweetheart, can my resources assist you in any way in the meantime?"

"I'll check in once I'm done with the angels. Until I have a shard in hand, I don't know what we're actually hunting or the pitfalls of possession." Bix eyed Sophia. "Are you fit to participate, or do I need to find a safe space to park you until we can end your curse?"

It would be my honor to help in any way I can. Redemption is my greatest desire. Sophia bowed from the shoulders. *As for my curse, humanity's ability to ground magic of all types helps minimize the effects.*

"Nice thing about the Primary Mid World, every superpower has a reason to be there." Bix wagged a finger at Sophia's attire. "But supermax prisoner accessories sort of limit our ability to blend in."

Ah, yes, of course. Shimmers of red covered Sophia from head to toe for the briefest moment, changing her attire from Consortium detainee garb to the black-and-white habit of a nun, her shackles disguised as belt and rosary.

"Of all the styles that carried across time… I'll be in touch once I have actionable intel. Good luck, all." Phobos vanished in a cloud of navy, sniggering.

Tobek started to say something but pursed his lips instead as a blush crept across Sophia's cheeks. Yeah, there was a story there.

Opening gates to the Primary Mid World, Bix smirked. She had the perfect place to interrogate a nun while waiting on an archangel.

CHAPTER 3

Electronica bass beats vibrated the bricks of the renovated church-cum-fetish bar Hella Fella in Southeast DC, Primary Mid World. Scantily clad club goers from the profoundly underage to the hoary wizened popped, swayed, vogued, and commendably contorted to the throbbing beats being spun by the DJ on the altar in the chancel. Colored exterior lights blasted through the stained-glass windows of saints in suggestively parted robes. Velvet-lined nooks filled with BDSM gear arranged in artful displays lined the walls. The choir loft above the main doors had been converted into VIP seating with table service.

Bix opted to arrive at the main floor bar. Its diamond-plated front panels reflected the strobe lights and black-light body paint. Every barstool was taken. Every gap wedged with the eager, the predatory, and the thirsty. It was a sweaty, smelly crush of joy, desperation, and straight-up horniness.

Perfect for a nun, right?

Why here? Sophia stared at Bix with pale eyes shimmering to mask the red pupils that identified a god.

"You've been out of commission nearly two thousand years. I doubt the ether offered you souls to feed on, just as I doubt the Consortium was sufficiently hospitable." Bix tipped her head toward the untethered souls drifting through and above the crowd. Certain lifestyles had high mortality rates driven by societal rejection and oppression, but the souls of the deceased still craved acceptance and belonging. Thus, gatherings like this attracted them.

Unclaimed? Sophia gasped. *So much has changed. This would never have been allowed before the ether went up. Gods used to rampage through villages to claim their dead, destroying civilizations if a single soul was missing.*

"The guild of psychopomps is into extortion these days, so they don't always take souls to the gods in a timely manner. The pantheons are a bit distracted of late too." Bix nudged Sophia closer to the dance floor as patrons aplenty took notice of the nun. "Go. Feed. Dance. Give these kids the thrill of their lives, and maybe earn yourself a convert or twenty. I warn you, most are high on any number of things, so don't expect their behavior to be rational."

To someone who'd been a prisoner, showing them kindness went a long way to loosening their tongue. Yes, Bix could simply rip everything she needed from Sophia, but the original Chimera had chosen this knowledge goddess from hundreds of other knowledge gods for a reason, so something made Sophia special. Maybe that something had to do with Tobek. Maybe that something had to do with why the Devourers had chosen Sophia to fetch the prism pieces instead of the six other captive shard holders. Whatever it was, Bix was keen to learn just how much Sophia knew about what had happened the day Bix had given up her mind and her magics. Bix had the patience to let the goddess get comfortable in her presence before pressuring her for details. Bix also needed time to sort the goddess's tells from the curse's triggers.

I thought we were here to talk to angels? Sophia gasped as a pair of freckled boys in schoolgirl uniforms patted her arm and gestured for her to join them.

"I'll grab you when we're ready for next steps. Shriek if you think you're going to explode, and I'll get you to safety." Bix motioned for the humans to take off with the nun. Their bleached-white smiles bloomed as they gently tugged the goddess, who could crush them with a flutter of her lashes, to the dance floor.

A cluster of Chweds glamoured as magnificent drag queens caught Bix's eye. One cleared a stool and patted it, while the others gestured for Bix to join them.

Bix took the offered seat. "Thank you, ladies."

"Our pleasure, mighty Chimera." One of the ladies in an enviable magenta fringe minidress gave her a crystal-studded wink. "You need anything at all, just let us know."

"You are too kind." Bix opened a small gate to a long-forgotten cistern that served as her isolated home and gathered an earpiece and smartwatch from a shelf overstocked with them. She had a bad habit of losing tech when she shifted forms. A simple text message over a secure network issued an invitation to an archangel.

The next song was barely into its chorus when the archangel appeared in a pulse of potent native magic and shouldered his way to Bix's side. Thick necked and hard bodied, Archangel Samael had dressed in second-skin black leather pants and a studded chest harness that exposed the wealth of his scarifications.

"Last time we were here, you severed my hand," he drawled on a breeze curling around her ear. In the Mids, angels controlled all things air, including atmosphere and sound waves. As an archangel, Samael could hear a snore in the UK Parliament from this noisy bar in DC if he chose. One of many fun features of being made from pure native magic and directly connected to a ley line.

"That was after you made me kiss the shellacked bar top." Bix grinned. They'd come a long way since that first meeting, absolute enemies to something resembling friends. Not actual friends, though. He might break out in hives at the idea.

Samael ordered a beer and faced her. A scowl fell across his square features as he glimpsed the dance floor. "What is the Holy Ghost doing in my neighborhood bar? And as a *nun*? Anyone tell her she missed Halloween?"

"Sophia? *She's* the Holy Ghost?" Bix searched for memories linking Sophia to that time frame, but they came up as a mishmash of gnostic texts and comic books. Nothing that gave her confidence in her recollections. "The Holy Ghost was the Angelic Host's go-to henchman in the emergence of multiple monotheistic religions. How is she not your greatest ally in the pantheons?"

"Crisis of conscience. She pissed off the entire Host. We gave her a hand up and out of mediocrity during her ascension to godhood, then we gave her a direct line to souls for her consumption once she became a goddess." He chugged his drink, slammed it on the counter, and ordered another. "After a few centuries of a good deal, she balked. Rebelled. Decided the religions created by the Angelic Host were bad for our creations and then tried to stop their spread."

Bix laughed. "Modern religions *are* bad for your creations. They promote guilt, shame, hatred, and depression, among other negative emotions."

"Which is exactly their point. Angels have to eat, and we eat negativity," he defended. "The Host lost our shit over Sophia's countercampaigns. Had all the texts in which she is mentioned pulled from canon. By then though, she'd overcome the ignominy of being a lesser knowledge god by bonding to an archangel."

"An archangel? Which one?" Bix asked, interest fully piqued.

He gave her a flat stare. "Your personal favorite."

"The former Chair of the Consortium? Oh, that explains so much," Bix whispered, beginning to understand why the original Chimera might've selected Sophia for watcher duty. Cunning, courage, and a sliver of morality. That last one was a rarity among gods. "Original me should've left her to be a pain in your ass, but I apparently recruited her to spy on the Devourers in the ether, so play nice."

Samael stared at her flatly, then barked with mirth. "What a special hell you gifted her. The Host will be thrilled to hear it."

"She's helping me gather parts of a prism that'll bring down the ether. The Devourers are trying to force her to steal them, but she's refusing to cooperate at great personal cost." Bix didn't divulge the whole exploding-body consequence of Sophia's decision. That kind of vulnerability didn't need to be shared. Besides, Samael had his own gruesome experiences being a prisoner of the Devourers. He could commiserate without the gory details. "I'm told I gave some pieces to the Host. Know anything about that?"

"The era of the ether is at an end, eh?" He raised his beer to the row of illuminated stained glass. "Once it comes down, the night will no longer be as dark as it is now. Days will no longer outshine everything beyond this atmosphere. I'll be able to walk down any street and see six neighboring Worlds. Moons will be revealed as the cosmic bumpers they are. Polytheistic religions will have a renaissance as the Uppers and Unders come back into view. The pantheons will regain footholds even as individual gods sacrifice autonomy. The influence of the Angelic Host will wane as we are once again viewed as minions of the gods instead of their peers."

"Is that a verbose way of telling me the Host doesn't want a future where they play second fiddle, so no, you will not help me find the shards?"

"Allies all the way through this mess, that's our deal. I'll honor it." He inverted his empty glass on the bar and ordered a third drink. "Besides, the Host fighting you instead of the true enemy is a luxury beyond our reach now. However, no one at the top enjoys the fall, so don't expect gleeful cooperation."

"Change is upon the Mids. It's not slow and comfortable, but it is overdue." Bix spun on her stool, taking in the dance floor and Sophia laughing and gyrating as the stuffing in a man sandwich. "The laws condemning humanity to ignorance about the magic surrounding them can't last much longer. Once they see the lies in the sky revealed, the Consortium is going to have all kinds of problems."

"We make humanity as a reflection of ourselves, an act of both ego and self-flagellation. We make them powerless because we fear our own propensity to abuse power. Yet humans consistently mine our weaknesses and still make us quake in our boots." He rapped his knuckles against the bar top. "We are weak, Chimera, we are fallible, and we are proud. Too proud. We will be paying the price for our hubris long after we rout the Devourers from our Worlds."

"Let's you and I focus on getting rid of the anti-gods first. Starting with the prism pieces. Since lesser angels are an offshoot of their archangel, thus suck at hide-and-seek, I'm guessing I handed the pieces to archangels. Did I give them to all of you? Some of you? One of you? I don't even know how many pieces I'm supposed to collect from the Host. All help is greatly appreciated." She'd only be this frank with Samael. His siblings? Not a chance. He was the archangel of the fallen and disavowed, which meant he did the Host's dirty work and the Host got to pretend he was the villain. Meanwhile, he'd been the first archangel to grok the danger the Devourers presented and been the first to work with her to do something about it.

"Three of us. You gave segments to three archangels." Samael bowed his head over his beer. "Give me a minute or two to set up a meeting, yeah? Finding a secure location is going to be tricky, what with the Devourers hunting us for food."

"Just like that? You know who I'm looking for just like that?" Bix snapped her fingers.

"Chimera, we've been awaiting this summons for centuries." Samael closed his eyes, but his smile was wry and his tone relieved.

"Why not do the handover here?" She waited for a response but got none. His eyes were still closed, but rapidly moving beneath his lids. Archangels could butt in to each other's brains if invited, and he was apparently having an issue with negotiations. "We're at the back door to the Consortium's chambers, and security has tripled with the new Chair taking the reins. Plus, there are lots of humans to ground whatever magic the shards hold."

"It's not as subtle as passing an envelope of cash." He opened one eye that rolled black, then white, then black again as he gave his siblings an eyeful. "Though you have a point about the humans grounding the magic. The shards are potent."

"Winter holidays are all about angels and miracles…and this *is* a church," she said in a singsong way. "A church of self-love and a good time, but still a church."

"And you're toting around a nun. Fortunately, I appreciate your twisted humor." He finished his drink and paid his tab. "National Cathedral is mostly empty right now. I don't have to draw you a picture, do I?"

As long as Bix had a clear mental image of a location, she could open a gate to it; she didn't have to be nearby. Heck, she didn't have to be on the same World.

"I know the alleyways of DC by heart. You can be damn sure I know the landmarks," she scoffed. With a passing thought, she opened gates, taking an archangel and a nun with her. Probably just as well the patrons of Hella Fella weren't remotely sober.

CHAPTER 4

Moonlight and floodlights shone through the Rose Window at the west entrance, casting blues, reds, greens, and plums across the limestone arches of the gothic National Cathedral, Washington, DC, Primary Mid World. Bix landed her cargo in the balcony overlooking the long nave, oddly empty without its columns of seating leading up to the crossing of the transepts. At the far end loomed the simply carved rood screen and the integrated dark wooden benches of the Great Choir bracing the ornate High Altar. Two hundred and thirty-one stained glass windows of incredible art added their colors to hard night softened to an almost watery Other Worldly ambiance. There were lots of negative things to be said about modern religions, but there was no denying the beauty created by passionate believers.

The sweet woody aroma of frankincense lingered in the cathedral. The infrequent shuffle of feet and the occasional crackle of a radio hinted at security patrolling the narthex. A low murmur of masculine voices drifted from the War Memorial along the southern transept. Voices escalated. A dispute of some sort.

"So much for mostly empty," Bix murmured as Samael and Sophia leaned on the rounded stone railing.

Samael laid a finger to his lips, his angelic black eyes dancing with amusement. A breeze cocooned Bix's ear, delivering the distant conversation with clarity.

"Look, Deacon, I served. I just want to pay my respects, maybe get warm."

"I thank you for your service, my son, but buy a ticket and return during business hours."

"A ticket? For a church? What happened to Matthew twenty-five, verse forty-one? That ring a bell, Deacon? The fate of the goats who refused compassion for the poor? Wouldn't you rather be a sheep and be rewarded?"

"Friendship Place will open in a few hours. I suggest you make your way there. They'll set you up with the resources you need. That includes a shower."

"Deacon, it's snowing, and dawn is hours away. Can't you just leave me here to pray? I promise not to be any bother."

"Son, for the last time, you cannot sleep here. Leave, or I will be forced to call security."

Sounds of a scuffle snuck along the breeze.

"Security. Security!"

The jangle of a utility belt and rubber soles slapping against limestone echoed as the security guard raced down the nave.

"Depart from me, you who are cursed, into the eternal fire prepared for the devil and his angels. For I was a stranger, and you did not invite me in." The voice warbled and pitched into tones altogether inhuman as it quoted the Bible.

A horrified shriek chased rapid footfalls, joining those of the security guard coming into view. A middle-aged man in a white cassock with a stole over one shoulder burst from the south transept. The inhospitable deacon, apparently. The guard caught the deacon and spun him around as they collided in the crossing.

"Mortals, repent," boomed a sonorous male voice from the High Altar. Icy blue light bathed the reredos of a hundred carved angels and saints. Before the Majestus sculpture of Christ, in all the rampant glory attributed in song and scripture, floated an archangel, features obscured by the brilliance of his glowing toffee-and-cream-colored wings spreading wide around him.

The deacon flung himself prostrate upon the steps of the High Altar. The security guard pulled a Taser from his belt.

"Do not join him in his sins," cautioned a vagrant shuffling from the south transept. His filthy desert camo coat, frayed olive sweatpants, and thin sneakers with duct tape wrapped around the toes screamed his destitute state. His oily hair was plastered to his face, and his scraggly beard didn't fare much better.

"Stay where you are," blurted the security guard, swinging the Taser at the vagrant.

"The deacon wants me to leave. You want me to stay. Whom am I to heed?" The vagrant advanced farther into the center of the cathedral.

"Fifty bucks says he shoots." Samael sniggered.

Men always shoot, Sophia quipped. *Mentally, fear makes the need akin to sexual climax. Their thoughts are racing toward a singular goal. He can't hold back. He can't deviate. There is no sport in this. Do not accept his bet.*

"Ready. Fire. Aim," Bix murmured wryly.

Sure enough, the guard shot the Taser at the vagrant. The traveling jolts echoed in the mostly empty church. The vagrant didn't so much as quiver. He did, however, sprout a pair of sand-colored wings. One pump of the mighty arches launched the vagrant above the balconies and knocked the guard on his ass. The guard scrambled back, whimpering, Taser abandoned.

"For doing no more than your duty demanded, you may go." The vagrant flicked his wrist. Wind carried the guard across the north transept and out to the patio, heavy wooden doors slamming open and shut.

That left the sniveling deacon.

Bix wasn't a fan of playing with one's prey when they were so far down the power hierarchy. She nudged Samael. "Really?"

Samael rolled his eyes. "If you fed on emotions, you'd notice the stole he is wearing has absorbed the negativity of hundreds.

We need that to fuel the ritual without breaking the Consortium's many laws about not revealing magic to humans."

Clerics' stoles were possibly the most cursed gift a mortal could receive from any superpower. They embodied the price of one angelic miracle, a price that could never be repaid across countless lifetimes. Woven from an angel's hair and feathers, a stole's debt passed to one's most hated enemy upon death with no option for refusal. They represented currency among the Angelic Host, but they were also an angel's weakness should they fall into the hands of a greater power who could use the stole to enslave an angel.

"I can't believe the Host hasn't rounded up every stole in the Mids to keep them out of the hands of the Devourers," Bix muttered.

"Calculated risk, admittedly." Samael hitched a shoulder. "They've proven to be useful weapons since conflicts are won by the actions of the little guys, not us assholes calling the shots."

You may wish to recall in religious texts, angels only fight themselves, not mankind. Sophia leaned toward Bix. *The greatest genocides are committed by men. Omitted from the texts are how many of those men possessed cursed stoles.*

"Gods are pretty effective mass murderers too," Bix reminded.

"Oh, is she playing the blame game?" Samael sneered at Sophia. "Too much a coward to accuse me out loud, eh? Well, let's not forget the five cities of the plains, the plight of Egypt's firstborn, or the fall of Jerusalem. You had a knack, oh Holy Ghost."

Sophia huffed and thrust her jaw to the side. *You can't feed off my shame, Samael, so leave your jibes where the Chimera doesn't have to suffer them.*

His chin went up, and he stepped back, slapping the buzz cut of his side fade. His gaze dropped to the illusion of Sophia's rosary, then snapped up to the goddess's face. "Get out of my head. You're not invited. Never were."

Bix studied the two superpowers facing off. Sophia's

expression remained placid, every bit a staid nun. Samael looked like a cat who'd just gotten a whiff of a pack of dogs. Samael didn't get prickly. He got sassy. He got snarky. He did not get prickly. Apparently, Tobek wasn't the only one sharing a curious history with Sophia.

"How about we back up to the part about a ritual that requires a lot of special angel juice?" Bix suggested as the two archangels at the far end of the cathedral arranged the deacon in the center of the crossing of the transepts and the nave. The human's appendages flopped limply as the archangels positioned him with legs outstretched and arms crossed over his chest. The fact the deacon's soul hadn't fled his suit said the man was unconscious, not dead. Yet. "Do I need to open gates or something to protect the masses?"

Samael pivoted toward her, leaning a hairy forearm on the railing and visibly relaxing. "I thought you had most of your marbles back."

"Five out of seven segments. Why?" Bix hated discussing her partial wits, but Samael had been helpful by hunting the gods in whom she'd stored her memories.

"We've got the shards. Let me emphasize the word 'shards.'" He faced the sanctuary and his brothers, who were standing stoically to either side of the deacon with wings arched high. "If you can't remember how to glue the pieces together, then I hope you brought a cosmic bucket."

You deliberately broke the containment prism into fragments that cannot be reassembled by anyone but you. Sophia offered a sympathetic smile. *I will do everything I can to fill in the blanks in your memories, but there are details you kept to yourself. If you do not have the memories to complete the reconstruction, then perhaps we would be better served collecting your missing knowledge before collecting the prism.*

"No," Bix snapped with more vehemence than she'd intended. Part of her knew they weren't being intentionally condescending. They were trying to be courteous. Still, it chafed. "Assimilating memories sidelines me for too long. We can't afford for me to do that, not with the Devourers also hunting the shards so they can weaponize them against the Mids. Once the pieces are in my possession, they can't be exploited by anyone else. We get the pieces, then we worry about putting them together."

She didn't miss the wary look exchanged between goddess and archangel.

"No objections from the Host, Chimera. I just hope you know what you're doing," Samael hedged. "Brace yourselves, ladies. It's about to get crowded in here."

Samael leapt over the balcony railing and landed softly in the nave. A few angelically long strides and he was standing with his brothers, taking position at the head of the unconscious deacon.

"Arrive, my choir," intoned the vagrant archangel.

A gust strong enough to force Bix to brace against the balustrade swept through the cathedral, rattling panes. An army of the derelict and downtrodden overfilled the south transept, curving to the rood screen and then into the nave.

Throughout time, Azazel and his choir have walked among the lowest and most oppressed across the Mids, not just humanity. He is an instigator as much as he is an instructor and builder of communities. Sophia watched the assembling choir with fondness softening her features. *Religious texts have not been kind to him, nor did he wish them to be.*

Bix refrained from comment, not wanting a thousand ears to overhear any questions that would expose her ignorance. Within her broken mind, angels occupied a plump bubble of very old memories without any emotional significance. However, her experiences with the Host over the last thirty years were quite contentious, to put it kindly. Being in the presence of this many angels set her teeth on edge.

"Arrive, my choir," echoed the second archangel. Without his holy light obscuring his appearance, it was easy to see his refined contrast to Azazel the vagrant. This second archangel wore a fine cotton kurta in copper, embroidered with ice-blue threads over ivory pajamas. His black Verdi beard was impeccably styled all the way to the curled tips of his mustache. His side-parted pompadour gleamed in the watery lights thrown by the stained-glass windows.

His choir arrived in an eerie cascade of whispers as they materialized, shedding forms of every race of Chwedlonol to assume their angelic natural state. This was the white-collar group, evidenced by their choice of business attire. They assembled behind their archangel in the north transept and similarly overflowed the space as Azazel's choir in the south.

Iblis. His choir is often found among the shaitan and djinn, seeking out the exploited and the exploiters. He favors the dreamers, the remorseful, and the regretful. Sophia's tone said she didn't much care for Iblis. *Many of his angels are Miracle Workers.*

Ah. Miracle Workers were the angels who dealt in stoles, thus the equivalent of Wall Street traders in the Host. No wonder Sophia didn't like their archangel. Bix pretty much shared the goddess's opinion on the matter.

"Arrive, my choir," Samael commanded, staring at Bix across the cathedral.

This time, Bix grinned as angels she recognized filled the nave, appearing as average everyday men and women. Much like their archangel, Samael's choir had an allyship with Bix and her team. When they weren't wheeling and dealing as a crime syndicate in the Crimson Market, they were protecting the select mortals for whom Bix cared. For all their interactions, she'd never once sensed Samael or his choir were protecting something Other Worldly.

She definitely sensed the presence of something not angelic now. Faint. Too faint to identify.

Three full choirs are far too many to fit inside this building. They must be amassing outside. I worry they are drawing unwanted attention. Sophia rubbed the beads of her rosary. Her narrowed eyes darted around the church. *We should be vigilant until the shards are fully in your possession.*

"When the Devourers started hunting us, it was assumed they did so solely because we are tasty in the raw." Samael rolled his shoulders and widened his stance, taking the hands of Iblis and Azazel. "Yet, as the Resen defense system has progressed, so have the Devourers' raids on our communities. Their interrogations of our captured kin have revealed their desperate search for the shards the Chimera entrusted to us centuries ago."

Bix glanced at Sophia. The goddess grimaced while her gaze continued to scan the cathedral, clearly unsurprised about the Devourers' desperate search. Then again, after having her own shard ripped from her and being cursed to retrieve the other pieces, why would Sophia be surprised? That part of the goddess's story tracked.

"The Chimera has called upon us to return that which is hers. Our compliance will usher in a change of eras, but change does not come easily nor bloodlessly. Our choirs are unique in that change forces us to excel where our kin falter. We are twice honored." Iblis took the hand of Azazel, closing the circle of archangels as he stretched his wings wide. Beams of icy blue light burst from the tips of his feathers and connected with one angel among his choir, then another, then another and still more, leaving a drunken zigzag in the restless night.

"The Chimera subdivided these sacred fragments into slivers so small, they'd be beyond detection by our peers and our enemies." Azazel also flared his wings. Muted blue rays connected to seemingly random angels within his choir. "We stored those slivers within the extensions of ourselves."

Well, that explained why Bix hadn't gotten the woo-willies around any of Samael's choir. Lookie at original her being smart. Possibly explained why she'd given seven pieces to seven gods but had only involved three archangels. Maybe. Or not. Until she actually held the pieces in her hands, it was too soon to know much of anything.

"If harm befell the shell of a shard, we extracted the shard and placed it in a new shell." Samael didn't have wings to display. He'd forfeited them after making a series of bad decisions. Instead, bold royal blue rays burst from the whole of his aura like a neon porcupine, tagging the third contingent of angels. "Thus, we have kept our promise to the Chimera and proven ourselves as caretakers of the Mid Worlds."

Eh, jury was still out on that last part for the Angelic Host as a whole. Samael's choir? Yeah, sure, they'd proven themselves.

"Rise, shards," the three archangels commanded in unison. At their words, their auras lifted the chosen angels to the lofty heights of the stained-glass windows. The chosen lesser angels unfurled their glorious wings, tipped back their chins, and stretched their arms before them with palms facing the archangels.

If there was an angelic rapture, this was probably what it looked like.

The three archangels' auras shifted hues until all three glowed with the same rich cobalt light of their cosmic creator. The archangels began to chant in tongues. The lesser angels threw their heads back and convulsed.

Slivers of pewter, so small as to be barely perceptible, floated from the sternums of the lesser angels and traveled the lights toward the archangels.

Windows shattered. Unholy keening filled the cathedral. Contorted, horned, boil-coated monstrosities rappelled down the walls, lunging at the unprotected shards. Long claws slashed through lesser angels. Angelic blood spurted and streamed as angels screamed in horror, then in rage. Every cry was answered by an Other Worldly screech.

Demons.

Demons not Devourers were after the shards.

CHAPTER 5

Vines of thorny night and shadows unwound from Bix's spine, chasing demons descending on the cathedral by the dozens with the preternatural speed of the divine. Sophia looped the chains of her shackles around the throat of a demon scrabbling across the balcony and planted a foot in its tailbone, pinning it against the balustrade. The knowledge goddess speared one hand into the nape of the demon. The demon flailed and writhed, screeching as ichor spurted over Sophia. Still, the goddess kept her hand within the demon's skull. The red of her pupils glowed. The demon ceased its struggling as its body desiccated, shedding its monstrous outer shell and leaving only the translucent husk of a once-beautiful male god.

The demon's transformation meant he and his cadre were not lesser gods. They were gods punished by their pantheons' leadership to hideous appearance while they worked off their sentence. A kinder punishment than the complete husking of everything but the seed of their divinity. Husking was as close as a god got to dying.

Sophia had just husked whoever that punished god had been.

Draining a god was a feat only a greater power could accomplish, which meant Sophia was a higher-caste goddess and more powerful than Bix had discerned. Was false weakness intentional on Sophia's part, or was it a side effect of the Devourer magic corrupting her?

The shards, Chimera, Sophia shouted into Bix's mind as the knowledge goddess tossed aside the husked demon to pursue the next. *Protect the shards. The Host and I will deal with the demons as we have throughout history.*

Angels arch and lesser rose with battle cries, weapons manifesting alongside angel fire. Demons lost limbs and burned as the angels went on the defensive. Alas, there were too many of everyone crammed within the limestone walls. Too close quarters for much more than inefficient hand-to-hand. The nave resembled a mosh pit more than a battlefield. Shards, unprotected and smaller than a pinkie tip, tumbled to and fro, knocked about in the struggle.

Bix let the shards fly, curious to see if any demon *could* touch them, and if anything adverse would happen to the cursed gods if they did. Could they claim something that wasn't meant for them? Had she, as the original Chimera, intended for the shard keepers to have to fight to protect the pieces? Was that part of some larger test of worth? Sophia had said the shards could be stolen, yet Bix had nothing but the goddess's word on that. Frankly, this attack was the perfect opportunity to put Sophia's story to the test. Besides, the demons weren't going anywhere, not until Bix dropped the gates she'd opened around the cathedral. The gates looped back on themselves, creating an invisible and impenetrable barrier.

A cluster of angels and demons scrambled after a shard that shot out of their hands a breath before fingers and talons could close around it. The shard gained speed with each avoidance until it zinged toward Bix, nicking Sophia's cheek before darkness gently captured the projectile. The goddess curled a lip but kept fighting, ignoring the ichor dribbling down her face.

Monstrous shrieking drew Bix's attention across the cathedral to a demon repeatedly flinging itself against open space in a shattered window, only to bounce off the nothingness of a gate. A shard gleamed in the demon's maw as its talons dug at that which could not be torn.

"Silly demon," Bix derided, extending a tentacle of shadow to engulf the damned deity. "Hasn't anyone told you not to steal my toys?"

The demon's hammer-like head swiveled from side to side, and its clawing became more desperate. It swallowed the shard. As if that would stop Bix from taking what was hers. Shadows pierced the demon and seized the shard...then lingered. Hunger needled her. It would take no more effort than a sigh to drain the demon of its essence. A twitch to take its memories. A smirk to reduce it to a husk. Alas, she was deliberately abstaining from feeding on gods since one and all were needed to fight the anti-gods. Politically, *she* couldn't be seen reducing the ranks of potential defenders without it blowing up in her allies' faces. It would be a complication that would further distract from the defense of the Mids, not something the collective could afford.

Sophia, on the other hand...

No, no, no. Not now, not now, the goddess cried in panic and pain, stumbling away from the raging conflict. Veins pushed up along the goddess's skin, mapping her face and hands in cursed light.

"Sophia, what triggered it?" Bix asked, withdrawing from the demon and taking nothing more than the shard.

Contact with a puissant artifact that I did not contain. The goddess whimpered, covering the wound that had already healed thanks to her divinity. *The curse wants me to hunt the shards, the shards are pow——*

An audible gurgle of agony burbled from Sophia's lips as the goddess crumpled, juddering.

"Samael, get your choirs out of here, now," Bix demanded louder than was probably necessary. She dropped the gates surrounding the cathedral. Angels might be hard to kill, but they were merely long-lived mortals. Bix wasn't at all confident they could survive Sophia's explosion.

Samael was too smart to argue as he combined a salute with

an elbow to a demon's face. The angelic retreat didn't come with the blasting of a holy horn. It was as subtle as a serpent's hiss. One moment, the clash and scream of conflict; the next, the befuddled chitter of thwarted demons.

Before the demons could give chase, Bix cast her darkness through the cathedral like a great tide, stuffing every nook and cranny while enveloping shards and demons alike. Her peeved muttering at the insolence of the condemned gods carried through her disembodied night, making it seem as if the cathedral itself mocked their presence. If a demon happened to be lucky enough to possess a shard, that demon was relieved of its burden before being punted out of the Mids via gates. Their expedited departure didn't hurt the gods, it just distracted them long enough for Bix to finish her business.

It was a nonce before silence once again filled the cathedral. The three archangels remained amid the ruins, protectors of the catatonic human deacon. Their auras offered a gentle illumination amid the solid night filling the cathedral.

Almost solid night.

Beside Bix, Sophia glowed like a torch, her curse burning through her nun's habit. The illusion masking her shackles faded. The knowledge goddess whimpered and groaned, her face and neck straining as she fought her curse. Bix opened gates around the goddess to contain the blast if the shackles failed. They also muted Sophia's screams and obscured her struggle.

It was easy to be unaffected watching Sophia suffer on a hologram. It was enraging to stand helplessly beside her, feeling the surge of Devourer magic corrupting the goddess's divinity. If Bix thought for one moment she could remove the curse without harming Sophia or anyone else, she'd do it in an instant. For now, the best Bix could offer was a fraction of dignity within the box of gates.

"Chimera?" Azazel whispered on a traveling wisp. "What can we do to help her?"

Bix shook her head. "This is beyond what Mids' magic can assuage. This is how the anti-gods try to break a god."

Surprisingly, and despite their history, the archangels murmured sympathies for Sophia. Samael hefted the unconscious deacon over one shoulder and carried him into the Children's Chapel, while everyone else waited for the writhing lights within the box of gates to dim. Once the box darkened, Bix removed one wall. Sophia lay curled in a fetal position, body whole, skin smooth.

The shackles held. The goddess rolled to her knees and manifested her nun's attire. *Thank you for the privacy.*

"Thank you for husking some demons. That they pursued the shards despite knowing I was here and could end them shows remarkable desperation." Bix offered Sophia a hand up. "I'm curious what they fear more than me."

What they crave more than they fear is the better question. Sophia again declined to accept Bix's help. Instead, the goddess clenched her fists at her sides and slowly regained her feet. *When we are done with the angels, I will unscramble the knowledge I took from my kith to find out why they were after the shards.*

"Divine criminals hoping to trade the pieces for early release?" Bix asked, while privately wondering if Sophia's refusal to touch her had more to do with the goddess's curse potentially reacting to the cosmic power contained within Bix's corporeal form than any personal slight. After all, Sophia had had no problems being in close contact with humans at the night club. Bix dropped her hand and made the mental note to stop putting Sophia in the awkward position of having to refuse Bix's help. Her attention drifted back to the nave as Samael rejoined his brothers in the crossing.

Stealing from you at this point in the conflict with the Devourers will only extend their sentence. Sophia unknotted her rosary shackles. *The leadership of all pantheons are cooperating with the new Chairman of the Consortium. Ogun has made it clear that any interference in your efforts to save the Mids will be swiftly crushed beneath the full might of the Consortium.*

"That's an edict that's probably never been issued by any Chair, ever. They might not have gotten the memo." Bix recalled the bulk of her darkness to her body, leaving only those thorns that held a shard to dance through the dawn peeking through the broken windows as she relocated herself and Sophia to the crossing where the archangels waited. The shards lunged at the archangels as if desperate to return to their keepers. "I don't think we're quite done with the handoff."

"Did the demons manage to get away with some of the shards?" Iblis blustered.

How could he stand in the heart of darkness and think anything escaped you? Sophia derided. *The arrogance of angels never ceases to stun.*

"No, this is about reassembling the pieces, Iblis." Bix caged the shards upon her thorns and tried to draw the glowing slivers together, triggering a repulsion like polarized magnets. "These are still drawn to you, as though you haven't released them."

Samael huffed. "Uh, abracadabra, we release you?"

"Funny. Let's figure it out." Bix moved the shards closer to, then away from the archangels, studying the way the pieces reacted to distance. "Why did original me choose the three of you to keep these shards and not your siblings? What makes you different from them?"

"Among the archangels, there is always one of us on the outside," answered Azazel the vagrant. "One of us tasked to be the contrarian, one of us duty bound to push back when the Angelic Host pushes ahead. This is not a permanent placement. There are six of us to whom the honor falls in rotation."

Iblis stroked his mustache. "You likely chose us knowing our experience being the disavowed had given us the fortitude to stand up to the Host and the Consortium if we believed the Mids were not ready to defend themselves without the aid of the ether."

Lucifer was departing the role, and the twins Harut and Marut were readying to take it. Samael, Iblis, and Azazel were unencumbered by the transition at the time the ether was created, Sophia explained. *You picked knowledge gods as watchers and keepers because we were your eyes and mind while your attentions were elsewhere. Your choice of these specific archangels similarly suits.*

Bix followed the path of memories unlocked by their

explanations. Since memories were relational not linear, she couldn't pinpoint time or sequence, but two themes repeated regardless. The words varied as languages do, but the concepts were consistent. The most contemporary application of the concepts…

"Parrhesia. Satyagraha," Bix said, overenunciating. The shards spun like dials seeking north.

"Parrhesia is courage in speech. Greek in origin." Azazel sidled closer to the shards. "Satyagraha is Sanskrit for truth held firmly."

"Both are linked to nonviolent civil disobedience." Iblis gestured to the pulpit, then to the counter-crossed corner and the statue within. "The Reverend Doctor Martin Luther King Jr. gave his final sermon at this pulpit. That was the message of his sermon."

"Speaking truth to power," Samael added dryly. "Mahatma Gandhi named his rebellion methodology satyagraha. He too popularized the notion of speaking truth to power. A bit too contemporary for a cosmic entity who'd checked out of existence at the time."

"I'm the High Executioner for All Worlds. I tend to ask questions before I decide whether things need to be permanently ended." Bix glowered at Samael. "The concept of speaking truth to power is nearly as old as the concept of power. Besides, Greek and Sanskrit were in use when I 'checked out,' as you put it."

"The Chimera is the power who seeks our truth." Azazel steepled his hands in front of him. "Which truth, I wonder?"

"The shards take down the ether, so our truth is tied up with the Devourers, Resen, or our general readiness for war against a foreign army." Samael leaned back as a pair of spinning shards repelled each other and one headed his way. Bix's darkness caught it before it went too far.

"My truth, Chimera: I don't trust the pantheons to defend us or these Worlds once they are truly challenged by the Devourers," Iblis stated, his tone cold. "I believe they will turn tail and abandon this collective to save themselves."

A third of the shards zipped toward each other like daggers, fitting together into a larger shard. The seams glowed platinum and tin. The pieces pulsed murky pewter.

Azazel and Samael stared at the larger shard, then at each other. Samael gave a curt nod. Azazel sighed and focused on Bix, black eyes gleaming as hard resolution took hold of his features.

"My truth, Chimera: I oversee the Host's armory. Once we discovered angel bones were capable of harming you, we slaughtered our own to stockpile. We were smug, confident. If our bones could hurt you, then they should annihilate any lesser entity regardless of origin."

Bix refrained from mentioning the window of opportunity for angel bones inflicting any notable physical damage to her had passed. The more of her memories she reclaimed, the fewer her vulnerabilities. It was the simple matter of growing into her cosmic self again.

"When the Devourers started to hunt us, we used the bones of our dead to defend ourselves and quickly discovered our presumptuous fallacy. Our weapons fueled our foes." Azazel paused. The muscles in his jaw twitched, and his lips pursed to a white line. Heartbeats passed before he spoke again. "We then created angels whose sole purpose was to be captured by the enemy and serve as beacons for us to locate enemy camps. We condemned them to the prolonged misery of being livestock for the Devourers. It is a delaying tactic and a fit punishment for us, the archangels, because we feel every indignity suffered by one of our angels. We are ashamed of our arrogance and of how far we fell from grace in our need to feel superior to you."

Half the remaining shards whirled, then affixed themselves to the larger shard. The bigger piece hummed softly; the undulations of dark pewter slowed.

"My truth, Chimera?" Samael rubbed his neck. "Once you signed the contract to create the ether, the Consortium never intended to build a defense. Instead, we committed our resources to finding whatever it was you wanted protected here in the Mids, so that we could exploit it and you to eradicate all enemies for us in perpetuity. We never identified the original Berserker as the target until your recent return from exile. It's my job to catalogue all your weaknesses—persons, places, ideals—for future use by the Host."

Sophia croaked a gasp. The weight of her gaze burned Bix's back as the final shards found their places in the greater piece. The seams faded, the colors stabilized, and the humming ceased, leaving a polished pewter isosceles triangle the length of Bix's forearm.

A chuckle burbled up Bix's throat. She knew what form the containment prism would be. Her sacred symbol. The seven-sided pyramid. Six sides and a base. However, Bix couldn't create something from nothing. That was a skill she would never possess, so she wasn't the manufacturer of the containment pyramid. Her siblings, however, were prolific creationists, and one of them had made this piece of the pyramid for her. Not one of the four elders with whom she'd become reacquainted. No, she knew their magical resonances now. That left one of the younger twins, the fraternal pairing of one brother and one sister. Both of whom had given her ample reasons to distrust them. She turned the triangle over and over in her hands as the resonance of this piece jiggled memories until a cluster came rolling into her consciousness.

Tempest. The daughter aligned to their mother, the Chaos. The instigator of Bix's torment in the ether after she'd given up her magics and memories. The perpetrator of countless mental and physical agonies.

Well, shit. This mission just got a million times worse for her mental stability. Her problems, though. She wouldn't allow them to become the Mids' problems. Eyes on the mission; it was the only way to get through this without losing control of her crazy.

"A correction to your catalogue, Samael. Tobek's not my pressure point." Bix wagged the triangle at her ally. She didn't bear him any ill will for his confession. She'd known from the get-go he was collecting dirt on her to be used at a future date. That's what allies did. It was part of the information game that shaped governments and influenced all players. Hell, it wasn't like she hadn't done the same to him, and she had more than dirt on Samael—she had his wings. Flap. Flap. "Tobek is immortal. He has, and will continue to, suffer great horrors inflicted by powers you are only beginning to imagine. However, should the Consortium seek to harm him in the future, it is not I who will hold them to account. It will be the foundational magics of the Mids. The very magics that enable the Host's existence."

That earned multiple looks of astonishment, some of which faded into perplexed scowls.

"For the record, what I wanted protected in the Mids was the collective itself. Same as I do now. Should the Host choose to be suicidal, again, then have at it. Pretty sure you will blink before I do." Bix took a page from the archangels' book and folded the triangle into her darkness, then folded her darkness into her corporeal state. The containment piece tickled like a butterfly's kiss. "And yes, Iblis, I am aware of those within the pantheons who will choose cowardice over courage, and that they are in no small number. Then again, the new Chairman of the Consortium is also aware of them. When mettle is tested, you and I may be pleasantly surprised by the gods who have been forgotten by the Mids, but who have not forgotten us. And, Azazel, as you say, you and the other archangels are already suffering the price of your sins. Let's hope the lesson sticks, for a few millennia at least."

Azazel bowed and tucked his wings into his back. "It has been an honor to be entrusted with the welfare of the Mids and to have our truths heard and fairly judged."

"An honor indeed, great Chimera." Iblis inclined his head. He kept his wings on full display as he assessed the ruins of the cathedral and the gardens growing from the blood of the wounded angels. All flora indigenous to the Mids began with the spilled blood of angels; the type of plant depended on the angel. The floral variety within the cathedral proved the demons had been earnest in their pursuit of the shards.

"Thank you for being honest and for keeping the shards safe

until I was ready to come for them. My condolences that your angels were injured in the process." Bix sent a message via her smartwatch, checking the location of her team members. "I'll leave the cleaning to you who possess the magic to repair the cathedral. Sophia and I are going to round up the rest of the shards."

Bix did a double take at the response flashing across her watch's screen. Her team was in the same place, waiting on her. At this hour? Something was up. Opening gates, she lingered when Samael tapped her shoulder.

"No matter what intel I've gathered on you, I would never offer up the mortals you care about. You know that, right?" he grumbled.

"They grow on you, those mortals, don't they?" Bix grinned and leaned toward him. "You excel in this role of the disavowed because you care about these Worlds and their occupants more than you care about accruing power, Samael. As the years stretch to centuries and beyond, and mortals come and go, you'll know deep in your bones that you and I want the same core thing. No amount of propaganda or politics will change that."

He stood straighter and rolled his shoulders, grunting with confirmation and the barest hint of a smile.

With that settled, Bix whisked Sophia to meet the team that would help them track down the remaining segments of the pyramid and figure out what—or rather who—was behind the attack of the demons.

CHAPTER 6

Built on the banks of the Potomac River across from DC and nestled between Reagan National Airport and Old Town Alexandria, the multiple buildings of the renovated coal plant sprawled across twenty-five acres that served as the base for Tobek's battalion of Berserkers. The beer hall on the ground floor of the main building bustled as early morning sun struggled through the long front windows that had been hand-painted to reflect the assorted winter holidays. Big burly dudes of a variety of skin tones, haircuts, tattoos, and casual attire filled the rows of heavy wooden tables and benches, while still more men pushed carts of food, swapping out empty platters for full ones. The aromas of seasoned meats, saucy vegetables, and warm breads added to the cozy welcome of jovial banter and loud guffaws.

Berserker brunch. It was a weekly bonding thing, kind of like game day and movie night. Attendance wasn't mandatory, but judging by the turnout, most of the guys living in the main building were here along with clusters from the other barracks on base.

Free food explained why the youngest member of Bix's team was crashing brunch with the boys; didn't explain why the other two were.

"Pretty lady," shouted the lone diminutive male among the overly brawny. Passed like a chunky baby over the heads of Berserkers from the far side of the hall to the doorway in which Bix and Sophia lingered, Gurp, the majordomo of the base, arrived in full mutter and grumble. Set gently on the ground again, he straightened his tunic over his potbelly. "He cook. I get?"

Gurp was referring to Tobek. Bix didn't blame the goblin for the assumption since she didn't usually butt in on the brotherhood unless she was up to something, which typically involved the battalion's commander. If Tobek was taking a moment away from planning Resen's launch to feed his troops, then he needed the mental reset as much as the physical reconnection. Leading from within rather than from a desk was one of the many traits she admired about her Berserker.

"And distract him from his stress relief? Not on my account. I'm here for my squad of hungry spies anyway." Bix waved to said trio sitting shoulder to shoulder amid the soldiers. The youngest of her team was chipmunking his food. Pale, unshaven cheeks strained to contain what might be cinnamon rolls. In his defense, his intense focus on the guy sitting across from him plus the pounding and chanting coming from his tablemates hinted at an eating contest. Boys. Pfft. "Sophia, this is the indispensable Gurp, master of all things."

Bix spared a glance for the goddess's reaction to the goblin. Goblins as a race were reviled for many reasons, most of which could be blamed on their diet of everything from overflowing trash dumpster—including the metal frame—to napalm. This goblin, however, was cherished by everyone in the compound for his skills, his loyalty, and his bond to Tobek. If Sophia got on her high horse, then the knowledge goddess couldn't read a room, which would make her a liability on the other stops the mission required.

Master Gurp, it has been far too long. Sophia curtsied before the squat goblin, presumably speaking into his mind as well.

Gurp cut the goddess a sly look and sidled close enough to

hook a pudgy finger in the rosary hanging from Sophia's hip. "I bring pictures. Help you better blend. Yes?"

You don't approve of my attire? Sophia feigned affront. *I assure you, I was quite the hit at the night club.*

Gurp chuckled hard enough his belly quivered. "Meet in clinic. Come, come."

Bix obediently followed the goblin down the iron-clad back hallway that connected the main rooms on the ground floor. Gurp detoured into the body-modification shop operated by the artists within the battalion. The shop was still dark. It was far too early to welcome the customers of the day.

A public space within a military base? Sophia cocked her head. *Seems that would invite trouble.*

"Closing themselves off from the surrounding community would pose more problems." Bix skimmed her fingers over the half wall that separated Tobek's stall from the others. "This shop caters mostly to Chweds who bring the guys the latest gossip while they have work done. Happy customers are, of course, happy to reassure the community that the Berserkers are a benefit to everyone's safety. Symbiotic."

Considering our close proximity to the Consortium, their staffers, and the guild masters, it's easy information gathering too. Sophia nodded, accepting a handful of tattoo magazines from the goblin. *I understand now.*

Gurp resumed the short walk to the stainless-steel morgue that also served as a science lab, medical clinic, and semiprivate meeting room at the far end of the plant. Hydraulic locks hissed, and the heavy door opened to two mortician's tables occupying the back of the cold shiny room and two padded convertible surgical chairs in the front quadrants. A long wall of freezers stood across from a wall of cabinets, autoclaves, and assorted machines. Monitors hung from the stainless-steel ceiling on mechanical arms. An orange drench shower in the rear corner offered the lone flare of color. Recessed lights dimmed to a soft amber prevented a harsh glare from bouncing off all the metal.

This is far more welcoming than the Consortium's clinic, Sophia noted, clasping the magazines to her chest as she inspected the morgue. *Though I admit I expected a barbershop, not a place to dissect the dead.*

"Pretty sure the guys are fluent in multiple uses of a straight razor," Bix quipped.

"They're opening a men's grooming salon in another building soon. All the beard and back wax a hirsute gentleman could need." Ashtad Ba'al, Bix's former team leader in the spy game and the premier broker of demigod challenges, strolled through the open door, rolling up the sleeves of his marled ivory cardigan. He leaned against a table, eyes narrowing on the nun. He cut a questioning look at Bix, then twisted sharply as the goddess slapped her magazines on the table against which he was leaning. Confusion fluttered across his face before he bowed. "*The* Sophia? Your reputation precedes you. It is an honor."

A young Ba'al. Sophia raked Ashtad with a mixture of pity and disdain. *Your imperiousness reeks like rancid oil. It'll get more pungent once you ascend. Unfortunate family gene. Your great-grandfather is downright putrid.*

Bix choked on a gasp clashing with a snicker. Sophia wasn't wrong; Ashtad was an elitist but strove to compensate for his bias. Sometimes.

"He is an exceptionally arrogant ass, I agree." Ashtad laughed outright. "Ashtad Ba'al, my goddess."

Sophia's eyes crinkled at the corners, and her rigid posture relaxed. *The decision to learn from the original Berserker rather than fight him is a wise one, young Ba'al. You will make enemies within your pantheon because of it, but you will earn greater opportunities as well.*

Ashtad tipped his head toward Bix. "Imagine what befriending the Chimera during my trials is doing for me."

Sophia cringed, then looked up. *That is an interesting quandary. The Chimera's influence on a demigod's trials have historically ended poorly for the demigod, usually because the demigod attempted to interfere in events far greater than their comprehension.*

"That's not reassuring." Ashtad glared at Bix.

Bix blew her dear friend a kiss. "Ashtad is one of the architects of Resen. He's clearer than most regarding the big picture."

The foundational elements of the Mid Worlds chose to heed a demigod? Sophia blinked rapidly.

"The other underqualified architect is guzzling milk to wash down his second-place finish of fifteen cinnamon rolls in five minutes. He will be joining us in a moment." Ashtad jerked his thumb over his shoulder.

"I'm here, I'm here." Cian, the youngest member of Bix's team, made a sterling first impression with a long belch to end his introduction. "Excuse me."

Sophia turned to Bix with lashes still fluttering. *A child?*

"A Sage," Bix corrected. "Recently aged to a legal adult by human standards. You two have more than acquaintances in common. The Devourers have left him with physical impediments as well."

Sophia swept to Cian with the speed of the divine, catching the kid mid squat above a rolling stool.

"Whoa. Hi there, Sister Space Invader," Cian muttered, but wisely froze.

The goddess's fingers curled over Cian's too broad, too solid, and too rugged shoulders, kneading his olive-green hoodie. The veins in her hands pushed against her skin, glowing from contact with the magic the kid was trying to hide. The crystals encasing Cian's shoulders pulsed in response, their gentle shimmer peeking from beneath the collar of his button-down. Sophia abruptly released the kid and stumbled back, staring at her hands. The threat of her curse faded.

"If you don't want to have a come to Jesus with a ley line, you'll keep your Devourer-tainted mitts off the herb nerd." An old man, liver spotted and crepey, moved with the Other World agility of the draugr inside him to push the stool under Cian with a baby-blue moccasin. "Sit, kid."

Anudrengr? gasped Sophia.

"Heya, Holy Ghost, been a while." The old man rolled Cian to the table, parking the kid across from Ashtad. "These days, it's Drew."

"Don't tell me." Ashtad wagged a finger between Sophia and Drew. "The Holy Ghost and Zombie Jesus."

Bix dropped her chin to mute a snorffle as her best friend mimicked Christ upon the cross and muttered something profoundly unchristian in Aramaic. With Drew's penchant for drama, Bix wasn't at all surprised to learn of his inability to resist residing within a celebrity of the age.

"Roomie, did you do it while he was still alive or wait until he was dead-dead?" Cian pumped the lever on his stool to raise his seat, eager interest animating his features.

"Dead-dead." Drew patted Cian on the head. "Souls like his aren't ones you want to provoke. They've been recycled a lot without being drained. You think you're going in for a box of Junior Mints and you wind up suffocating under a mountain of York Peppermint Patties."

Drew's stunts were canonized. Sophia chuckled. *The Angelic Host overlooked the involvement of an Other World creation in the second wave of their monotheism because the stories were crowd favorites.*

"The Host sent Mostly Ghostly here to evict me from their martyr, but she and I managed to claim a few days of wild and crazy before the suit lost its suitability." Drew hopped up on the mortician's table and grabbed a magazine. "If it's those chains you need to hide, Sophia, I suggest the goth punk look. The attire gives you more flexibility to do whatever it is Bixie has brought you in to do."

Everyone gathered around the same table and stared at Bix expectantly.

"In a nutshell, we're on a scavenger hunt." Bix unfolded her darkness from her spine, withdrawing the first of seven panels of the containment pyramid. The faint resonance of her sister's magic skittered over her skin.

Wards within the walls responded, gleaming silver and green and streaming spells. Alarm lights flashed blue and green. A sonic siren pitched above inhuman hearing wailed.

A cage of magic slammed around Bix.

CHAPTER 7

Had Bix been a god or lesser entity, the attacking magics of the cage would've dropped her in a heartbeat. Since she was who she was, the assault felt like a damp loofah, and the cage couldn't actually contain her. She stayed by choice on the off chance this was a system glitch and the guys watching up in Ops needed it on the record.

Gurp slapped his hands over his ears and glowered at a security camera. Perplexed silence held her team until a low guffaw drifted through the doorway. Tobek sauntered into the room, his hair in a net and a drying towel over his shoulder.

"Sorry about that, sweetheart." Tobek laid his palm against a wall. Hunter-green magic built around his hand and shut down the alarms. The cage faded, and with it the reminder to refresh her shower supplies. "I suppose I need to fine-tune things a bit more."

Bix reached across the table to pass the fragment to him. Cian's crystals sang out, and the kid leapt from his seat, flattening himself against the wall of freezers. The ginger stubble up his neck curled and burned away from the flare of his crystals.

"Okay, yeah, that's n-n-not good," Cian croaked.

Tobek closed the fingers of his prosthesis around the piece still held by Bix. The amalgam of plastic, rubber, and machinery crumbled into dust. He changed hands, cautiously gripping the triangle. The ink of his heavily tattooed arm and torso illuminated through his T-shirt. The green of his pupils lit, and the vibrant blue of his irises followed.

"Let go, Tobek," Bix quietly urged.

"I'm learning its resonance." His voice sounded as though it was rising from a deep well. "Cian is correct. You cannot store this in the Mids. It's more dangerous to all native life than the ether."

"Well, that's interesting, because original me scattered fragments of the remaining six pieces across the Mids." Bix tugged the panel, but Tobek held fast.

Five pieces, Sophia corrected, flipping through magazines. *The sixth is with gods who are prisoners of the Devourers in the ether. The seventh is there in your hand.*

Drew and Ashtad leaned warily on the table, getting closer to the piece remaining inert in Tobek's hand even though the Berserker himself was in full-blown woo. Gurp stayed way the hell away from the table, which was odd for the goblin, who prided himself on being a walking forensics lab. He busied himself checking on Cian, which wasn't odd, come to think of it. People first when it came to Gurp's great big heart.

"Chief gave us the heads-up that you're removing the ether so we can push Resen live." Ashtad got his hand within six inches of the triangle before he snatched it back with a wince. "If Resen was active, we could track the fragments by resonance, but…"

"Anything that's powerful enough to contain the magic of titans is going to be detrimental to any collective, not just the Mids." Drew succeeded in touching the triangle but lost half his hand as a result. Fortunately, the senses of a dead suit were minimal, so pain wasn't a problem and neither was viscera. "Makes sense the Devourers want the completed containment unit. What's stopping them?"

"The shards I gave to the Angelic Host were no bigger than a fingernail." Bix tugged the triangle again. "Could be that they can't sort the resonance of the fragments from Mids' magic."

"That's why they cursed Sophia." Tobek finally released the triangle and turned to the knowledge goddess. "Your tenure as the Holy Ghost taught you a lot about the variables in Mids' magic, meaning you *can* find the pieces, but you've chosen captivity instead."

When the game wants to use you as a pawn, you have to take yourself off the board. The personal cost be damned. Sophia glanced at Bix a beat too long before returning her attention to the magazines.

"Amen, sister. Bixie, babe, hit us with the rules of the scavenger hunt. You know I loves me a quest." Drew propped his chin on his mangled palm and batted his lashes.

"Seventeen hundred years ago, I divvied up the containment pyramid among the superpowers, the Chweds, the humans, and one other party." Bix folded the triangle within her darkness, then within her corporeal self. The balance of magic in the room settled and thrummed within normal parameters. "We have the angels' piece. I'm going after the dragons' next. Cian, can you take lead with the Fates?"

"He's got Resen to launch, sweetheart," Tobek reminded.

"I can make time between scripts and tests." Cian rubbed his neck and rejoined the group at the table, his crystals inactive now that the triangle was within the confines of Bix's person. "Don't suppose you can point me to the field of haystacks you're hoping to find that needle in?"

Bix stared at Tobek, wondering yet again why he didn't know more about this. He'd been her confidant and consort when the ether went up and centuries thereafter. Something didn't sit right. Tobek staring back at her with an inscrutable expression didn't give her warm fuzzies about the sitch either.

"Contrarians," Bix said, tearing her gaze away from her Berserker. "I need you to find the contrarians among the Houses of Fate. Who among them has the audacity to tell their leadership when they're wrong?"

The whole room snorted derisively. They all had history with the Fates, some more complicated than others. Cian, however, was a Sage questing to become a Fate, so the more he learned about them, the better his odds of passing his trials.

To whom would the leadership listen when being corrected? Sophia added, lining up three opened magazines on the table beside Drew. *You're not looking for opponents. Think advisors, the ones who aren't openly or regularly consulted.*

"Oh, like those CEOs who meet with psychics on the down low so the board doesn't find out." Cian bobbed his head. "Yeah, I get it. I get it. I think I know where to start."

"Good." Bix reveled in a pang of pride for the kid. The most mortal among them, yet he didn't flinch from the challenge that could instantly kill him if he exploited the wrong resource. "Drew, can you hit up the Chimera Fan Club? See if you can pin down gossip about artifacts that would've been introduced when the ether was created?"

"Seventeen hundred years is a long time, Bixie, even for Chweds. We're talkin' three cyclical wars when the Mids burn and society resets." Drew poked the center magazine and pushed it back to Sophia. "Whoever you gave the bitty-bits to back then ain't likely to have them now."

"Same problem with the humans," Tobek pointed out.

"I know. It's a toughie." Bix grimaced. "I don't have much detail to give you. You're not looking for a completed triangle like the one I showed you. You're looking for fragments of it that aren't the same shape, size, or smell. I didn't lick them to know about taste. I can tell you they repel each other until a unification rite is completed."

They also repel magics of all kinds. Sophia danced her fingers over the magazine image. Other World magic fluttered through the room as a copy of the page built atop the original. *The larger the piece, the more potent the power. I'd suggest asking after cumbersomely expensive artifact wards. The more despicable the person, the more likely they needed broad protection, the higher they drove the value of the shards.*

"Meaning they would've been traded in the Crimson Market and sought by the spy guild." Drew tapped a moccasin against

Ashtad's arm. "That's you, Sparky. You're the only one of us still employed by the spooks."

Ashtad nodded. "I'll check in with the Director, see if I can take a tour through the warehouses. That'll take time, though."

"Start with protection items we were sent to obtain," Bix suggested. "Both the team you recruited me into and the team Drew and I were on. Odds are the Fates knew about the shards and tried to put them in our paths to see if they'd trigger my memories in any way."

"Fair point. If I can at least find one shard as a guide, then I can ask the Director for resources to assist in locating others within the guild's possession." Ashtad inclined his head toward Tobek. "I can tag team with Cian on testing Resen so we don't lose momentum there."

The demigod should join me in hunting the demons who are also after the fragments. It will be beneficial to his trials. Sophia closed the magazines and restacked them.

"Demons?" Drew and Ashtad echoed in unison. The draugr looked repulsed, the demigod intrigued.

"Whose demons?" Tobek asked, detaching his fried prosthesis.

"Indraja's?" Ashtad imbued the goddess's name with notable vehemence merited by his time as prisoner of said goddess's turncoat flunkies. "She's a greater goddess with a history of enslaving lesser gods. She was behind the corruption of the Consortium, she's in league with the Devourers, and she's got a big bone to pick with you, Bix."

"We'd be fools to think it was anyone else, especially since the pantheons are supposedly in lockstep with Ogun now." Bix pressed her fingers into the cold steel table, quashing the urge to lash out at the mere mention of the greater goddess who'd been eluding her for months. For the harm Indraja had done to the Mids and Bix's friends, the goddess would suffer, but not before Bix exploited Indraja's connections and insights into the Devourer hierarchy. Bix wanted the Devourer leader who could call off this and all future invasions, and she needed leverage to get said leader to comply.

Indraja would've sent Devourers, not demons. She has neither the faith in nor the respect for her own kind. If she is behind this, then her alliance with the anti-gods is crumbling.

"Your acquaintance with her, is it recent or…?" Bix cocked her head, which was better than slapping her forehead. She should've guessed this earlier. It was so obvious. Sophia had been a prisoner of the Devourers and the Consortium, both of which had been corrupted by Indraja. Of course Sophia knew the damn greater goddess.

She is the means by which the Devourers caught your watchers, Chimera. Sophia spoke without intonation as she met Bix's regard. *She's been feeding gods to Devourers since our old foes began their occupation of the ether. Her familiarity with the old foes predates that, however. She was once a prisoner of theirs.*

"Are you telling me *she's* the reason they're here?" Tobek growled. "Did she offer up the Mids in exchange for her freedom?"

Sophia seemed to contemplate the question before slowly shaking her head. *I believe she followed them here. She fled this galaxy a very long time ago under a cloud of shame.*

"What better revenge than to use the old foes as the weapons against those who wronged her?" Drew grunted with a head bob and triple snaps.

What better revenge than to teach the enemy to hunt and thrive within a place where the pantheons discard their husked membership, thinking it a sanctuary?

"Fish in a barrel," Tobek harrumphed.

"No," Bix groaned. "Do *not* tell me she's hiding in the ether. All this time I've been hunting her?"

The ether was seemingly endless if one was inside its perimeter. Bix had wandered for years, even centuries, without setting foot on a border. There were no landmarks, seasons, or sunrises. It was vast pitch-black nothingness. Bumping into any other form of life was more coincidence than not—encounters with certain cosmic entities excluded.

She absolutely has a bolt-hole there, separate from the Devourer camp.

Sophia inclined her head. *I would bet all my knowledge on it.*

"It makes sense." Ashtad puffed a curl from his eye. "You've cut Indraja off from all other resources, Bix. You've turned all pantheons against her, husked her allies, dismantled her networks, and destroyed most of her Worlds. Where else could she hide?"

"Those Worlds of hers you've left intact, you're having monitored." Drew patted Bix's hand. "Got to admit, she would find a certain petty satisfaction claiming refuge in the very thing you created to protect the collective."

"All the more reason we need to retire the ether." Cian scratched his forearm and looked at everyone with wide-eyed eagerness. "Like soon, right?"

"Which returns us to the topic of the demons and the shards." Bix bumped the kid with her elbow. "Plan A, we use the shards as bait to lure Indraja out of hiding."

"Plan B, we use the demons to track her to her hiding place in the ether, then drag her ass out." Drew crossed his arms and scowled at his maimed hand. "Pantheons should be cleaning up this demon mess, not us."

"Sophia, you said they were cursed gods not lesser gods, right?" Ashtad leaned back on his stool as Sophia nodded. "That likely made them prime pickings for Indraja to recruit them to her cause. Now, if we can turn them against her, Drew is right, we can use them to get to her and to her base within the ether."

"And her base will lead us to the Devourer staging area," Tobek added.

I've deciphered the minds I took from the demons. They were punished gods, yes, I can confirm that, but I didn't spot Indraja in any of her guises within their memories. Sophia scowled and shook her head. *Again, if—and I must emphasize* if—*Indraja is behind this, then we're dealing with middlemen, possibly layers of them before we get to her.*

"Oh, come on. Who else would these demons follow? Indraja can remove those curses and help them get revenge. They clearly fear her more than me, because they gave zero shits about me being in the cathedral when they attacked the Host." Bix caught

Drew eyeing her oddly and Tobek watching her too intently. Tone. Too caustic? Emotions swinging too far to the contemptuous. Had to be. Damn it. "Sorry, I didn't intend to sound so dismissive."

Sophia kept her chin down but cast a furtive glance at Tobek. Tobek, however, only had eyes for Bix as he scratched his Eternal Knot buried beneath the layers of ink on his pec. Yeah, Bix was definitely getting a citation from the tone police. Awkward silence fell upon the room, until Sophia cleared her throat.

These demons exist on the fringe of divine society, which suggests whoever is calling the shots is also a fringe dweller but charismatic enough to unite them.

"That describes Indraja and a hundred other gods." Ashtad sighed. "However, Indraja has means, motive, and an abundance of opportunity."

"Not to mention a track record." Drew huffed.

They knew exactly what they were looking for, which means they have or have had a shard in their possession. We need all the pieces; thus, we need the demons' leader, whoever it might be. Sophia stepped away from the table. Ribbons of red light swirled around her. When they dissipated, the nun had become a fetid, tusked, scaled, and weeping-boils demon.

"That is so cool." Cian rolled closer to the goddess but kept his hands to himself. "Is that an illusion, or did you really change? Like insides out? Or is it like a latex suit?"

"Forgive him, Sophia," Drew blurted, shooting Cian a scornful glare. "He doesn't know that's an indelicate question to ask a god who is, of course, an expert shapeshifter."

The hunger of a young Sage for knowledge is dear to me. I take no offense. Sophia thoughtfully considered Cian. *Gods are quite vain. Our transformations are limited by our narcissism. However, my time imprisoned by the Devourers taught me to enhance my skills. They are, as a race, better at shapeshifting. For instance, I learned from them to root this change within what makes me a god rather than in the form my parents chose for me.*

"Your parents decide what you—"

"Later, herb nerd," Drew interjected as Ashtad snickered. "I'll explain the divine version of birth to you later. Suffice to say there's no standard like human births."

"I'd like to send some of my men with you, Sophia, to back you up and to run interference with mortals should the need arise." Tobek chucked his prosthesis to Gurp, who proceeded to inspect the damage in the way of goblins…by eating it.

"I volunteer, Chief," rasped an eavesdropper.

Tobek didn't appear the least surprised. He didn't even bother to turn around as Hywl, one of his lieutenants, rolled around the doorframe. Built big like his fellow soldiers, the Welshman had eschewed his usual casual attire of flannel and faded jeans for a Berserker's blue-and-black combat uniform. Hywl's vibrant blue eyes fixed on Sophia. A wealth of emotion flitted behind his lashes as the goddess pivoted toward him.

"Hywl?" Sophia croaked, her voice cruelly broken.

Taking two steps, the black-haired Berserker clasped his hands around Sophia's demonized waist and hoisted her in the air. He spun her around with a broad smile, cooing something unintelligible. In a slick move befitting any romantic movie, he set her on her large talon-tipped feet and tilted her over one arm to plant a kiss on her whelk-coated mouth.

Ashtad turned away, fist to his lips and cheeks puffing. Cian covered his eyes and rolled away from the couple with a groan. Gurp chortled and winked, wagging a piece of prosthesis at the pair.

"Aww," Drew squealed, fluttering a hand over his chest. "Love. Nothing else would explain kissing that. Nuh-uh. Nopety nope. Gotta be twu wuv."

Sophia curled a monstrous hand around Hywl's head, keeping him close.

Bix couldn't help staring. Not remotely the pairing she expected…except maybe? Hywl was an angel hunter. His successes as a regular guy had gotten him recruited into the ranks of the Berserkers. Sophia had been on a quest to stop the Angelic Host's spread of monotheism. Imagining them crossing paths didn't take much effort. Imagining how they'd progressed from there did.

Tobek ambled to Bix and tapped a finger under her chin, closing her thoughtless gape.

"I thought it was you two who had the history," Bix admitted.

"We do, but not that kind." Tobek draped an arm across Bix's shoulders. "Finding me to either kill me or learn from me is a rite of passage among demigods. Has been since I traded my divinity to the Fates. You own the blame for their introduction, however. You were the stars he followed at night, and he followed you to her."

"Was that intentional on my part?" Bix searched for those memories. Flashes of gore and spatter amid agonized screams answered. She pinched the bridge of her nose hard, the discomfort necessary to force those memories to retreat without further examination. Those sounds and visions were too close to her experiences in the ether, and she wasn't remotely prepared to face any part of that.

"Couldn't say." Tobek kissed her temple, then cleared his throat, loudly. "All right, Hywl. That's a fine welcome. Why don't you round up green team and get them ready for demon hunting?"

Sophia released the Berserker as Hywl set her upright to tower over him in her demonic form.

"On it, Chief." Hywl saluted Tobek, tossed a wink to his demon, then loped to the beer hall.

If Sophia was the least bit embarrassed, it didn't show. In fact, she simply gathered the copy of the magazine image she'd made, folded it, and slid it beneath her scales. *I'll wait here until they're ready. We'll need a gate back to the cathedral, if you would, Chimera? Parking lot will do. Each demon had a different rendezvous spot with their handler, but they were all here.*

"In the Primary Mid World?" Tobek asked.

In the greater metro area. They've been recently summoned, though by whom is still a question. I'll get to the middlemen, then to the top. You may leave it with me.

"Gurp and I will plug the guys with trackers before they ship out," Cian offered, rolling to a computer station. "We'll triangulate, see if we can't come up with the demons' hiding place."

"Nasty nest." Gurp waddled to the wall of cabinets to prepare a tray of injectable trackers.

"Bixie, if you can drop me at my favorite shop, I'll pick up a new suit, then hit the local branch of the Chimera Fan Club for leads on the Chwed bits." Drew stomped his feet and tossed Bix a smile. "I'll be in touch via comms. We'll find your lost toy, babe, don't you worry."

"Thanks, Drew." Bix opened a gate to a District hospital morgue, and Drew dropped through it.

"Bix, if I could get a gate to the Smithsonian Metro, I'll set a meeting with the director of the spy guild, then recruit some demis to help with the demon hunt." Ashtad clapped Cian on the shoulder. "Send me green team's location when they deploy, would you?"

Cian gave Ashtad a thumbs-up.

Bix provided the requested gate. Once Ashtad was clear, she closed it and eyed Sophia. "You don't mind the other demis tagging along, do you?"

As long as there are gods, there will be Devourers. They exist to be our cosmic balance. You told me that when you asked me to be a watcher. You wanted me to study my foes, to understand them as I understood humans, to become an expert who could educate my fellow gods. Sophia stared with curiosity at Cian's computer screen while his rapid typing sent code scrolling in a blur. *Knowledge is of little use if it is not shared, thus I welcome the participation of the pantheons' youth. It pleases me that so many are involved in the fight against the old foes. Those who survive and ascend will be leaders in the next war and the ones after that.*

More questions died on Bix's tongue as green team thundered down the hall and burst into the clinic, eager grins abounding and mixing with triple takes at the very large demon in the middle of the room.

"Green team, you know how to reach me if you need me," Bix said, creating a gate to a stand of trees behind National Cathedral and leaving it open in case of emergency. The coal plant's wards would block any unauthorized users. "Good luck, all, and thank you."

The team's unified, "My lady," accompanied salutes. With a wave, Bix dropped herself into the basement of the building. She had a meeting with some dragons to arrange, and a desire to brush broken stained glass out of her hair and cleavage.

CHAPTER 8

B ix stood in the middle of the very girly teal bedroom Gurp had rebuilt for her in the northwestern portion of the modern-industrial-antiquarian-chic basement of the coal plant that he and Tobek called home. Scents of sandalwood and cedar wafted on drafts from the exposed ductwork in the high ceiling. Cozy lighting came from lamps, reflecting off the translucent sigils painted over dark matte-gray foundation walls. Originally, Gurp had built her a pink room, but events had happened that had forced her to move out. The teal was his way of acknowledging the changes they'd all gone through since he'd first built her haven of femininity amid all the masculinity. One of a thousand reasons she adored that goblin.

Bending at the waist, Bix dusted debris from the cathedral conflict from her bra, then shook out her hair. Glass plinked as it scattered along the concrete floor. Pinpricks of anticipation rose up the back of her stocking-clad thighs and fanned across her backside.

"Even though we're no longer connected, I can still feel your presence." She peered through her legs at her big blond Berserker leaning against the cubby shelving that comprised the walls of her room. His smile was one of appreciative intimacy that made her blush until her ears burned.

"Gurp's filled your closets and provided a wide assortment of shoes, as you can see. He's anxious for you to move back in. As am I." Tobek picked her dress off her bed and crumpled it in his big mitt. Magic glowed around his fist. A moment later, a new black dress hung from his finger. This one more suitable to the winter weather of the DC area. "I thought you were looking forward to coming home. Did something change?"

"We did." She straightened and took the dress he offered. "We severed our bond. You can't protect the guys from me in my unstable moments anymore. Until I can do that for myself, it doesn't seem fair to jeopardize Gurp or them by making this my sanctuary. Let's face it, I risk them enough with my crazy missions and the fact I can't stay away from you when I sleep."

"If that's all it is, then I understand." He tucked her hair behind her ear. "Take the time you need to be more confident in yourself, but know that you are wanted. Wherever I have a home, it will always be your home too."

"Nice answer, Mister Smooth-Talker." She shimmied into her dress and presented her back to him. She hated being alone; she'd spent her formative years in forced isolation. She was the only one of her siblings without a twin. She, well, she genuinely *liked* people. Tobek knew it, but he wouldn't push. He wouldn't smother. Some women might question their lover's commitment and desire in similar situations. Not she. Not with him. He showed his feelings for her repeatedly in actions big and small. It could be unnerving, how he refused to falter in his steadfast devotion, but there was no greater comfort than knowing he was there for her.

"We may not have a direct link to each other's emotions anymore, but we've lived together long enough for me to be fluent in your body language." He zipped her in and kissed her nape. "The merest reference to the ether and your hackles go up. For example, upstairs at the briefing and right now. Talk to me. We promised each other we would learn to communicate like normal couples, right? I'm holding you to that."

"Don't you have a defense system to launch?" She reached over her shoulder and tweaked his beard.

"Nothing is more important to me than you." He slid his hand around her waist and tugged her against his chest. "We've never spoken about your time in the ether. We should. What happened?"

She really, really, really didn't want to go there, but she couldn't cope with all the bad on her own. Baby steps. She could sort of do this. With him. Yep. Maybe just a little seep of the emotional storm front brewing inside her.

"I was in the ether in this corporeal state, not my native." She leaned against him, drawing on his stability, her forever rock. "This form is vulnerable. It feels pain and bleeds and breaks and starves. There was a whole lot of that going on once I regained consciousness. Most of it wasn't self-inflicted."

"Oh, sweetheart," Tobek groaned with a wealth of pity. His broad hand stroked her side, the slow friction reassuring.

"That's the first of many things that don't make sense, you know?" She thumped her head against his firm muscles. "How, if I didn't know my ass from my elbow, was I able to hold my corporeal form? How could I be utterly unaware that it wasn't my base state? How did I not automatically revert to midnight and starlight when I gave up my marbles?"

"Good questions," he conceded.

"Most of all, why did I do it?" She flailed her hands in mounting frustration. "Why did I give up my memories? Why did I give away my power, my knowledge, and my place in the cosmos? Why did I run away from my life with you? We were told it was to reinforce the ether, but Sophia debunked that. So what the hell really happened?"

He inhaled slowly. Too slowly.

She pivoted sharply to face him. "What? You're not cursed to silence anymore. Tell me."

There was such sorrow rolling off his entire body that her breath caught.

"Tobek?" She curled her fingers over her heart as fear spiked.

"What happened to us? Why did I leave you?"

His hand trembled as he wiped his mouth. He looked away, his eyes brimming with unshed tears. He chewed his cheek and shook his head. At length, he finally whispered, "That's not a conversation we can have until you remember. That's not… I can't… We…"

She laid a hesitant hand on his arm. "Tobek?"

He pulled her close, burying his face in her hair. "When you remember, know that I am here with open arms. When you are truly ready to talk about it, we will finally talk about it. But we can't discuss why you left me until you remember. It will do more damage than good."

She shivered from the vehemence in his rasp. She knew she had the answer, that it was part of that blister of roiling memories she kept walled behind thorns of malice within her mind. She knew her family was involved. She knew Tobek was involved. That was all she knew with confidence. Until she was certain she had the whole story, she wasn't going to poke it, and she sure as shit wasn't going to do it in any populated area. Every breath she drew warned her that she would end Worlds once she ripped open that festering sack.

"Can we talk about the creation of the ether instead?" she mumbled into his pec. It bothered her that he was so clueless about something that had altered all lives in the Mids, including his.

He huffed softly. "Yes. That's fair game."

"Did I consult you at all?"

"Initially, yes. We disagreed over you hearing the Consortium's plea for help, much less giving them aid. I was of the opinion that if the Consortium wasn't under pressure to act, they wouldn't."

"Well, you weren't wrong."

"Yes and no." He loosened his hold, allowing her room to breathe. "In the past year, we've pushed not only the Consortium to change, but also native magic itself. Hell, we've pushed ourselves to be greater than we were. So, in hindsight, I don't think we *could* have been ready to face the Devourers all those centuries ago.

Your gift of time to the Mids was arguably the right choice."

"And conceiving the ether, recruiting the watchers, dispersing the containment prism, I cut you out of those conversations too?" She leaned back to see his face, to see if he was angry about any of it. "I thought we were a team back then."

He laughed. "Oh, sweetheart, I wasn't qualified to participate in the brainstorming of the ether. Altering the *galaxy* in which we exist? To this day, such a concept wouldn't cross my mind. If you consulted anyone, it would've been your brothers. As for the rest, you didn't need me for that. Studying the Mids in all its microdetail was your hobby. It's what you, great cosmic entity that you are, did to relax. Besides, I think I was deployed to an Undine uprising at the time."

It was almost absurd that she'd been dealing with a World-collective issue while he'd been battling a national one. Macro and micro, one no less important than the other and no less distinct in skills and scope. "Our gross differences, they weren't a…thing?"

"A problem? Not after our first millennium together, my dear warden." He brushed his nose against hers. "Our relationship was, is, successful because we respect each other. Respect that was hard earned, mind. You have your life, I have my life, then we have our shared lives. We've had eons together to hammer out the finer points."

He'd never had the choice to leave her. He'd been her prisoner, chained to her by bonds emotional and magical. Frankly, *she* had problems wrapping her head around their relationship being anything more than aggressive Stockholm syndrome. He was free now. But that was super recent. There was no small part of her waiting for him to bolt and dreading it.

"Do you ever get mad at me? Or feel like I'm taking advantage of you?" she asked, half teasing. He seemed to be doing the bulk of the heavy lifting in their relationship these days, probably because she was afraid to remember the challenging parts.

This time, his laugh was full body. "I spent far too much of my life hating you to waste another breath being mad at you. Do

I ever disagree with you? Yes. Do I ever think your approach to something or someone could've been different? Yes. Am I ever hurt by your words or actions? Occasionally. But angry *at* you? No. Enraged by circumstances? Oh, yes. I am a very old curmudgeon with an abundance of free will, after all."

"I don't know why you stay with me, but thank you for doing so." She looped her arms around his neck and pushed up to her toes to plant a kiss that started as chaste but heated up as he demonstrated just how much he loved her…until her smartwatch vibrated in his ear. With a groan, she pulled back. "And now I have a meeting with a dragon queen. Good luck with Resen."

He watched her go, eyes crinkling at the corners and a wicked grin firmly in place.

CHAPTER 9

O ronoco Bay Park followed the curve of the Potomac River out of the touristy section of Old Town Alexandria into the residential. Clouds prevented the late morning sunshine from being too bright as it bounced off the ice creeping along the river. Snow covered the grassy park areas and turned the paved walking trail slick. Big fuzzy dogs in their thick winter coats bounded and frolicked in the plowed banks while sleek hounds in knitted couture lifted their noses to the scents of grilled meats and fresh baked goods rolling out of the restaurants and shops. Pet owners bundled in puffers and furry boots laughed and danced around each other, trying their best to keep leashes untangled and their coffees from spilling.

A lazy holiday happiness filled the air and extended to the pair of dragons in humanoid form ambling along the path. The dragon queen ascendant carried herself with confident refined elegance that had nothing to do with the lavender peplum coat tastefully embroidered with her royal crest, the perfectly tailored ivory wool slacks, or even the way the halo of her natural curls framed her sharp features. It lived in the unrushed movements and the unburdened kindness with which she greeted the World. Raspoine Dreigiau was simply majesty personified.

Raspoine's twin brother, on the other hand, seemed an unyielding monolith of unfun, stoic and taciturn. As his sister's enforcer, Rummir exuded peak Don't Fuck with Me energy, highlighted by the deep jewel-toned swirls inking his dark skin from nail bed to broad brow that branded him dragon royalty. Even the snow avoided falling on his tooled black leather coat. Mud didn't dare spatter over the ghost flames on his shit-kicker boots. For every passerby who looked a little too long at Raspoine, they found themselves stumbling away in haste once Rummir entered their line of sight.

"Raspoine, Rummir, thank you for taking time away from your Consortium obligations to meet with me," Bix greeted as the twins joined her on a small wooden lookout jutting above the rocky banks of the river. Across the Potomac, the full Consortium was in session, Ogun having summoned the representatives of the superpowers and their minions to do their damn jobs. The mixture of magics potent and lesser coursed outward from the District in invisible tides.

"Chimera, we are honored you have requested our aid in this time of the Mids' great need." Raspoine held out her hands and smiled beatifically. "How may the Dragon Horde be of assistance?"

"It's time for the ether to end." Bix squeezed Raspoine's hands, grinning as the dragon queen's pastel markings shimmered at her touch. Back when Bix had been nothing more than a burned spy on a desperate mission, the twins had provided insight and support, risking the censure of the reigning dragon queen and the corrupt Consortium. Once the presence of the Devourers and their Mid World collaborators had been confirmed, the twins' enviable political finesse had resulted in the surgical dismantling of the network of traitors within the Consortium. Where Archangel Samael operated outside the purview of government, the dragon twins were in the thick of it. They were probably using their lunch break to meet with her, so she didn't expect to have their attention for long.

"Finally," Rummir muttered, his serpentine plum eyes in constant motion.

"The Angelic Host will not be pleased," Raspoine said, casting an amused glance at her brother. "The Horde, however, will celebrate."

Dragons were natural rivals to angels. The two extremes constantly strove for superiority, which kept the Mids in balance. Where angels feasted on negativity, dragons gorged on positivity. Where angels owned the atmosphere, dragons controlled the terrain.

"You guys weren't fans of me doing it? Putting up the ether?"

"We had our reservations." Raspoine tipped her head, violet gaze taking in Bix from toe to crown. "The ether denies a view of the Worlds beyond ours. It bolstered isolation of more than the collective. It extended to the souls of mortals who exist here, down to an individual level. Forced sequestration feeds the seeds of hopelessness and depression. It stifles dreamers and limits imaginations."

"Feeding on that is how the angels amassed too much power," Bix guessed, extrapolating on the obvious. "Meanwhile, the Horde suffers?"

"Magic's potential is suppressed whenever imagination is. All magic, not just native." Raspoine looked to the clouds. "The gods bring chaos. In so doing, they expand the very concepts of unknowing while stringing along the hope of understanding. That fosters innovation, which is born from imagination. Think of creativity not rooted in desperation but in unencumbered potential. Wild. Boundless."

"Where each small success is a cause for joy untainted by fear. Joy amid oppression is a fleeting, despairing joy." Bix nodded as guilt tweaked her conscience. "The Dragon Horde's been eating tainted food for the last two millennia thanks to me."

Raspoine neither confirmed nor denied it. The dragon queen ascendant was too polite to do more than hint that the original Chimera had screwed over the Horde. No wonder most dragons didn't like Bix. She didn't blame them.

"I want to put an end to that. To do so, I need help locating dragons who would've been privately regarded as honorable opposition to the court of the Dreigiau back when the ether was created." Bix paused as Raspoine's attention cut to her brother. Rummir said nothing, but his scowl deepened. "Advisors, perhaps? Infrequently consulted and likely in secret."

"May I ask what they have to do with the ether?" Raspoine folded her hands in front of her, long fingers lacing.

"I gave them parts of a containment device for safe keeping. Large pieces would be fairly potent and act as magic repellants. Slivers might go undetected."

"Foreign magic?" Raspoine sighed when Bix nodded. "Then these keepers have been ostracized by the Horde. Possessing foreign magic causes atonal discordance in one's magical resonance, in a dragon's personal song. The Horde as a whole is a symphony. A wrong note can be corrected, but being perpetually out of tune cannot be abided."

Wow, Bix had really done a doozy on the dragon keepers. Good thing she was noncombustible, because she had a feeling she was going to be more than roasted when it came time for them to speak their truths.

"You're looking for the Seventh Sons," Rummir announced, his Danish accent incredibly thick compared to his sister's nearly imperceptible lilt. "They're a fraternity of the younger sons of the queens' enforcers. They believe it is their duty to live outside the queens' court among the lessers of the Horde and the Chwedlonol. As first-generation blood relations to an enforcer, they're raised amid the court, then depart when inducted into the society as adults. An enforcer might seek their counsel to introduce perspective when the court gets too myopic or too insulated."

Every dragon queen had an enforcer, a Rummir of their own. However, Rummir was an anomaly as the only dragon sibling of a queen. Queens didn't have mommies and daddies. They were born from pure native magic alongside an archangel and a ley line. Had the Dragon Horde not been an immutable matriarchy, Rummir would've been its lone king by right of birth. Nonetheless, he'd long ago made his decision to stand with his sister as her enforcer, rather than fracture the Horde by demanding his turn to rule. Not every dragon agreed with his choice, but they were in the minority for now.

"How do I get in touch with this secret society?"

Raspoine laughed brightly and held her hand up to her brother. Rummir raised his hand to meet his sister's, mirrored without touching. In the small gap between their palms, pastel magic built against jewel-toned magic. Music played, complex and beautiful, evoking joy and contentment with its allegro tempo as it swept from pianissimo to forte.

Except for a cluster of clattering and bleating that was nearly drowned out by the symphony, yet was undeniable if one listened for it.

"Shh," Raspoine urged, and the beautiful music quieted, allowing the rabble to be heard clearly.

Five sounds similar in tone rang out in clarity amid the discordant chorus. Like clowns in a tiny car racing through the orchestra pit, out of tune and out of time with the greater composition.

Raspoine pulled on the air above her fingertips, extracting five twists of purple magic as if plucking the clowns from their car. Faces took shape within the twists. Dragons in their natural form. Not looking happy at all.

"Rummir…" Raspoine whispered with a wealth of concern.

"I feel their distress too." Rummir honed his attention on the five images. "One more moment. I've almost got their location."

"Chimera, it is good you called on us when you did," Raspoine said far too calmly as anger ruffled her regal composure. "They are under attack."

Wrath surged against the confines of Bix's corporeal form, causing her skin to ripple and writhe. Gods damned demons. She'd gone too easy on them in the cathedral trying to work within the confines of politics. She hadn't broken Indraja's hold over them. Fine. Screw politics. She'd do it now.

"Show me," Bix demanded quietly.

"No time." Raspoine clasped her brother's hand.

"Trust us as you have before," Rummir urged as the bubble of dragon magic grew to encompass the platform.

The twins gripped Bix's wrists and whisked her away on a torrent of song amid streaks of lavender and plum.

CHAPTER 10

The Dragons' song of transport faded, and the din of physical battle took its place: the thudding of large bodies colliding, the grunts and bellows of vocalized effort. The tinny tang of blood and ichor lingered on the thick haze obscuring wherever the royal dragons had landed with Bix. It wasn't the Primary Mid World. It emitted a wholly different resonance. Bix might not have been able to see past her hands, but she could feel dichotomous magics and null spots.

Null spots meant humans were here, about a thousand in clusters forming a great big circle ten miles wide. They, however, were not her immediate concern. That belonged to the mirrored-surface portal hovering in the cloudy sky above the center of the humans' ring, disgorging Devourers by the baker's dozen. Devourers, not demons, were in pursuit of the shards. Long black hair streamed around crowns of pewter horns atop towering gray bodies in bronze uniforms. Devourers dropped from the gate into the haze carrying gruesome weapons that looked like patinaed copper but were far more indestructible. Battle cries doubled in volume, bestial and desperate.

"They dare," Raspoine seethed.

"Not for much longer," Rummir snarled.

Native magic surged on either side of Bix as the dragon twins shed their human forms. Bodies expanded with the depth of their breaths. Clothing unraveled seam by stitch by weave, reverting to tufts of raw fleece and sheets of tanned hide. The twins' innate magic lit the pastel and jewel-toned scrolls stretching along their skin as their flesh hardened to scales and their bodies distorted, elongating, bulking, growing fivefold until they shivered into their natural states of massive magic-breathing dragons.

Bix held perfectly still, not wanting to be crushed between enraged royalty.

The twins' shimmering leathery wings arched high into the cloud cover. With unified roars that unleashed plum and lavender flames, the twins swept their wings downward, propelling their bodies upward. Pure native magic ripped apart the haze to reveal a battlefield of puce and mauve mountains that formed the high sides of a bowl around a golden lake. A dozen gods armed with divine weapons spread around the shores of the lake. Vastly outnumbered by the Devourers, the gods fought as though their immortal lives depended on winning. Limbs lost to the Devourers' weapons and their flesh broiled by the spatter of the anti-gods, the gods refused to cede ground. Alas, their dragon compatriots weren't as resilient.

Humongous corpses of dragons spilled blood and intestines down the slopes of a mountain across the lake. Two wounded dragons raced to aid a third pinned down by Devourers. It was to that point of skirmish the royal twins flew. Their interlaced magics raised the mountains, shifting the terrain and increasing the slopes, causing Devourers to tumble like bowling pins toward the gods.

Dragons couldn't kill Devourers. Nothing made from Mids' magic could. Devourers consumed all types of magics. Fleshy bodies, plants, rocks, it didn't matter what form the magic held; all of it was edible to a Devourer. Gods, on the other hand, could kill anti-gods. Oh, gods would suffer in the process, but that was a price some happily paid for the thrill that broke up the monotony of immortality.

Bix, however, could end them all: dragons, gods, and anti-gods. High Executioner for All Worlds was a title that represented a mere fraction of her duties to the greater existence, but it was the title by which most of the Consortium members knew her. They expected her to kill both them and their enemies without mercy or concern. That wasn't quite how she operated. She didn't believe screwups should lead to death. This horror, this gruesome devastation, this sickening loss of life playing out around her was the consequence of the Consortium's screwup. Sure, the superpowers were fighting back now, when it was clearly too late. There were hundreds of Devourers teeming over the mountains and more still streaming through the portal.

It would be easy for her to exterminate the anti-gods. Messy, yes, but easy. Alas, Devourers served a purpose in the larger scheme of galaxies and gods. They, like the gods, were also her food source, so annihilating them was out of the question. Letting them destroy the Mids was also not going to happen.

For all that she was an executioner, she was far more an entity of balance.

A cosmic entity. One who really, really liked this collective of Worlds that her sisters had made specifically for *her*. *Her* playground. *Her* sanctuary. If she wanted to keep it, she had to empower the Consortium to be the caretakers her sisters had chosen to maintain this sanctuary. That meant she had to stay on mission: collect the shards, assemble the containment device, remove the ether, and support Resen's launch.

If Resen had been operational already, the Devourers' portal in the sky couldn't work. Enemy technology wouldn't keep belching more troops to overwhelm the few gods who remained standing. Once activated, Resen would repel the lesser foes, restrain the midlevel, and track the greater. If Resen was live, this small cooperative of dragons and gods could've successfully defended this World.

Yeah, but it wasn't, and it wouldn't be if she didn't put the kibosh on the Devourers adding the dragons' segments of the containment pyramid to those they'd stolen from the gods. The more pieces they amassed, the greater their weapon of cataclysmic destruction. That the Devourers hadn't yet used what they already possessed was either due to them not having enough parts or not having enough knowledge to use the broken bits. Bix didn't like either case being all that stood between the safety of the Mids and a calamity that could make the 1st century eruption of Mount Vesuvius seem like a mere dumpster fire.

A shudder of alarm violently wracked Bix, sending chills and goose bumps along her skin as anxiety pushed a frightening thought into her consciousness.

What if the Devourers took the shards out of the Mids? Beyond the ether? That would be disastrous. The anti-gods might not yet know how to use what they had, but it didn't erase Bix's need to complete the containment device. What if the anti-gods decided to lead her on a merry goose chase across galaxies while their other troops gobbled up the Mids? Thanks to Indraja and the knowledge gods they'd captured, the Devourers knew Bix wanted the shards. They probably also knew that as long as they kept the fragments beyond Bix's reach, they could delay the launch of Resen indefinitely too. If they took the shards beyond the Mids, Bix had no clue how she'd find them—the thieves or the shards.

"Focus, girl. Focus on the mission," she chided herself under her breath, hating how her wild emotions spiraled at the worst moments. How the hell had Tobek managed to function all these eons with her crazy slamming through him with such extremes? She had to be better at managing her mental state. She was a seasoned pro. She knew better than to let emotions interfere with an operation.

With a tsk of annoyance at herself and a hard mental shove to stow her feelings in boxes, Bix reverted to her native state of midnight and starlight. As the seventh child of the primeval Chaos and Cosmos, her presence defied boundaries. Larger than galaxies or as tiny as an electron, she could thrive wherever. Constraining herself to a defined size required a passing thought, one so insignificant that before the dragon twins rolled the tops of mountains around enemy troops like a Bûche de Noël, Bix had covered the World as a blanket of sentient night.

The first thing to go was the Devourers' portal. That, she simply knocked out of place, which caused the mirrored surface to ripple and bubble before collapsing in on itself, then winking out of existence. The troops that were halfway through didn't survive the collapse. Not her intention, but not something that would cost her any sleep either.

That left the anti-gods on the ground, the ones ducking and crouching as she pushed her amorphous self down from the atmosphere, over the mountains, and into the valleys. Militaristic to their tarry cores, Devourers nonetheless responded like the prey they were, shrinking from her predatory presence. Gates opened, swallowing the anti-gods and dumping them across the ether. If they arrived near wherever their greater army was staged, it was a fluke.

Next, she stretched her senses, verifying the absence of Devourer resonances. Native magic and null spots answered her query. Ah, and the quivers of divinity, some stronger than others, came from the gods sinking to their knees on the banks of the lake and roughly peeling their armor from their maimed, but rapidly healing, bodies.

There was something curious about the lake, a mixture of magics native and Other World. As much as Bix wanted to investigate, flutters as faint as agitated moths alerted her to the locations of the containment shards cocooned within burrlike prickles of native magic moving slowly along the mountains. Two dragon soldiers prowled around a third. The third dragon was grievously injured, the tingle of his magic less than the others. A problem not unnoticed by the royal twins, but not prioritized either.

Soaring above the mountain range, Rummir zigzagged north to south, while Raspoine flew east to west. They wove webs of purple magics that healed the land ruined by battle and buried the soil stained with Devourers' tarry blood. The twins glided through Bix's night, sure and strong, confident they had nothing to fear from the cosmic bogeyman.

They didn't, of course. Bix would never intentionally hurt either of them. So while they completed their care of this World, she compacted her form to something comparable to dragons in their natural state. Bix allowed her upper half to assume the shape of femininity without the defining flesh since she had a real hang-up about corporeal modesty. Her tentacles of night curled and coiled into a proper starry cloud as she settled beside the one dragon unable to rise.

"The night has chosen the form of a woman," the dragon gasped. Blood dribbled over the muted iris scales of his lips, adding to the pool running in cruel contrast beneath his body of pale thistle and wisteria. He lay on his side. A deep angry gash bled without signs of clotting from haunch to shoulder. The black bubbling edges of the wound confirmed a Devourer weapon had caused the damage. "Joyous praise to the eternal feminine."

The eternal feminine was Bix's mother, the Chaos, but Bix accepted the prayer with a smile nonetheless as she opened gates around herself to shield the dragon and his injured protectors from her overwhelming presence. The last thing she wanted to do was add to their discomfort.

"You have come for them, then?" one of the prowling dragons asked, his body so large, he had to drape himself over the ridge just to bring his head close to his fallen kin.

"Is it time at last?" The third dragon curled his body along the midrange of the bowl and hung his barbed tail down toward the lake. Though he lay behind Bix, he took pains to bend his long neck in such a way as to rest his chin beside her. "Will the poisonous blindfold of our hostage collective be removed?"

"The ether? Yes. It is time." Bix studied their fearsome wedge-shaped heads, their wide-set serpentine eyes, and the scutes that grew from their cheeks and brows. All different. The most wounded dragon had a horn like a rhino squarely between his nostrils, while the ridgeline dragon had an array of spikes more like an overgrown hedgehog. The dragon stretched beside her had spiraling horns that reminded her of her eldest brother.

Memories kept in networks of stars and aurorae flared and shifted within her, searching for the past that married the present. She didn't have all her wits, but she had five out of seven segments. There was a fair chance a recollection or two of these brave Seventh Sons...oh, ah. There. A cavern beneath a sea. Moisture had beaded on the walls, adding to the shimmer of crusted jewels waiting to be discovered. Faint light had come from the young dragons, from beneath their scales, from their mortal cores as they hummed a low song. The song had been a debate. Their own secret code. They'd thought she wouldn't understand their special language. She'd allowed them that false belief. She hadn't been there to school them; she'd been there to recruit them.

There had been five dragons in that cavern, not three.

She looked to the mountains surrounding the lake with intention this time, spotting the royal twins on opposite sides and noting how their wings sheltered corpses. In the haze of conflict, the dead dragons had blended in with the mountain range, but now there was no mistaking the hacked-up remains and entrails still gleaming with blood. If she'd had a physical heart in this state, it would've shriveled. First, from sorrow, then from panic, before settling into wrath.

"How did the Devourers know to find you here?" she asked, her voice barely a whisper as she fought to employ logic amid the onslaught of emotion. "How did they know which of you to pursue?"

The worrisomely injured dragon coughed more than sputum, and the ridge dragon shushed him before answering, "There's no way they could've known about us before they slew Jepp. They were crawling all over him, consuming him like a flock of vultures when they encountered his shard."

Bix didn't believe for one moment the Devourers hadn't known precisely who and what were here. Not with the anti-gods having the gods' shards. Not with Indraja's demons recently attacking the archangels. The timing was too coincidental. It was as if someone had tipped them off, as if someone had told the anti-gods to hurry up and get to the dragons before Bix did. But who? Who could've known that these specific dragons had the shards? Who would've known how to find them?

"The foes arrived as a company," the dying dragon wheezed with a slight convulsion. "After they met the gods' opposition, their reinforcements increased to a full regiment. That's when I called my brothers for aid. That's the only reason the five of us were in the same place at the same time."

"The five shard keepers," Bix clarified as certainty settled within her, feeding her shadowy thorns of malice and making her cloud of night a bit prickly. Either these dragons didn't see that they'd been tricked into coming together, or they were hoping she didn't notice they'd fallen for the ruse. "The second of your dead, he was also a shard keeper, yes?"

"Yes, and they took his piece too," the dragon beside her hissed, exhaling aubergine smoke. "We were helpless to stop them."

Damn it. The Devourers *had* gotten to two of the shards before her. She'd been too…too what? Too late? For sure. Too clueless and careless? Obviously. She'd broken the first rule of conflict: she'd underestimated the enemy. She couldn't afford setbacks like these. The Mids couldn't afford for her to make another mistake that would put more pieces of the containment device in the hands of the anti-gods. It'd be nothing short of a miracle if the Devourers kept the shards close to the Mids.

May the Powers That Be help her, she was actually hoping the anti-gods had cosmic weapons aimed at the Mids just so she'd know where to look for the lost pieces. How low she'd sunk, and this was only the second of seven segments.

Gah.

"To the Devourers, you are livestock. Be proud that you survived. The odds were not in your favor." Bix reached to stroke the dragon's snout, but her hand slid through the layers of gates, an invisible reminder of the threat she posed to her chosen champions. She silently cursed herself and the thieves. There was some component of this sprint to collect the shards that she was missing. Some unknown player was passing out cheat codes. It didn't bode well for the Mids or for her.

"Their original target must've been the Resen data center at the bottom of the lake," the ridge dragon insisted. "Why else would they be drawn to an otherwise unremarkable World?"

Resen was at the bottom of the lake? *Resen?* Someone was definitely spying on her team. Resen *plus* shards *plus* timing? None of this was a coinkidink, it was a godsdamned message.

Who was the sender?

CHAPTER 11

"Resen? Here?" Bix sighed, eyeing the lake once again. "Did the Consortium submerge the data center to mask it from enemy forces or from human curiosity?"

A Resen data center readying to come online would explain the magical oddities she'd sensed when she'd arrived on World. Security for a data center explained the gods fighting beside the dragons instead of haranguing each other. Neither of which explained *who* was working with Indraja to dispatch the Devourers on a shard-intercept mission. That the Devourers were involved confirmed Indraja's involvement, but Indraja and the Devourers had needed Sophia to track the shards of the containment device. Sophia wasn't cooperating with them, so who else had Indraja recruited? Who else could hunt the shards? Another cursed shard keeper? Bix could either track down the shards or track down this new player; she didn't have time to do both, not successfully. Damn it.

"To leverage physics." The dragon beside her twitched the tip of his barbed tail along the shore, earning an indignant cry from the god recuperating nearby. "The hope is that water will diffuse the heat generated by the machines integrated into the physical structure and from the anticipated direct connection to the network of foundational elements."

The foundational elements of Resen were the ley lines woven together with yarns of Fate that lay as a huge net around the collective Mid Worlds. At the moment, the elements communicated among themselves. The data centers were the mortals' means of interacting with the elements to register, restrain, or reject Other World entities from existing in the Mids. Resen's launch involved firing up the data centers to connect to the elemental network. There were hundreds of data centers across the Mids to load balance the influx of magic a direct connection would generate. A web within the net. Lots of humans were needed at every data center site to ground the magic of the connection. If Cian and Ashtad were incorrect in their load and grounding calculations, the result would be the explosion of a World. No pressure or anything.

"That means the humans I sensed earlier are here to ground the anticipated influx of overwhelming magic." Bix couldn't see a single man, woman, or child in the restored landscape. She felt them, though. "You hid them?"

"Refugees are all too familiar with taking cover," the dragon beside her said with a wealth of sadness. "The Seventh Sons have long been embedded with those discarded by society. We are the protectors living in their midst when the cruelty of the Fates forces them to flee. We keep the overpopulated ferry from sinking. We divert the mudslide racing for the camp. We create the spring of clean water amid the drought. We are unseen until we need to be seen."

"You still serve the greater good despite the Horde disowning you?" Bix's voice quavered with a surge of pride and humility. "Despite your service to me corrupting your personal song?"

"We serve Mids' magic, with or without the permission of authority. It is our duty and our honor." The dying dragon drew one curved talon along his throat. More blood spurted.

"Einar, no!"

Bix jerked her attention skyward as Rummir dove at the dying dragon, roaring the younger dragon's name again and again. The ridge dragon launched at the royal enforcer, knocking Rummir off the path of intervention.

"Let him do his duty, Onkel," the ridge dragon bellowed, slamming into the larger royal repeatedly as Rummir corrected his trajectory. "Let him finish what was begun when the queens couldn't be bothered to think of the least among us."

"I will not let him die under the delusion of martyrdom." Rummir rammed the ridge dragon, sending the smaller dragon spinning into the horizon.

"Brother, come, witness bravery with me," Raspoine beckoned gently. Her voice carried like a chime from the far side of the lake. Under the oranges and pinks of a twilight sky, her form shrank, her scales softened, and her body transformed to the statuesque human woman Bix had met on the banks of the Potomac River. Stepping through a shimmer of lavender song, the dragon queen ascendant took her place with the group of living shard keepers. Raspoine seemed so small standing in the loop of Einar's tail, a choice full of unspoken meaning, no doubt. Her humanoid hands laced in front of her as her gaze narrowed on the gruesome damage to Einar's side. "Please, Einar, do not let our guilt interfere in your journey."

With a roar of frustration, Rummir yielded to his sister's example and reverted to his humanoid form. Grumbling, he arrived on the high side of Bix, nearer Einar's head.

"We admit our ignorance and our failure," Rummir said flatly, his human features puckering in concern to belie his tone. "And when this is done, we *will* take you home to heal and rejoin in the song of the Horde. All of you."

The last was said as the ridge dragon returned to sprawl along the mountaintop, a snort of derision his only response.

Einar plunged two talons into his soft flesh. A gooey slurping sound preceded a pop. Behold, one long copper sliver radiating the magic of a First Child. It wasn't Tempest's magic. There was no abundance of chaos like that which had built the angels' portion. No, Einar's fragment pulsed with the primeval power of order, a very specific strain of order that identified Tempest's twin as its maker. Interesting.

Rummir grumbled a curse and stepped back. Raspoine grunted softly and her scrolls lit, but she didn't retreat. Along the shores of the lake, gods assembled, curious yet quiet, drawn by the power of the unguarded shard.

"Einar the Timid they called you, mistaking your lack of boastfulness for a lack of courage. They didn't understand how much you despise accolades for merely doing your duty to native magic." Bix smiled as bittersweet memories coalesced. She extended her hands of night beyond the cover of her gates as her darkness extracted the angels' panel from her form and set it on the cloud of her lap. "So I will not insult you with words of gratitude. Instead, I ask only for you to tell me your truth, Einar the Honorable."

"My t-truth," Einar gurgled. His shard hummed, awakening a honeyed glow that was answered by the pewter triangle in Bix's lap. "The Mids is not ready to stand against the foreign enemy. We will die because we, the superpowers, demanded to be *paid* to preserve our home. Avarice is our transgression against native magic. We, the community, will not learn our lesson without suffering tremendous personal tragedy. A brutal end at the hands of a race as uncaring as we have proven to be is precisely what we deserve."

Bix bowed her head, letting a tear fall for each wet gasp breaking up Einar's confession. His ending sigh sent his shard tumbling tip over end, past Bix's hands to fit itself at a slight angle to the completed angels' piece.

"Your truth has been heard, Einar the Honorable," she said with reverence. "The casualties will be staggering, as you have foreseen. That can no longer be avoided. What we have preserved is hope. Hope that from the ruins, a true cooperative will arise and propel the Mids into a harmonious future."

"Chimera, I offer my truth." The dragon lying beside her dragged his talon under his jaw and pulled free his shard.

Bix pivoted slightly to face him. "I will hear your truth,

Svante the Sure. You are slow to pass judgment, choosing instead to see all sides of a situation before forming an opinion. A trait undervalued, particularly by the long-lived and immortal."

"My truth is that the foreign army attacks us in ways that are horrific to every sense and sensibility of the Mids." He paused and licked his shard, wiping it clean of his blood. "It is a punishment, no doubt, but it is not meant for us. As you said, we are beneath the enemy's regard. Thus, the gruesome manner of our deaths is a punishment intended for you."

His shard flew to join to Einar's in the containment pyramid, while Bix's hand flew to her cheek as if she'd just been slapped. Svante's confession didn't make her mad, it just made her...think. She knew Indraja had a bone to pick with her, but according to Sophia, Indraja hadn't sent the Devourers to the Mids. The greater goddess had simply exploited an opportunity. Could Indraja's new shard hunter be this higher-ranking punisher? Yet another reason Bix needed to get her hands on the shot callers of the Devourer army. If someone was arrogant enough to think they could castigate her, the High Executioner for All Worlds, that someone was... Thorns of malice sharpened within her cloud of night and stars.

Later. Thoughts for later.

The purpose of the shard keepers' confessions was to gain *their* perspective on the future of the Mids. For the original Chimera to judge whether the collective was truly willing to fight for their continued existence. That last bit came to her in a rush of certainty.

Willing to fight.

Not necessarily ready, but willing. Together. All of them. Even the less magical races. That was why she'd given shards to humans and Chweds in addition to the superpowers. Everybody had to be on board. Everybody had to be willing to fight together for the future of their home. Man, she'd had some high expectations. Seriously.

"Thank you, Svante the Sure. Your truth has been heard and your point considered. Your insight is valid and useful."

Svante inclined his head as his body rippled, compressing. The grinding of his scales echoed the grinding of his bones as he assumed the form of a human man and revealed the flesh and muscle missing from his left leg, likely consumed by Devourers.

Raspoine gasped and reached for Svante, but stopped herself when the younger dragon stiffened.

"My apologies," the dragon queen ascendant murmured. "Now is not the time. The rite must be completed first. Forgive my intrusion."

Bix wasn't sure which of the male dragons appeared most stunned. Probably wasn't every day they heard a queen apologize. That was one of the things Bix liked about Raspoine—the queen ascendant blended compassion with authority.

"Malthe the Rigorous," Bix called to the ridge dragon. "Your truth, if you are ready to give it?"

"My truth, mighty Chimera." The ridge dragon stood upon his hind legs, spine straight, head framed by the clouds. He sliced under the scales protecting his armpit and produced his blood-coated shard. He shook the shard, spraying his blood—rather deliberately—over Rummir.

Rummir turned with a scowl. A flick of his middle finger over his shoulder and the spatter vanished. "Don't let my presence deter your confession, Malthe."

"Never has, Onkel." Malthe's sneer started in the muzzle of a dragon yet cemented in the face of a human neither young nor middle-aged as the dragon assumed the smaller form. "Chimera, my truth is that tradition should never be an excuse for exclusion."

"Here we go," Rummir muttered, crossing his arms and earning a searing look of reproach from his sister.

Bix gestured to the shard vibrating in the younger dragon's hand. "That is not the whole of your revelation. Be frank with your truth to power."

"The Horde is a matriarchy, resistant to evolution. Yet it is our duty to native magic to help all magic evolve." Malthe limped downhill, wincing. He turned to stand toe to toe with Rummir, exposing the raw, blistered skin across his lower back that extended below his waistband, possibly down the backs of his thighs. Likely caused by a blast of Devourer magic. No wonder he'd chosen to sprawl rather than sit. Ouch. "The ley lines could not have been clearer with their desire to have at least one male dragon sit in rotation of rule over the Horde."

"We've been through this," Rummir hissed. "It's not a matter for the Chimera."

"She asked for *my* truth, Onkel. Mine." Malthe cut his lilac gaze to Bix. "The males of the Horde are not asking to have the only voice in determining our future. We don't wish to overthrow the matriarchy. However, to evolve as a species and to push native magic to evolve, our gender should have an equal voice."

Bix refrained from glancing at Raspoine. The males' efforts to destroy the dragon matriarchy was no secret. Nor was it Malthe's actual truth. It was grandstanding before an audience who wouldn't take him to task as long as she was here.

"Satyagraha, Malthe," Bix sighed with annoyance creeping into her tone. "The shard has been a part of you for over a millennium. It has tuned to the truth of your heart. It will not join the other pieces without you setting it free. Without your contribution, the ether stays, and the Horde continues to feed on tainted happiness. Magic will only evolve so far with the Horde suffering malnutrition."

"Fine." Malthe closed the distance to Bix, stopping just shy of her gates. He eyed the invisible barrier with suspicion before exhaling loudly. "My truth is that the punishment Svante noted has devolved into a siege by design. Our prolonged torture is intended to gain your compliance in some unknown matter. It's an old-school tactic, straight from an enforcer's war book, just on a grander scale. You told someone no, so they're slaughtering your villagers until you say yes. History is full of examples of how well this strategy works."

At that, his shard spun free of his grip and soldered itself to the other pieces. Bix stared at the partial copper panel, dumbfounded. Could the dragon be right? It was a perspective she hadn't entertained at all. She looked again at Einar, who nodded and wheezed. Svante also nodded, resignation etched into his features. Rummir rubbed his hands over his face, muting whatever diatribe was stewing. Raspoine met Bix's look full-on.

"We will fight the enemy we can see, Chimera," the queen assured. "The rest is beyond us."

Raspoine was right, of course. The higher up the cosmic food chain these enemies of the Mids were revealed to be, the more the burden of defense shifted to Bix. The pantheons were capable of handling the Devourers when properly motivated. Gods and anti-gods existed as a cosmic yin and yang, just as dragons balanced angels within the Mids. However, a siege targeting the High Executioner? Who would have the temerity? Someone with a death wish, that was for sure. A part of Bix was mightily concerned about this nameless punisher and the lengths to which they'd gone to motivate her. On the other hand, there was a not insignificant part of her that relished an impending fight. Alas, the more of her innate magics she got back, the less justified punching down became. But maybe delivering *one* punch wouldn't be so bad. Would it?

"Malthe the Rigorous, your truth has been heard. Your insight and experience will prove beneficial to this collective and beyond as it seems the fight for the future of the Mids involves entities yet to be defined." Tucking the containment piece within her amorphous state, Bix inclined her head to Malthe, then to the queen ascendant before focusing on Einar. "Young Einar, your death in my service is not desired."

"If the Chimera would oblige, we would take our lost sons home to heal the wounds physical and familial." Raspoine danced her fingers through the twilight, painting a picture of a sea rich with bold, breathtaking hues.

Bix tested a destination gate, and it vibrated in readiness. Addressing her former shard keepers one last time, Bix calmed her quixotic emotions and steadied her breath.

"Find your personal songs, my brave keepers. Let them tune to the symphony of the Horde while you welcome your united family into your existence. Allow them to atone for their transgressions. Allow them to restore your health and your hopes. Thank you for your service."

An origin gate connected the wounded dragons to the colorful sea. A rich chorus of numerous voices came through the opening. Einar, Svante, and Malthe dropped into the distant World. The royal twins followed, reverting to their dragon states before they hit the water.

Bix held the gates open an extra moment, reveling in the curative embrace manifesting within the song of the Horde. Raspoine must've been silently coordinating the kumbaya while the Seventh Sons aired their truths. Then again, Bix wouldn't put it past Rummir to whip the Horde into action. The Horde under Raspoine's rule with Rummir at her side would be a marvelous thing, especially with all the changes converging on the Mids.

Releasing her form to once again blend with the night, Bix drifted higher into the atmosphere. Wonder shivered through her as the corpses of the two dragons the Devourers had killed came into view. What was once bone and viscera was now verdant hills, the bodies merging with the landscape to nurture the new lives calling this World home. Around the golden lake, human children, small and shrieking with glee, charged from their shelters into the water at the encouragement of gods fully healed and dressed not as warriors but as everyman. Slowly, beneath the canopy of starlit night, more humans emerged from nooks and caves within the mountains. Tiny fires sparked to life as refugees from the Primary Mid World set about making this new World their home.

Bix didn't dare linger for too long, not with a third party somewhere out there possibly guiding Indraja through the siege and straight to the remaining shard keepers. Bix needed to return to Tobek with haste and let him know about the attack that might or might not have been on this data center, but had definitely been on the dragons stationed here to help with the refugees' relocation.

He was, after all, in charge of Resen. Plus, he was experienced at waging wars against the very mortal and the insufferably divine. If someone was using the Devourers to lay siege to the Mids in order to push Bix's hand as Svante and Malthe had suggested, then Tobek might be able to help her work out the who and the why.

Additionally, she still had the larger mission to complete, which meant collecting more shards of the containment pyramid. Yes, the Devourers now had the gods' complete set and two of the five dragon shards that they'd stolen from Jepp and his brother before Bix and the twins had arrived on World. She had the complete angels' set and three of the five dragons' shards. That left Fates, Chweds, humans, and the unknown seventh shard keeper as her next steps. She had to get to them before the Devourers...and the demons. Couldn't forget about Indraja's demons.

Gah.

CHAPTER 12

Tobek wasn't in the basement of the coal plant nor on the main floor. The shove and clutch of his magic against Bix's came from the same floor as the ops room, but at the opposite end. Bix drifted along the corridor ceiling in her native state, keeping clear of the Berserkers hustling up and down the carpeted hall with strange-looking equipment that could've been tech, artifacts, or hybrids. A watery green glow emanated from the otherwise dimly lit room. Gurp must've remodeled this half of the floor, because the end-cap room didn't use to occupy this much space. Then again, the last time she'd been up here, the Berserkers had still been part of the Mid World Army. Now they were the inaugural team of the Resen Immigration and Defense Division. RIDDers. Yes, she had way too much fun with that acronym. Yes, her team was having T-shirts made for the guys. Yes, Drew was ensuring the shirts would absolutely be NSFW. It was the least her crew could do to show their support for the guys' new endeavor.

Bix contained her state within the frame of the thick crown molding into which complex antispying wards had been burned. That Tobek needed these wards in addition to the ones already embedded throughout the compound was…interesting. The walls within the large room were modular—some clear glass, some dry erase, some matte black. Live maps and scrolling data streams accounted for the green glow spilling into the hallway. In the center of the room, Gurp sat atop a huge wood-and-glass table built like a plus sign. Stacks of papers and sticky notes filled the wooden portions, while more data feeds illuminated the glass portions. The backlit floor was a geometric masterpiece of storage beneath a thick layer of glass. Berserkers added, moved, or removed thingamabobs from the floor cubbies based on Gurp's direction.

Never underestimate a Berserker's ability to follow orders, nor a goblin's uncanny workflow optimization.

Tobek stood in a corner, studying a video feed playing a familiar battle scene over a matte wall. He raised his natural hand high above his head and waggled his fingers. Bix uncoiled a curl of midnight and wrapped it around his hand.

"Alarms went off in the data center on the World you and the royal dragons just cleansed. I'm reviewing the reports now. The Devourers never touched the lake. Did you notice that? They didn't adjust the position of their portal to deliver their troops directly into the water." He tapped the video wall with his prosthetic hand, pausing the feed at the point Bix had encompassed the World.

"I think they were after the shard keepers, not the data center." Bix whispered, but it carried throughout her state, which caused a few of the Berserkers to pause and look up with surprise that quickly faded to mild amusement as they resumed their work.

"Agreed." Tobek tapped the wall again, rewinding the video. "This is the part you'll find interesting. Devourers need a portal to get in and to get out, right?"

"As far as we know." She streamed down Tobek's arm and assumed a shape and size more typical of her corporeal form, making sure she didn't give herself too much definition. Humanly naked in a room full of men was not going to happen.

"They deploy one portal. The same one you removed. Yet they only *enter* the World through that portal. They don't use it to depart. How, then, did two platoons vanish into thin air just as you arrived, eh? Down to the nanosecond. Watch." He split the videos into three wedges of a pie to run the gruesome death scenes of the two consumed dragons and the spot on which Bix and the dragon twins had arrived.

Despite the thick haze covering the mountain range and the lake, the data center's World-integrated security system had managed to record the scenes with a clarity only magic could explain. A deep charcoal-gray ripple undulated about six feet above the ground, piercing the Devourers' chests, then dragging them through the fissure. All at once. Like some monstrous millipede. Only the two Devourers holding the shards screamed. The rest seemed too stunned. The fissure closed at the same time the royal twins' gateway opened.

That explained why Bix hadn't noticed the disruption when she'd arrived.

"Could you back it up to the moment the Devourers are impaled, please?" Bix asked. There was something in that action that niggled at a memory. The recollection didn't come easily, so she didn't chase it. Her brain would make up shit to form a false memory if she pushed too hard. She couldn't afford to do that for a whole lot of reasons.

"Are we thinking Indraja?" Tobek rewound the videos to the requested frames. "A greater goddess like her would be able to do that, no problem."

"There's potentially a new player in the mix, someone capable of locating the shards before we do. Another greater god or an equivalent Devourer, perhaps?" Bix shrugged her barely defined shoulders. "Possibly the same one who cursed Sophia? An ally to Indraja, for sure, more likely to be the one who *brought* the Devourers here, not followed them like Indraja."

Tobek pivoted toward her, a playful grin twitching his thick beard. "You don't have to hide it, you know. It's healthy."

"What?" she asked defensively.

"Your desire to pick a fight. A real fight. A hand-to-hand split lip, spitting-teeth kind of fight," he goaded. "I lead a battalion of Berserkers. You think I don't recognize your tone? You think I haven't used it myself? Often? I do like the novelty of hearing it from your lips, though."

"The higher the rank of the Devourer, the more powerful they are," she supplied, ignoring his bait. "Those shards are too powerful for a foot soldier to touch, so whoever ripped them from the dragons' bodies has to be more powerful than a dragon enforcer's son."

"At least a colonel in a divine army, which far outranks the gods I have stationed at the data centers." Tobek scratched his beard. "I need to alert Ogun to the problem."

"I guess that explains why Indraja is using both demons and Devourers to gather the shards. If the shards or their keepers are protected by a deity, her demons will be husked. So she deploys Devourers of greater standing because she has access to higher ranking Devourers through this new-to-us leader." Bix crossed what passed as arms over her semblance of a chest. "What are the chances we have midlevel or higher gods protecting the shards given to the Fates, Chweds, and humans?"

"Slim to none." The answer came from a live stream video that popped up on the glass wall abutting the matte wall of tragedy. Cian's face came into view. Judging from the abundance of workstations and Berserkers behind him, he was down the hall in the ops room. "I have Drew on the spy line. He's located the Chweds' shards. Okay to patch him through? It's audio only."

"Go ahead," Tobek allowed and tilted his head toward Bix. "Are we placing bets on the body your dearest friend has purloined?"

"Bixie? You there?" Drew's whisper was feminine with the sort of lisp that hinted at long fangs. The background noise of multiple languages from multiple sources, most of which were terse and unpleasant, did not convey the usual conviviality of a Chimera Fan Club party.

"I'm here. You've got Tobek too."

"Excellent. We're going to need him."

Tobek's brow shot up. His playful grin turned lecherous as he leveled it on Bix. She tugged his beard coyly.

"Turns out the Chwed pieces aren't a secret," Drew mumbled. "They're part of Chwed lore with many names. We've passed them dozens of times throughout our official careers and felt their heebie-jeebies imbuing us with a deep foreboding."

"Really?" Bix looked up at Tobek, who met her questioning expression with one of his own.

"Eleven pieces for eleven doorways," Drew sang under her breath. "Eleven eyes to see the Worlds. Eleven guardians to protect those who bend the magics to support the lives and livelihood of all Chwedlonol."

"Guild Hall," Bix and Tobek groaned in unison. The saying was incorporated into the mosaic floor of the grand foyer at the political seat of the Chwed guilds. There were eleven doorways leading into the central rotunda where all the assorted guilds of the Mids haggled over contracts, membership, territory, grievances, etcetera. The number eleven was believed to represent a connection to higher wisdom and an awareness of cosmic truth.

The irony did not escape Bix.

"The doorways are in the shape of eleven heroes from Chwed lore." Tobek harrumphed, probably having known said heroes. "The magic contained within those guardian doorways is said to come from the ashes of the heroes themselves."

"Ashes plus the shard they were carrying, probably," Bix scoffed. "When was Guild Hall built?"

"Not long after you vanished," Tobek said.

"Touch me again, rat breath, and I'll drive your teeth straight out your asshole," Drew snapped loudly.

Soft snickers came from the Berserkers still filing in and out of Tobek's latest lair. The tone of Gurp's inimical opinion didn't need translating.

Drew cleared her throat and resumed her muffled update. "Sparky must've gotten through to the director of the spy guild, because the guild masters have added you two to today's schedule of petitioners. Pretty sure they weren't planning on telling you that, since you're supposed to be here in ten minutes."

"Clock," Tobek called out. Instantly, a clock counting down ten minutes appeared next to Cian's feed.

"Both of us?" Bix asked as she looked again at the paused video of the gray millipede yanking Devourers out to…to where? The ether, presumably. Hopefully. That was where Indraja and the Devourers were hiding. Yet, if that was the case, why didn't ether seep through the fissure that was the millipede? Why hadn't there been seepage after the fissure closed? Fissures were sloppy and permanently marred the protective layers around the World.

Souring in Bix's unformed gut radiated throughout her ethereal state. What if the other side of that fissure wasn't anywhere near this galaxy? What if the goose chase had begun? No. Stop. She couldn't let her mind go there. The best course of action was to first pursue the shards where she and her team could confirm the locations. Phobos had taken point on the gods' shards the Devourers had stolen. She had to let him do his job, just as Drew was doing her job right now. Teamwork was the only way through the mission. Any mission. She might be more powerful now, but she still needed her team.

"Mmhmm," Drew grunted over a muted chuckle, drawing Bix's attention back to the current issue. "They want the head of Resen to dance attendance. Bixie, word of your imminent arrival has this place packed to the rafters. Might want to wear your best RBF."

"Resting Bitch Face? Guess I should put on clothes, then." Bix cast an absent glance at the starlight churning within her midnight as broken memories sought the connection to the millipede. No. No searching. No confabulations. No. Stop it.

"Uhm, did I interrupt some sexy fun times? Finally?" Drew screeched through a quiet exhalation.

That earned another round of commentary from the goblin in the middle of the conference table and wolf whistles from the Berserkers.

"Well, I also need to affect skin and a body, so…" Bix purposely did not look at Tobek. She didn't need to. His wicked grin had grown and added unholy mirth to his bright eyes, all of which were clear in his reflection bouncing off a lot of surfaces.

"Resen can't launch with the ether still up, and we can't get the ether down without the guilds' containment pieces, so I will make the time to answer the summons of the guild masters," Tobek drawled in such a way as to cause a smart man to beg him to reconsider.

"Expect us shortly." Bix tweaked Tobek's hand in gratitude. "Oh, and Drew? Demons or Devourers, if they're not there yet, they will be soon."

"Goodie. Maybe we'll luck out and it'll be both at the same time. Make a memorable entrance, you two. Full floor show," Drew snarked, then cut the connection.

CHAPTER 13

Guild Hall was in a loud, noisy industrial section of Prince George's County, Maryland, a skip downriver from the District. Barbed wire and twelve-foot chain-link fence made the half dozen flat-topped sprawling warehouse buildings resemble a prison compound. What looked like gang tags on the greige concrete walls were a mix of guild sigils and protection wards. Closed loading bay doors displayed individual guild identifiers in patterns of rust or chipped-paint logos. Deep potholes in cracked, sun-faded asphalt held oil-slicked runoff from brown snow berms. The revolting stench of diesel fumes and hot brakes stained snowflakes before the frozen water hit the ground. Dump trucks and flatbeds rumbled past the single gate and guardhouse before kicking up loose gravel as they shoved their way into gridlocked traffic on the main drag.

Bix wrinkled her nose and grimaced. "Have to give the guilds credit for hiding in plain sight."

"The Drivers Wanted signs are a nice touch. Lure a desperate human into signing what they think is a standard employment contract, only for the human to discover they've indentured themselves and their family to the guilds." Tobek drew sigils in the air with the hunter green of his magic spilling from his fingertips.

His long exhalation blew the spells across the area, revealing the grid of diverse Chwedlonol magic blanketing the whole compound. "The Hall extends a mile and a half underground, as does their protection network."

"Aye, Chief, establishing a three-hundred-yard surface perimeter," crackled over the comm piece Tobek wore. Bix had forgone her comm since she wasn't planning on staying corporeal.

Berserkers in well-worn and work-dusted construction attire took up positions in idling work trucks parked on the road shoulder or in overgrown abandoned lots to either side and behind Guild Hall. If demons showed up, the Berserkers would move in.

"Anything you can add to reinforce the Chweds' protections?" Bix asked, reaching out with her senses to search for magics not belonging to the Mids. The butterfly flutters of order denoting the containment pieces made by the youngest of her brothers were easy to locate now that she knew what she was looking for. They had the same resonance as the pieces she'd reclaimed from the dragons, which meant the youngest pair of twins had created alternating panels of chaos and order to contain the volatile magics of titans that had built the ether. The balance was necessary. She couldn't explain why she'd asked those siblings to make the containment pyramid for her, but it did explain how they'd known where to find her in the ether after she'd ruined herself.

The festering pustule of memories shielded by thorns of malice throbbed behind her corporeal eye, making it twitch. Okay, not the time to start pondering family problems, not when she had to go face the guild masters who'd shit on her repeatedly and tried to capture her frequently when they'd believed she was nothing more than a gatekeeper. Only one of them had known she was a spy…until the spy guild had burned her and publicly outed her as the Chimera.

Yeah, good times. Good times. Actually, some of them really had been.

She glanced up to catch Tobek watching her with curious amusement.

"Didn't hear me, did you? I said I dare not add anything to the guilds' defenses for fear it would draw unwanted attention from the demons or the Devourers." He rubbed his thumb against his finger, and a penny appeared. "Penny for your thoughts?"

"The past year, I've been so focused on the superpowers, clearing traitors from the Consortium, defeating Devourers, and helping heal ley lines and whole Worlds that I've lost touch with the everyman. I'm beyond curious as to what the guilds' truths will be." She plucked the penny from him and dropped it down her cleavage, earning a lascivious brow waggle from her Berserker. "Thirty seconds until the floor show. You ready?"

He gave her a chaste kiss as his magic rippled around him, changing his attire from denim and a Henley to a blackish-green suit with a Berserker-blue shirt open at the collar to give a peek of his tattoos. He kept his hair down, except for a few thin braids woven with colors that seemed to mean something more than a style preference. He'd opted to forgo his prosthetic arm, likely in case of a clash of magics causing it to go haywire. Thus, the exquisite tailoring of his suit accommodated his partial arm by banding a proper cuff under the bulge of his bicep.

"No uniform?" she asked, curling her fingers around his bicep, just above his amputation scars. She was a huge fan of a man in a suit, but Tobek in uniform was a sweet, sweet delight.

"Not in the army anymore," he reminded. "We haven't settled on the Resen uniform design yet, so civvies it is."

"Strangely enough, you still cut a suitably imposing figure," she teased, then pushed up to her tiptoes to speak into the comm piece he wore around his ear. "All right, boys, we're going in. We'll try not to blow up anything."

There were comments, most of which made her snicker as her darkness wound around Tobek and her, engulfing them completely in a Gordian knot. She could use gates to connect to the underground rotunda at the heart of Guild Hall, a place she remembered all too well from her days of undercover work trailing the movers and shakers of the guilds. However, Drew had requested a floor show, and there was nothing quite like filling a crowded sanctuary with complete and total darkness. Thus, she reverted to her native state and connected her darkness to shadows spreading within Guild Hall, taking her Berserker with her.

Bix's darkness filled the mile and a half multilevel compound that comprised the many offices of Guild Hall, touching every life-form and letting them feel a hint of her true self. Since Tobek was the cosmic sponge who sopped up her magical excesses and prevented her from destroying the Mids, his presence protected the Chweds from her while simultaneously allowing her native state to make direct contact with such fragile beings. When fully corporeal, she was safer to the masses, her magic mostly concentrated within her. Native state, however, she was far more fee-fi-fo-fum femme fatale. Once the Chwedlonols' fear amplified to a flavor her insubstantial state could actually taste, she allowed her starlight to shine and drift, creating a light show that twisted fear into awe. She chuckled softly, letting the sound ripple throughout her, as her darkness found Drew within the suit of a wood nymph in the grand foyer poking at her starlight. While the Chweds marveled within the vastness of Bix, she studied the containment shards.

Drew had been right, of course. Eleven containment shards were embedded in eleven carvings of individual guardians that framed the towering arched doorways leading into the rotunda at the very center of Guild Hall. The repulsion of the shards pulsed against her, soft as a sleeping baby's heartbeat. If she'd been a rank-and-file angel or dragon, that power would've been strong enough to physically repel her across the grand foyer and into the soil layers beyond the bunker walls. The shards must've tuned to the magics of the guardians, much as the shards would've tuned to their truths, protecting the Chwed guardians from greater magics. It pained her, but she had to give her siblings' credit for very clever engineering.

Satisfied that the shards were here and that there was no trace of demon or Devourer, she began consolidating her form within the Gordian knot of shadowy tentacles and thick, thorny vines. After she added flesh to form, Tobek added fabric over flesh, redressing her. Within the protection of her shadows, his dark green pupils glowed with his evolving magic, making his bright blue irises appear teal. He leaned down and brushed his nose against hers. She gently tugged his beard, then took her place at his side.

The hostility within the rotunda of Guild Hall was palpable. The cries of indignation were almost as loud as the gasps of wonder as she made a grand show of untangling her Gordian knot of darkness. Some of her shadowy appendages uncoiled as aggressive tentacles, quick to snap at the oiled oak balconies overflowing with Chweds of assorted races. Other shadows manifested as writhing vines that slithered among the feet, hooves, and paws of Chweds gathered behind half-wall barriers of carved oak showing the dents and gouges from agitated crowds. The final threads of her knot wound themselves through the legs of curved tables that formed a half circle from east to west at which the masters of three dozen guilds sat.

Acrid body odor, pungent perfumes, and acute halitosis permeated the space located three-quarters of a mile underground. One would never know they weren't topside, not with frame-lit frescoes, ceiling-to-floor fountains, and abundant greenery ringing every column. Someone must've pissed off the sprites, though, because the air wasn't moving. Then again, allowing the heat and stench of overcrowding to build was likely an intentional means of passively encouraging folks to keep their business presentations before the masters short and to the point.

At the masters' table, in the seat aligned with true north, sat the Obermeister, the master of the guild masters. Bugarda Steelsplint, a dwarven woman with a plush red beard and eyes befitting her surname. As a spy, Bix had done her level best to steer clear of Steelsplint. Bugarda was a woman with an uncanny talent for spotting a weakness and exploiting it.

To Bugarda's right sat the director of the Cross-World Intelligence Guild, aka the spy guild. He was Bix's former big-big boss and Ashtad's current boss, the guy who'd arranged to put Bix's name on the schedule. His hulking Beelzebub build, complete with crimson skin and a black pompadour, required him to sit farther away from the table than his peers. Sitting in the shadows suited him and his calling. He and Bix had a volatile history, but he'd come around to her side once the Devourers had started targeting his spies.

To Bugarda's left sat the guild master of psychopomps. Bix didn't know him, her, uh, them, but the trident of small hooks on the back of their left hand identified them as a soul transporter. Their predecessor had met a rather unfortunate end, so Bix had zero history with the new honcho. Alas, all psychopomps had an axe to grind with Bix ever since she'd unleashed the Reaping Winds that randomly collected souls the psychopomps used to extort the living. Bix had never locked the Winds away, so they were still out there, gutting the illegitimate revenue streams of the guild. Incredibly, the new guild master was very busy ignoring Bix and making moon eyes at Tobek. Bix couldn't find fault with that. Tobek was commandingly handsome.

The rest of the guild masters had thick dossiers Bix had helped fill, so if she'd wanted to make them squirm, she could. Ten years ago, she would've done it. Begun her greeting to the masters by airing salacious and borderline career-ending secrets of each of the folks currently judging her from behind the perceived safety of an oak table. Hell, even a year ago, she might've done it. Today, though, she regarded them for what they were: frightened minor life-forms, ignored and taken for granted by those who'd created them. A tragedy on many levels.

"It has come to my attention you desired an audience, Obermeister Steelsplint," Tobek said, breaking the uneasy silence that had settled within the rotunda. "How may I be of assistance?"

Steelsplint dragged her attention away from Bix and huffed. "I want to know why the Consortium took the Mid Worlds' most accomplished and levelheaded military general and demoted him to a glorified immigration paper pusher."

Bix hoped she schooled her features before the incredulity made it through her starlight to her skin.

"What you see as a demotion is, in truth, a challenge. After all, it is far more difficult to wield the pen than the sword." Tobek gestured to his amputated arm.

A few titters from the masters and the gallery could be heard.

"A pen isn't a challenge for you, Chief. We all know better." Steelsplint turned something over in her teeth and sucked, a tin wedge, probably. It was the dwarven version of tobacco chew. "What are those self-absorbed ley-line fuckers hiding from us? What has the Consortium so scared, they've got you building a different kind of army? Why isn't the Mid World Army good enough to defend us?"

Tobek opened his mouth, but the master of psychopomps cut him off. "Don't bother with the evasion. My guild has seen the deaths of too many Chwedlonol discounted by this new race that feeds on dragons and angels. These strangers have no interest in us. They don't even acknowledge our existence until they want to replace one of ours with one of theirs. We've sent overtures to their camps. Our messengers don't come back."

Whoa. Talk about flagrant stupidity. Sending a Chwed, any Chwed, to a Devourer camp? It was like tossing a tiny gourd into a den of starving tigers. The director of the spy guild knew that. Unless, of course, the Consortium security oversight committee had forbidden him from sharing the intel? He had two bosses, the Consortium and the Obermeister. The Consortium controlled the job, the Obermeister his employees. It was an unenviable balancing act.

"Obermeister, you have the remit of my organization in your possession. Get to the point of why you asked me here." Tobek's tone lost all trace of congeniality.

Gasps and whispers abounded. Guild masters fidgeted in their seats. The director of the spy guild rolled his bright yellow eyes and pursed his lips. The master of the psychopomps cut a cold glare at Bix and curled a lip.

"This." Steelsplint leaned forward over one arm and wagged a finger in Bix and Tobek's direction. "I wanted to see the two of you together. The original Berserker and the Chimera."

It took a beat for Bix to adjust her perspective. To her team of spies and his battalion of Berserkers, Bix and Tobek's relationship was no secret. Most of the Consortium had likely figured it out by now too. But to the Chweds, the Chimera was a myth they'd only recently discovered was real. To those who had known Bix over the last forty years, she'd been just another midlevel magical being. She hadn't known she was the Chimera at that point in her amnesic existence—why would any of the Chweds? Tobek, on the other hand, was a fixture consistent throughout their histories, a guardian of the Mids who'd been around longer than most of the Worlds in the collective. While there was probably a thick tome of conjecture over his intimate partners, there had never been so much as a suspicion that the original Chimera had intimate partners. They probably thought she wasn't physically capable of it.

Cat was out of the bag now. Not that she cared. Doubted he did either since he made no movement away from her.

"Tabloid curiosity is the reason you're wasting my time?" he whispered, and his eyes faintly glowed with dawning rage.

All but the Obermeister and the director of the spy guild squirmed in their seats.

"The Chimera is about to make an ask of us. Your relationship with her factors into our decision." Steelsplint pressed her fingertips into the table and slowly stood, never looking away from Tobek's ire. "Why is the man who built the Mid World Army only now given permission to organize a foreign defense? The ether's been up for hundreds of years. She created it to protect us because the Consortium wouldn't."

Conflicting grunts of hostility and support came from everywhere. Bix wasn't at all sure where this was headed. Were they blaming Tobek for the actions of the Consortium? He'd never been the Chair. Were they just searching for an audience to air their grievance? Hearing their concerns went hand in hand with getting the shards, which again, why vent their angst to him when Bix was standing right in front of them?

"They've waited until now to cover their asses," Steelsplint raised her voice, addressing the gallery. "There's never enough bedsheet to cover us too, though, is there?"

Shouts of "No" echoed with enough force to cause the fountains to spray and the plants to sway. The Obermeister cut a gimlet glare at Bix.

"The Consortium doesn't give a shit about us, and you come here, now, when enemies even they can't defeat are picking us off? You want to take away the most powerful magical protections in all Chwedlonol possession?" Steelsplint shook her head. "I'm sorry, Chimera, but you will not hear our truths. We do not believe we will be safer without the gifts you gave us."

Tobek's brows rose to his hairline, and his rage shone brightly in thousand-watt blue. "You would deny her?"

"We have to look out for ourselv—"

Screams of pain echoed amid the whistles of flying arrows. Chaos erupted. Tobek spun to cover Bix. Starlight brightened within her.

She stepped out of the flow of time.

CHAPTER 14

Time was a function of order. Order was the purview of the Cosmos, Bix's father. Being equal parts Chaos and Cosmos, Bix could access time. She couldn't go forward since that required multiple acts of creation, and she wasn't a creationist. She could go backward, though. Downside, her chaotic half would erase the timeline as she went, thereby reestablishing the present as wherever she stopped. That was a bit drastic for the circumstances. Besides, her interest wasn't in changing time, it was simply to linger in this moment. To understand. To figure out what the hell was going on.

She detected no divine resonances, neither demon nor Devourer. The only powers greater than divine in the chamber belonged to her, Tobek, and the shards.

Bemused, Bix untangled the tip of an arrow from the curl of her hair and repositioned the fletching about to scrape Tobek's eye. Weapons weren't allowed in Guild Hall for reasons just like this, so someone had smuggled them in. Who, what, when, why, how? Firstly, who were the targets? Secondly, who fired the weapons? Or maybe vice versa. Whatever.

Threads of shadows unfurled from her spine to align with arrows paused midflight, then continued on to establish trajectories from beginning to end. She was accustomed to absorbing information from thousands of sources simultaneously, so deciphering what her shadows told her about the hundred-odd arrows in various stages of progress was easy. Some arrowheads were made of iron, some silver, some of metals not from the Primary Mid World. Not every Chwed was vulnerable to the same thing. Some metals were painful, while others highly poisonous. The choice of arrowhead depended on the target, which made it easier to figure out which guild master was the intended mark of which arrow. Knowing the masters' weaknesses was yet another benefit of having contributed to their dossiers for the spy guild.

She flashed a toothy smile at her old boss, appreciating the ridiculous expression of his face frozen midbellow.

All masters were the intended targets. Each had three arrows shot from three different locations on paths to kill. Interestingly, neither she nor Tobek had been in the paths, or rather, Tobek hadn't been until he'd moved to protect her. Silly goose. He knew anything made from Mids' magic would just bounce off her like grains of rice. Maybe he was worried about ricochet? It was close quarters, after all.

Targets confirmed, she switched her attention to the shooters. They'd positioned themselves in hidey-holes that spoke of more than a passing familiarity with Guild Hall. Some of those crannies required quite the contortionist to get into. What a mishmash of races, guilds, ages, and genders. Nothing immediately visible linked them together aside from the bows in their hands. The lack of quivers said they were single-shot shooters with perfect aim. All of them? Hunh. That definitely required more investigation. Alas, not the kind she could pursue, not covertly, at least. But there was someone on the premises who could.

Giggling, she enfolded Drew in her shadows and relocated the wood nymph with the draugr inside. Much like playing with a doll, she wrapped Drew's arms and a leg around one of the shooters in such a way that the draugr would get the hint…after the initial moment of shock, probably. Drew would either read her the riot act later or beg her to do it again. Her bestie really was the best when it came to rolling with the unexpected.

Bix brought her shadows back to the arrows and debated what to do. The easy answer was to do nothing. To let the arrows find their marks. If this really was a Chwed-on-Chwed uprising, she had no business interfering. On the other hand, the timing of the attack was suspicious. Right when Steelsplint was telling Bix to kiss her ass? That sort of stunk of something relating to Resen or the shards…or Tobek, even. After all, he was the one about to grab the Obermeister by her stacking swivel and scream into her eye sockets.

As much as Bix's history with her old spy boss should make her rejoice at his demise, she needed him alive. He knew the sitch with the Devourers and was tracking the anti-gods who'd infiltrated his organization to get more intel on them. He also allowed Ashtad a whole lot of leeway, which included feeding Bix top-secret intel. Thus, she repositioned two of the arrows to hit his chair and the third to wing him.

Then there was the master of psychopomps. They should've seen this attack coming about thirty seconds before the first arrow had launched. That was part of their deal with the gods and Fates. Psychopomps needed the heads-up to be in position to collect the soul when it vacated its dead body. Speaking of whom, where were the psychopomps who should've been here for the masters' souls? Were the shards keeping them out, or was their guild in on the assassinations?

So. Many. Questions. Damn it.

Sighing, she turned to Tobek. "What would you do? Keep them all alive? None of them? Some? How much would you meddle?"

He didn't answer, of course. He wasn't out of the flow of time like she was.

If only this had been a clear case of a greater power punching down, then the decision to save everyone would've been easy. She really needed to pay more attention to what was going on in her Worlds. Based on what she knew…this wasn't her fight. The shards weren't being stolen, nor could she steal them. She had no justification to interfere. She ought to let whatever confluence of events the Fates had woven around this moment come to fruition. They knew more about the future than she ever would.

Yeah, but… She did know what was about to happen. Even though Steelsplint was withholding the shards and even though this was Chwed-on-Chwed violence, there was the inescapable fact that it was all going down with her literally standing in the middle of it. Once upon a time, she'd vowed to protect the Mids from enemies foreign and domestic. This was definitely a domestic problem.

With a sigh of surrender, she nudged the arrows off course. There would be injuries aplenty, some life altering, but none life ending. Close as she could get to a compromise.

Recalling her shadows to her body, Bix returned to the timeline.

An arrow plinked off her shoulder, then clattered to the ground. Tobek yanked her against him as arrows found their revised marks. Blood spurted. Masters lurched and slumped. Souls remained stitched into their bodies. Chweds responded with diverse magics, turning on each other.

Bright copper magic flared from the shards above the doorways, sending Chweds slamming against walls, then to their knees screaming. Magic native and Other World swelled within the rotunda spawning swirling nimbi of blue, purple, and green. An eerie song pitched far beyond normal hearing drifted above the din.

Resen. The foundational elements were responding to the activated shards.

Oh shit.

"Get us out of here, now," Tobek growled in Bix's ear.

Bix met the Obermeister's confused yet resentful glare as Steelsplint yanked an arrow from her side. Bix didn't feel anger towards the Obermeister. Disappointment in the Consortium for alienating the races they were supposed to protect? Sure. She'd have to approach this bargaining table a different way to get the guild masters to part with the shards. She wasn't too sure which way. Perhaps the other shard keepers could give her a clue as to how to quickly change the minds of a violently terrified people before the Devourers or demons showed up.

With a parting glance at the rising chaos, she opened gates.

CHAPTER 15

The gate to the coal plant basement kitchen closed, leaving Bix and Tobek in the forced-air silence. He kept her pinned against his chest. His irregular heartbeat thundered against her back. His cheek rested against her crown. The blue floodlights of his Berserker rage illuminated the wall of cabinets and high-end appliances. He huffed like a bull readying to charge. She crossed her arms over his and waited. Something had awakened his fury. Resen? The shards? The attitude of the Obermeister? It couldn't have been the archers—that sort of attack was old hat to him.

"Red team, report," he growled.

"Magic storm dissipating in the skies. A couple of fender benders on the roads, but all quiet on the surface of Guild Hall, Chief," came the answering snarl over his comm. His men were directly linked to his rage, so Berserkers across the Mids got insta-angry whenever he did. He was the source of what empowered them to be faster, stronger, and tireless whenever their rage was triggered. Now was not a good time to push any of their buttons.

"There's a riot inside. Many are wounded, magics are wild. Do not breach. Defend the perimeter only," Tobek ordered.

"Aye, Chief. Understood."

Bix rubbed her cheek against Tobek's bicep, still waiting for him to calm down. It took a while. Longer than it usually did. Eventually, the blue glow faded from the kitchen and his hold on her loosened, a teeny bit.

"Will Resen kill them? The Chweds?" she whispered. Technically, Resen was the defense system as a whole, but it was built upon the sentient ley lines and the Fates' weave. The foundation of Resen was very much alive, aware, and communicative—assuming one had the wherewithal to comprehend and withstand an exchange of its raw power. So far, Tobek was the only one who could directly interface with Resen. Bix couldn't because she was too powerful. Alas.

"Now that we're gone? Unlikely. The foundational elements recognize their creations." He stroked her upper arm. "My presence there, however, exacerbated their response. Without the defense system up and running, the elements use *me* as a focal point. Had we lingered, Resen would've come through me to attack the shards."

"The clash of magics would've vaporized Guild Hall and probably everything else within a ten-mile radius." Bix thought about that for a moment. A cold shiver of dread snaked down her spine. "If Indraja uses her shards to attack the Mids, Resen will use you to respond."

"After what just happened, I think you're right."

"You may be immortal, but that just means you'll *eventually* recover after the foundational elements turn you into an overpowered laser cannon." She twisted in his hold and curled her fingers in his lapels. "You'll still feel your cells coming apart. That's going to be unpleasant, even for you, Mister I Have an Extreme Pain Fetish."

"Do you think I'll become a liquid or a gas?" His eyes crinkled at the corners.

"Ew." She shoved him with a cry of disgust. "I will not let them do that to you. You're the champion of the Mids, not a singular weapon to be exploited."

"Neither of us has a say in that now, do we? Those are sentient powers beyond our control." He let her go, chuckling. "I notice you didn't take the shards. Thought that was the mission?"

"It does me no good to steal them. They'll try to return to their owners unless given to me willingly during a ritual of truth. Learned that from the bit of thievery that interrupted the angel retrieval." She ran her fingers through her hair, dislodging a feather from a fletching. "I'm sorry to ask this, but can we keep your guys on guard duty until I can figure out how to convince Steelsplint to part with the shards?"

"The shards can be stolen by others, just not by you? That complicates things." He peeled out of his suit jacket and tossed it over the quartz counter. "Yes, of course, my men will stand watch over Guild Hall in case demons or Devourers show up, but I can't send my men inside unless a third party attacks the site. The guilds would not thank us, and Resen needs the guilds' support resettling the humans in territories that are hostile to them. Otherwise those human colonies will be ripe for enslavement or slaughter."

"Fair point." Bix straightened her bangs, swiping the errant strands from her eyes. "Original me must've felt getting everyone's buy-in was more important than acting alone with regards to ending the ether."

He notably didn't comment on that part. "How do you want to proceed?"

"Let's wait to hear from Drew about the attack on the masters. The archers held their fire until Steelsplint told me no. Coincidence or cause?" Bix drummed her fingers on her hips. "Assuming Drew got my message before the shards activated, we should hear from her soon."

"You toyed with time, didn't you?" He gave her a chastising look. "I wondered at the inaccuracy of the shots. Could've sworn they were aimed true."

Before she could blurt the quip forming on her lips, yellow alarm lights flashed and the low drone of a siren cranking up made the glasses in the kitchen cabinets vibrate.

"Medical alarm. Green team must've returned." Tobek ran

his hand over his chest, dragging magic that changed his attire to second-skin T-shirt and denim. Battle-axe patterned clogs replaced wingtips. His hair coiled itself into a man bun, and his beard rolled into a tight knot under his chin.

If Hywl's team was setting off alarms, then their demon-hunting mission had not gone well.

Gates to the upstairs clinic opened.

CHAPTER 16

The clinic glowed vibrant blue while enraged, bloodied, and maimed Berserkers carried comrades through the gate left open at National Cathedral. Hywl screamed through clenched teeth as his men helped him onto a surgical table. He looked as if a grizzly bear had sliced him up his front and down his side. Clothes lay tattered. Bones gleamed between severed muscles and veins. Glimpse of an organ here and there. Hywl's men were fractionally better, but not by much. Most of them still had their insides inside, but there wasn't an unbloodied patch of uniform anywhere.

It'd been a while since Bix had seen Berserkers get their asses handed to them. She wasn't a fan. Alas, when it came to healing anything, she couldn't. The best she could do was stay out of the way until someone told her what to do. She pressed her back against the wall of morgue drawers as Tobek assisted placing one of his men on the second surgical table.

Gurp and a cluster of healthy Berserkers entered the clinic from the hallway. The goblin did a head count as the men who'd remained at base wordlessly helped their wounded peers.

"Pretty lady?" Gurp called, pointing to the door. "Beer hall. Men go. Yes?"

Gates shortened the walk of the wounded from the clinic to

the long tables in the beer hall. Overflow. Thank the Powers That Be for the boys being in the throes of a magical evolution alongside their fearless leader, otherwise Hywl and company would've been going in wooden caskets instead of on wooden tables.

"Sweetheart, those carts too, if you please." Tobek pulled a prosthetic arm from a cabinet and angled his chin at a fleet of surgical carts being loaded up by a pair of medics. Medics tapped the carts and gave her thumbs-up as they finished their task. When the carts were done, she moved the medics too.

Her attention kept drifting back to the cathedral gate. She hadn't realized she was holding her breath until Ashtad staggered through with a barely conscious Berserker across his shoulders. She didn't think, her darkness simply unwound from her to relieve Ashtad of his burden.

"Chair," Tobek barked with distraction as he leaned over Hywl.

Bix's shadows gently placed Ashtad's soldier in the surgical chair and pushed the Recline button. More shadows curled around Ashtad as his one good knee buckled, catching him before he pitched face-first into a cabinet.

"I'm the last. Close the gate, Bix," Ashtad groaned, relaxing into Bix's shadowy support. "Close it now."

"Where's Sophia?" she asked as gates closed before placing Ashtad into the second surgical chair.

Hywl started convulsing on the table.

"I let you go on one date with the goddess who broke your heart, and this is what happens." The long-suffering chastisement entered the clinic before Runjit, the battalion's lead medic and Hywl's battle buddy. A team of medics filed in behind him in scrubs and gloves, immediately descending on the occupants of the other table and chairs. Runjit paused beside the Berserker in the surgical chair and murmured instructions to the attending medics before joining Tobek at the table with Hywl. Runjit studied his battle buddy with increasing worry deepening the wrinkles forming around the edge of his turban. "Your balls aren't supposed to be up with your spleen. Do I need to review the birds and the bees with you?"

"Fu-fuck you too," Hywl wheezed, spewing blood.

Runjit's expression brightened, and he caught Tobek's eye, exchanging a chin-high smirk before affixing medical masks. Apparently, Hywl would live. Praise be. The uncomfortable panging of Bix's heart lessened a little. She was awfully fond of the angel hunter…and he was awfully fond of a certain knowledge goddess. A goddess Bix really ought to locate for a whole bunch of reasons.

"Sophia let herself get captured," Ashtad said quietly, waving off the medics who tried to tend to him. "We were ambushed. Our numbers divided, then picked off. They weren't a ragtag bunch of demon miscreants. They were divine soldiers well trained and expecting us."

"Sophia read the demons' minds when they attacked the angels. Why didn't she mention they were soldiers? Why put our teams at an automatic disadvantage?" Every question was rhetorical as Bix's infamous temper spun up.

If Sophia had encountered Indraja's new shard hunter on this failed intercept mission, then the knowledge goddess sacrificing herself to spy on the bad guys made sense. Like the Devourers, demons could take the shards out of the Mids and stymie the assembly of the containment pyramid. Sophia would've implicitly understood that and perhaps had deemed surrender necessary for mission success. Sophia was probably still operating with a prisoner's mindset of having survived the horrors once, therefore designating herself the best choice to do so again. Bix understood that desperate need to prove oneself useful to the team. Not too long ago, Ashtad had been her team leader in the spy game, spending a lot of time and effort teaching Bix to rein in that same desperation and to trust in their teammates. Now, Bix was the team leader and Sophia was trusting her to make the sacrifice worthwhile.

Bix might not have been able to appeal to the leadership of

the Devourers to stop their thievery and to rescue Sophia, but she could appeal to the leadership of the pantheons. Make that their recently elected leader.

She clenched her gargoyle pendent and seethed. "Ogun."

Tobek glanced at her, one brow arching as he scrubbed in. A less wise man might've objected, possibly even misconstrued her actions as going over his head. Tobek, however, kept his focus on patching up his men and not picking an unwarranted fight. He was in charge of Resen and the Berserkers. It wasn't his job to keep the pantheons and their members in line. That burden belonged to the Chairman of the Consortium.

"Ogun," Bix repeated, applying a bit of force to the call. Ogun had made the gargoyle to keep tabs on her, but that connection worked both ways, particularly when she was the stronger power.

A hologram of the Chairman streamed through her fingers, taking shape against the wall of cooler doors.

"Bix, I do not like to be summoned."

"Gods of war, Ogun, you'd best do an accounting of who is where and commanding which operations in the Primary Mid World, because one of them is allied with Indraja and has unleashed his demon army on my targets and my teams." Bix let go of the pendant and willed her wrath to calm. "I am trying very, very hard not to diminish your troops in this time of war. However—"

"However is understood," Ogun interjected, slowly pivoting to take in the clinic. "Where is Sophia?"

"Taken by the traitors. I want her returned to me with all haste," Bix said, imbuing those words with all the aggravation bubbling through her.

"Good. Her shackles are my creation. Consider the issue addressed." With that, the hologram of the Chairman of the Consortium winked out of existence.

"Do you think Sophia's working for Indraja too?" Cian asked from the doorway, nervously spinning a tablet in his hands as his wide green eyes fixed on the surgery underway on Hywl.

"I think she's hoping her curse will incapacitate the demons long enough for our side to capture them and any shards they may have." Bix forced a smile and prayed it resembled something reassuring. "Hywl's in good hands, Cian. He'll pull through."

"Yeah, I know. I, uh, I think I found the consultants for the Houses of Fate." He waved his tablet but didn't come further into the clinic. Poor kid. The scene probably reminded him too much of what had happened to his mom.

"Here. Let me see." Ashtad winced but extended his arm.

Cian didn't approach, instead he slid the data to the monitors in the clinic that weren't being used to display the vitals of the patients. Nine monitors displayed nine different Mid Worlds.

"Mom used to say the worst thing for an Oracle who'd failed her trials to Fatehood was living long enough to be overcome by her visions to the point where an Oracle's mind could no longer support her body. To any outsider, she'd be a vegetable, locked in her head. That means she'd require care." Cian tapped his tablet screen, and green dots appeared on the displayed Worlds. Views zoomed down to city level or city equivalent. "Now, the Houses of Fate never really abandon their failures. Failed Oracles who can still communicate are too risky to leave unattended. Who better to attend them than younger Oracles who are in possession of their wits and who are highly trained combatants due to the nature of oracular trials?"

"They're not soldiers, no matter what they think," Runjit objected, wielding a pair of clamps over Hywl's guts.

"Right, they're not. They're individuals. They're not trained to work together, which is what made these nine purported elder-care facilities stand out." Cian tapped his screen again, and exotic landscapes surrounding austere architecture filled the screens. "Small human populations on Mid Worlds other than the Primary was unusual until recently, but these facilities are old, old, old. Date back two thousand years, just before the creation of the ether."

"Because the Fates would've foreseen the need for those sites." Ashtad took a steaming mug from a medic and mumbled his gratitude as they angled his surgical chair toward the monitors showing Cian's intel.

Tobek glanced up at the monitors, then resumed mending Hywl's insides. "Locations are isolated and easily defended, assuming the Oracles have been properly trained."

"Cian, when did you learn how to track Oracles?" Bix asked with a touch of pride.

"When you sent me undercover in the spy guild." Cian blushed a bright shade of bubblegum pink. "You know how they like to recruit my kind."

"Good job, kid." Ashtad sipped his drink and moaned happily. "Failed Oracles remain human, living eighty to a hundred or so years. Bix, if you did give pieces of the containment device to failed Oracles of yore, then there's been a line of succession."

"True, and there's the question of where the Oracles keep their pieces. Angels and dragons embedded them in their bodies, but the Chweds baked them into architecture." Bix studied the images, testing gates. Six gates worked, no problem. Three required multiple attempts at farther distances from the structures. That didn't bode well. "Oracles are human, and the pieces are potent, so I'm guessing the shards aren't on their person."

"Then we need the shards *and* the women to whom they're keyed? Is that how it works?" Cian ruffled his hair and offered a sheepish grin. "How do we know how many pieces and women there are? These nine locations stood out to me, but I can keep digging."

"Nine is the right number," Bix assured, feeling more confident than was probably merited. "Three pieces to the angels. Five to the dragons. Seven to the gods. Eleven to the Chweds."

"Fates are either the missing nine or the missing thirteen." Ashtad levered up on his heavily scarred leg. The damage from an old op ran from midthigh to midcalf, thus locking up his knee unless he applied some draconian measures.

"Or the missing one, but my gut says it's nine to the Fates. Nine is a sacred number used by prognosticators in some cultures. Since the Fates are the only ones who can see the future, I suspect original me was attempting a sense of humor." Bix gestured to the monitors. "Cian, are there interior images of the care facilities?"

"Interior and additional exterior images already sent to your smartwatch." Cian stared pointedly at her naked wrist, then pulled a smartwatch and ear-clip communication piece from his hoodie pocket. "Once you put it on, you'll have the mission pics."

"It's like he knows your bad habits." Ashtad laughed and shook a finger at her.

"Yeah, yeah, yeah." Bix grinned, grateful for the infusion of levity. She took the watch and the comm clip from the kid. "Thank you. Drew's still at Guild Hall trying to get to the bottom of the fiasco there. When she calls in, put her through to me, okay?"

"You're not going alone," Tobek said through his face mask, still working on his patient.

"I'm not volunteering more of your men to be god fodder. I warned Ogun. That fulfilled my political obligation," she scoffed, buckling the watch around her wrist and clearing the security protocols. She was having second and third thoughts about the safety of the Berserkers stationed outside Guild Hall. She didn't voice those concerns because she didn't want to insult the guys or their commander. However, evidence of the demon army's advantage was still dripping onto the floor of the clinic.

Yes, minimizing the risks to her larger team stood directly at odds with her need to protect without punching down. She hadn't figured out when to be hands-on and when to take her hands off, but her instincts said she had to get directly involved in this fight. Whoever Indraja's new shard hunter was, whoever had brought the Devourer army and this demon army to the Mids, they'd also brought a whole new level to the game. Bix had to shut that shit down. Right? Cosmic überentity or not, she was still part of a team and had the obligation to watch her team's backs.

"All well and good for the *one* location where you will be, sweetheart, but there are eight other locations on different Worlds." Tobek nodded to Runjit and carefully removed his bloody gloves. A pair of medics stepped in to assist Runjit in his stead. "We know there is a god of war with his demon troops and an army of Devourers trying to beat you to the shards. How the opposition is getting their intel on the locations, we don't know, but we have to assume they are on their way or there right now. Time is of the essence, even for you."

"You have men in surgery and a defense system to launch," she reminded, trying again to avoid having a spat about the capabilities of his battalion in front of an audience. She didn't know if the Berserkers had evolved enough to take on demons and Devourers. Evade and annoy assorted castes of divinity? No doubt. But Devourers had deployed *by the hundreds* to get the dragons' shards. The dragons had had gods aiding their defense and still had suffered. Then there was Hywl's team, bested by a demon ambush because there was another elite army after the shards that her side hadn't known about. The risks were too high. She couldn't keep asking the Berserkers to die for her causes, even when her causes were backstopping the Consortium and its screwups. She was the godsdamned cosmic entity. She was the greater power. She would put the demons and the Devourers in their proper places.

"Sweetheart, I have the manpower you lack and a better-than-passing familiarity with Oracles." Tobek tossed his bloodied gloves into a biohazard bin and ripped off his face mask, chucking that in the bin too. "Xipil? Get me nine teams ready to deploy."

Tobek's second-in-command appeared on a monitor with the ops room in the background. Flat nose. Wise eyes. Youngest by appearance, but actually one of the oldest Berserkers, Xipil was the master of resource management. "Calling up teams now, Chief."

It was a good thing Bix was acutely aware that all areas of the compound were heavily monitored—with the exception of the basement—or Xipil's sudden appearance might've unnerved her. As it was, she was simply peeved that Tobek didn't seem to get that she was trying to protect his men.

"Tobek—"

"Sweetheart," he interjected with a look that spoke volumes of understanding exactly where her head was. "We need to test our new boundaries, and when better to do it than with you standing ready to catch us if we overestimate ourselves?"

Oh, he had to go and play that card, did he? She stared at Hywl's mangled body and the medics working diligently to put him back together. Once upon a time, Berserkers had had restoration clauses in their Cycle of Souls contracts with the Fates, but they didn't have those contracts anymore. The contracts had been voided when the men had evolved beyond humans into this new type of undefined entity. How fast and how well would Hywl and the green team heal now?

"I'm coming too," Ashtad announced before Bix could pull the guys from the mission. "I want a second chance at those demons."

"You're barely upright," she objected.

"I'm a demigod with a demigod's swift healing." He chugged his drink, then wagged the mug at her. "Plus, I'm your friend, not your direct report."

She looked helplessly between Ashtad and Tobek, two men she trusted implicitly, two men who…well, who needed her to let them step up while she stepped back. Her challenge was knowing when to do that, and they were telling her. Plainly.

"Fine." She caved with a sigh. "Grown men can make their own decisions. Cian, you want in?"

Every lucid man in the room scowled at her, except the kid, who looked equal parts apprehensive and excited. In for a penny, in for a pound, Bix figured. If the other guys were going to test their abilities, Cian should also be afforded the chance. The entire to-do with the containment pyramid was about equal opportunity regardless of magical caste, after all.

"Yeah," Cian yelped, then cleared his throat. "But what about Drew and Resen?"

"We'll monitor the draugr from here," Tobek offered, glancing at Bix quizzically. "Our men are on-site anyway, should she need them."

"The foundational elements made it known at Guild Hall that they'd very much like the shards gone, so think of acquiring the Oracles' pieces as a critical step in supporting Resen's launch." Bix turned away from Tobek lest he spot how her nerves were at war with her temper. She didn't know which brand of Indraja's minions would attack the Oracles, and with this many allies shipping out for the mission, being unprepared had her on edge.

"I don't want to be a bu-burden," Cian stammered, his attention returning to Hywl.

"You're a team member, never a burden." She studied the images loading on her watch, the routine of mission prep helping to calm her. "You'll travel with me. Worst case, you get bundled up in starry night and suffer a bit of disorientation. Risk you're willing to take?"

"To meet biddy Oracles who still have the Houses of Fate's ear? Yeah. Definitely in." Cian clutched his tablet to his chest. "Unless my being there messes with the plan. What is the plan, by the way?"

"Gather all the shards and their bearers in one care facility. It's easier to defend a single location against whoever is coming," Tobek said before Bix could.

"After that, there's a rite of truth involved in handing over the shards to me. As a Sage, you ought to bear witness firsthand. You might be the Houses' only source for posterity." Bix hooked her arm around Cian's and had her watch project nine location images along her sleeve.

"Nine teams ready to deploy in the beer hall," Xipil said from his spot on high.

"Comms and cameras on all?" Tobek asked.

"Aye, Chief, Gurp's fit them up," Xipil confirmed, eyes flicking to monitors at neighboring stations. "Cian, waiting on connection to your team's feed. Drew's in good hands."

Cian glanced at Bix for approval. Bix nodded.

"Xipil, give me the live feeds of the team leaders so I can keep the gates moving with them, please," Bix requested as Tobek and Ashtad hustled down the corridor connecting the clinic to the beer hall, gathering weapons as they went.

"Coming through…now," Xipil confirmed.

Left with the medics and the wounded, Bix let the weight of consequences settle along her shoulders. "Runjit, I'm sorry Hywl was hurt helping me."

"He was harmed in the line of duty, Bix. To apologize is to devalue his contributions." Runjit suctioned fluids from Hywl's insides, sparing a glance at her. "We'll get the injured to their beds and reset for more incoming wounded, just in case. Deliver them to the beer hall, okay? Tabletops."

"Got it."

Squeezing Cian's arm with hers, she opened gates to a periwinkle tropical island in the middle of a magenta sea.

CHAPTER 17

Chartreuse raptors keened against the echoes of pitch-black owls riding currents of cool air on a balmy night. Shadows of feathered wings cut through soft green lights framing the seaside entrance of an exotic garden filled with pale blue broad-leafed trees, orange bushes, and multicolored flowers. Subtle, sweet, and delicious spice ebbed and surged with the crashing of the tides against high crags. A pollen-dusted pink walkway led Bix, Cian, and their assigned team of Berserkers through the heart of the garden, under arbors of sweeping vines that tickled cheeks and nibbled hair. Moonlight bounced off curved-tile roofs of longhouses built in a giant X that provided views of different gardens and unblocked sea. Strumming guitars and beating bodhrans blended with women singing and laughing, the lyrics growing more distinct as Bix's team approached the mouth of the garden.

Thirty human women of various ethnicities whose ages ranged from their fifties to well beyond sat on fat logs in seats worn smooth by use and time. The logs formed a large vee within the lee of the longhouses facing the garden. Canes and walkers rested against each other like rifles in a stacking swivel, while wheelchairs of rattan remained parked closer to the buildings.

A small fire crackled in an elevated trough, its light just bright enough to highlight the oracular markings of abundant moons in different phases that covered liver-spotted torsos and rose to frame wizened visages. Shawls and blankets woven with patterns of meaning covered shoulders and laps.

A wolf whistle cut above the song, causing the verse to end in gales of laughter.

"Whoowee, I'd forgotten how pretty these Berserker boys can be," one of the younger women hooted. Lecherous comments in many languages answered from the other Oracles, escalating with vividly filthy descriptions as if the women were determined to outdo the dirtiest sailor to sail any sea. Ever.

They succeeded in making the Berserkers blush.

Cian looked to Bix, his horrified expression full of questions. Apparently, exposure to biddies who had passed the age of having any care for anyone's opinions had not been included in his education. He'd been raised by an Oracle, but his mom hadn't been the most social of women. After her death, he'd been embraced by the brotherhood of the Berserkers. Bix and Drew were probably the most consistent feminine influences in his life right now... which maybe didn't bode well for his future. Maybe she ought to look in to correcting that after Resen launched.

"Hey, hey, hey, quiet, quiet, quiet," shushed a hunchbacked woman near the point of the vee. Firelight reflected off her cataracts as she lifted her chin and sniffed the air. "Did we get *her*, though, eh? Did we get the Chimera?"

"I am here," Bix answered.

"Ha, I told you she'd come to our island and send the men to the others." The blind Oracle held out her hand to a woman seated next to her. "You owe me three."

The woman next to her rolled her eyes and fished in a shawl pocket. Loudly, she counted out three pieces of hardtack candy as she placed them in the blind Oracle's hand.

"Oracle of the Future, you know why I'm here." Bix felt the tickle of her brother's magic emanating from where the longhouses intersected, revealing the sorting method as to which race had gotten which siblings' pyramid sections.

Fates, long believed to be agents of chaos, were actually creations of order meant to minimize the chaos wrought by gods. Oracles strove to become Fates, thus they'd received shards of order. Dragons were creations of her sister Music, who was also aligned with order, thus they'd been given shards of order too. Bix had already seen the copper shards of order at Guild Hall. That meant she'd be hunting shards of pewter chaos when it came time to claim the pieces given to the humans and stolen from the gods by the Devourers. However, that sorting didn't shine any light on the seventh piece or who might have it. Dang it.

"And you know where the piece is, but you can't have it until I tell you my truth, and I'm not going to do that until the others are here." The Oracle of the Future waved her fist full of candy. "Well, let us have a look, then. Open the doors to the other locations. Let us see how those beautiful men are faring corralling our sisters."

Seeing being relative—particularly to Oracles who often sacrificed their actual sight to their visions of the past, present, or future—the blind Oracle's cackle warned that Tobek's men were likely not having an easy time. Bix glanced at the feeds from the team leaders playing along her sleeve, confirming the Oracle's caution. A sweep of her hand—more for show than necessity—opened eight doorways curving along the garden.

The three sites to which she'd had trouble opening the initial gates were nothing but ruins. One smoldering still, one coated in tarry gunk, one razed as if giant bulldozers had crushed every plant, building, and...person. Still, the Berserkers assigned those Worlds searched for survivors, digging through the rubble and triple-checking corpses for pulses. The men didn't do anything half-assed, not with Tobek as their leader.

Bix's guts didn't sink. They didn't clench. They wavered between corporeal and insubstantial as malice fed her personal chaos. Indraja's new shard hunter had beaten Bix, yet again, to another trove of containment pieces. How were they doing it?

What advantage did they have that kept them ahead of her and her team?

"Xipil, why am I not getting the audio from the guys?" Bix muttered under her breath as the Oracles still capable of normal sight crept from their seats towards the gates.

"All teams running radio silent," Xipil answered from the coal plant. "Locations are compromised. Suggest you verify you are alone with the Oracles, Bix."

Caution morphed into predatory anticipation as Bix stretched her senses through every stalk and frond, down the cliffs and into the sea. There. Beneath the tides, swimming closer, demons.

How deliciously interesting.

The Oracle outposts that had been burned and razed could've been done by either demons or Devourers. However, the tarry gunk at the third destroyed outpost was indicative of Devourers. Yet to this outpost, Indraja had dispatched her demons. Why the difference? The targets were the same, so why send Devourers to one outpost and demons to another? Bix was missing something important from the equation. What was it? Or was the better question Who?

"Oracles," Bix sang out, "who are the uninvited guests at the other locations?"

"So many possibilities," the blind Oracle of the Future hedged.

"Oracles of the Present, help your sisters clarify their visions, or tonight's entertainment will be very short-lived for the mortals among us," Bix encouraged with a lick of annoyance while her shadows lay in wait for the demons swimming closer to the island. More darkness unraveled from her body and headed for the eight gates to the other outposts.

"Chimera, some battles are not yours to fight, now are they?" the hardtack-doling Oracle challenged before popping a piece of candy in her mouth.

Tentacles stopped on the thresholds.

Tobek had wanted this mission for his men. Needed it, in fact, for them to test their new abilities. *He'd* asked for *her* help. The role reversal was nice, but there was a lot at stake here. Which did she value more? The shards in her grubby mitts and securing the Oracles, or her long-term relationship with the Berserkers? If she lost the shards, she'd take another run at them, bobbing across the galaxy with the other stolen shards though they might be. If she lost the respect of the Berserkers, it would cause irrevocable damage to her relationship with Tobek. Relationships like theirs gave meaning to her unending immortal life. Tobek was more important to her than the shards, no contest.

Bix willed her malice to chill and all but one tentacle of shadows to return to her. The outlier pooled around Cian's feet. Safe, not sorry.

She forced her lips to curl into something resembling a smile and turned to the Berserker team leader watching her intently. Hywl normally got stuck with her when Tobek had to lead the troops, and the fact the angel hunter couldn't be here because of what demons had done to him and his team…made it really, really hard to step back from the action. But, much like the Consortium, Berserkers couldn't rise to the challenge if she wouldn't get out of the way.

"Demons advancing from the sea," she said, heeding the advice of the hardtack Oracle. "They have the island surrounded. Let me know if you want me to intervene."

"That will not be necessary, my lady," the Berserker team leader grumbled as his eyes brightened. Hand signals dispatched his men around the longhouses. The metallic song of Berserkers drawing weapons was echoed by the scraping of the younger Oracles tugging free their weapons from stash spots around the fire trough.

The blind Oracle of the Future patted the vacated seat beside her. "Come, Chimera. Join me as the trials arranged by the Fates play out."

Fates. Trials. A convergence of circumstances. Bix felt like an idiot for not expecting this cluster of fuckery.

With a bit of rueful peevishness, Bix nudged Cian to the open seat next to the candy-doling Oracle. The kid was smart enough to ask permission of the hardtack Oracle before sitting. He received a clump of candy, a pat on his thigh, and a coo of approval for his display of manners. Bix settled between the two senior Oracles. Shadows unthreaded from her spine and hovered behind those women too decrepit to join the imminent fray.

"The Houses of Fate arranged for you and yours to be killed, maimed, or captured. Why?" Bix smoothed her skirt and laced her hands in her lap. Her nails dug into her skin, the discomfort keeping her mind centered on the moment. She wanted nothing more than to surge through the outpost gates in her native state and rip apart anything that sought to steal the damn shards. She wanted to drain every last thought and memory from the enemy and glean the identities of their leadership and the new shard hunter. This race against lesser beings was crawling on her last cosmic nerve. Unfortunately, the rite of parrhesia and satyagraha hampered her, that and the need to let the Mids' defenders actually defend the Mids.

The more of her innate magics she regained, the less fun the limitations of being the greater power became.

The Oracle of the Future cackled and slid a piece of hardtack over her lips before tucking it against her cheek. "Same reason the original Berserker insisted on picking the fight instead of letting you at it. The Berserkers need the practice, and the Houses need the knowledge about their new and improved soldiers."

"Not their soldiers anymore," Bix reminded.

"Bah." The biddy dismissed with a flick of her wrist. "As long as the Houses control circumstances, they control the Berserkers, contracts or no."

An explosion on one of the Worlds spat tangerine ash and debris through a gate. The senior Oracles on the logs tittered and cheered.

"Was that demons or Devourers?" Cian asked with panic in his tone.

"That's our girls blowing their sanctuary, dearie. No need for us to be separated now that the Chimera has come to reclaim what's hers." The candy Oracle held up her hand and counted down from five, curling a finger with each descending number until she reached the number one, which she then pointed at the gate.

Oracles covered in bright orange ash bolted through the gate, calling to others behind them. Ashtad hobbled through, bracing a wounded Oracle. Bright-eyed Berserkers carrying the rest of the infirmed brought up the rear. The tingle of another shard made Bix uncurl her nails from her clenched hands, slightly.

A Berserker with more bars on his uniform than the others gently set his liver-spotted Oracle on a log and nodded to Bix. "That's all of us through, my lady."

Bix closed their gate. "Encounter any uninvited guests?"

"A sky portal opened just as we found the Oracles." Ashtad handed off his wounded woman to a pair of residents.

"Good thing the ladies were expecting us." The Berserker responsible for the shard keeper tucked a blanket around his charge, failing miserably at hiding his disappointment in missing a battle against the Devourers. He started to say something more, but as one, his unit stiffened. He let loose a series of sharp whistles, followed by hand signals.

As quickly as they'd arrived, they left to join the first team of Berserkers defending this island against the demons.

"I *will* call if we need you, Bix, promise," Ashtad assured before taking off after his assigned team of Berserkers.

Bix extended a few thin threads of shadows over the edges of the cliffs, not too far down, just close enough to strike if summoned. *Only* if summoned, she had to remind herself. She was accustomed to processing thousands of data inputs simultaneously thanks to her ethereal appendages, so keeping multiple eyes on the boys while entertaining the Oracles wasn't an issue.

"I smell burning kiwis and rotten petunias," the blind Oracle of the Future griped. "If we lost that World, it was a favor to anyone with a nose."

"One World safe and three Worlds gone to the enemy, yet you're cracking jokes, you old bat?" carped one of the recently arrived Oracles as she slid along the empty seats until she bumped into someone in an occupied seat. As she moved, so did the tickle of a shard. "We were only supposed to lose two if she came here first."

"Ezichi, is that you?" The Oracle of the Future patted the open air, searching.

"No, Benilda, it's the ghost of your lost virtue." The newest Oracle reached across the body separating her from the blind Oracle.

"And a miserable ghost you are, Ezichi." Benilda the blind gripped the outstretched hand of her friend and beamed. "Two Worlds lost was always too optimistic. We'll be lucky if half of us make it through this reckoning."

As if summoned by the words of failure, three teams of Berserkers emerged downcast and grim from the ruined Worlds to which Bix had had a hard time establishing viable destination gates. Unit leaders caught Bix's eye and shook their heads before leading their teams through the four remaining gates to aid their brothers.

Three shards lost to the competition. Three care homes with, what, three dozen human women at each home, just…gone. Probably not painlessly either. An acceptable loss to the Houses of Fate who could've simply sent a representative to Bix to tell her where to go and when. But nooo. They wanted the demons and the Devourers to have stolen segments. They wanted freakin' weapons of cosmic destruction in the hands of goons who did not have good intentions with regards to the Mids and the mortal populations. Why did agents of order insist on making things complicated and why was death inevitably involved? Bix didn't know whether to scream or shrug.

Grappling with her infamous temper, Bix forced herself to focus on the video feeds from the Berserkers fighting the good fight and to keep the gates moving with them as they advanced on the remaining care facilities.

"The deaths of our sisters were bound to happen, Chimera. The only question was when," the candy-dealing Oracle murmured. "This way, they got the mercy of dying before their bodies further failed them. They got to die in the name of glorious defiance. A last battle against foes that weren't their own minds."

"The rush to embrace mortality is no excuse for the Houses to arm enemies of the Mids." Bix widened a gate as Berserkers hauling ass with women thrown over their broad shoulders evaded demons chasing them on four, six, or eight legs. Bix opened a gate between the demons and the men, sending the demons tumbling into the ether.

She wasn't supposed to intervene. Eh, sue her. The boys weren't fighting the demons, so there was no battle skill to test. But there was a third shard to collect. Shard and keeper joined the other two on the log. A younger Oracle was quick to locate a tank of oxygen on wheels within the longhouse and bring it to the newest arrival.

Three teams remained in action.

Twinned blinding flashes of copper. Harmonized choruses of "Holy shit" and "Run, run, run," heralded the breathless arrivals of two other sects of Oracles and their Berserker escorts. The shard keeper of one contingent came through piggybacking on a younger Oracle, while the second came seated on the shoulders of a Berserker. Both keepers held their picket-shaped shards above their heads triumphantly. As they crossed paths on the safe side of the gates, they clinked shards and laughed with the zeal of narrow escapes.

"Tricked those sorry sons of bitches into using magic," one of the shard keepers jeered, sliding off the back of her ride and onto a log seat next to the Oracle breathing oxygen through a mask.

"Demons are dumb once you get hold of their ego." The second triumphant keeper giggled like a schoolgirl as her Berserker hefted her off his shoulders as though she weighed less than a feather pillow before making a grand production of putting her on the log in the seat Cian quickly vacated. "Chimera, good to finally meet you. Oh, and you brought the young Sage. Good, good, good. All on plan, then."

"Moira, Uki," Ezichi somewhat chastised, rolling her cloudy eyes. "Still a pair of loons."

"What the hell else are we going to do in our dotage? The weirder the better, that's my motto." Moira bumped elbows with the senior Oracle puffing away on her oxygen. "Did they lace it with the good stuff, Gin? Toes tingling yet?"

That earned a wink and a double puff from Gin the Oxygen Oracle. Snorts and good-natured ribbing from the rest of the Oracles of Moira's and Uki's Worlds followed the women into the longhouses where the sounds of furniture being dragged into new positions accompanied the hearty greetings of old friends reuniting.

Five scattered enclaves of Oracles brought together. Three that would never be. One still in question.

Tobek's contingent.

What was taking him so long?

CHAPTER 18

Bix allowed herself to breathe and acknowledge the flutters of plain happiness rolling off these women, who'd seen more in their many decades than the greatest adventurers of any World could fathom. For seventeen hundred years, mortal women who had been denied the reward of full Fatehood had kept safe, at great personal cost, fragments of the Fates' containment panel. Passing down, from generation to generation, a sliver the size of their hands. Knowing that should they be chosen as a keeper, they would never ascend. Still, they retained their pieces. They hadn't traded, sold, or misplaced them.

Respect. Bix certainly owed these Oracles and their predecessors that much. She didn't blame them for the machinations of the Houses of Fate. Looking around at the abundance of hugs and backslaps, Bix sought balance amid the sorority of the Oracles and the fraternity of the Berserkers.

"Xipil, put me through to him," Bix said quietly, closing all gates but the set Tobek's team needed.

"Connected," Xipil answered.

"Tardy to the party, Tobek," she teased, somewhat, keeping her voice low. "You don't get bonus points for being fashionably late."

"There is some question as to where they placed the shard," he responded with exasperation. "Earthquakes over the years apparently caused it to shift its location."

The candy-doling Oracle beside Bix hooted a note of mirth, then tugged Bix closer. Her eyes turned white with the arrival of an oracular vision. "Tell those carb-loaded fools, it's under the pizza oven, about three feet."

"Did Priya lose it?" Moira slapped her thigh. "Oy, tell the Original to clear the room, then aim a blast at the floor. One short burst. It'll bite back. No digging required."

"Tobek," Bix started to say, but his droll groan said he'd heard.

"It's not the *shard* biting back that worries me," he reminded.

"We've had two instances of individual shards activating without annoying the foundational elements," Bix countered, gesturing to Cian and his tech. The kid nodded and started tapping away. If Resen was going to react to Tobek and a shard being in the same place, maybe Cian could give him a warning. "Chweds had all their shards rebel at once. Potency matters to the foundational elements."

"Or proximity," he said, as if reading her mind.

"You wanted to know what would happen," Bix taunted. "I am standing by for a quick body snatch. Or bodies snatched, to be more accurate. Just say the word."

The words he said were orders to his men to fall back. Bix waited with bated breath.

Around her, a rising din of masculine voices overrode the higher tones of the Oracles as Ashtad and the two teams of Berserkers defending this island from the seabound demons finally returned. They were soggy, bleeding, covered in ichor, and plucking clumps of demon flesh from their clothes. Yet, triumph screamed through their swagger as they clasped forearms with their drier brethren.

Gods in any form couldn't die, but they could be beaten, mauled, and bullied into retreat. Bix pushed her threads of darkness into the water to verify the demons had gone and not just popped out to lull the Berserkers into false serenity. Marine life stirred, but nothing divine. Still, she left her threads to bob in the deeps. If the demons did come back, she would have a snack before anybody was the wiser. She scratched her stomach. Her emotional roller coaster was making her hungry.

A bestial growl rumbled across her connection to Tobek. Berserkers damp and dry huddled together with the Oracles in the courtyard on her island. Everyone watched the scene unfolding outside a single-story square Mediterranean-styled compound with whitewashed walls and high arches around verdant gardens. The sun was setting on Tobek's World as Tobek's team of Berserkers and the last group of Oracles in need of rescue gathered outside the building.

A half-second burst of deep green flashed against the plaster walls. A disproportionately huge copper explosion answered. Walls cracked and crumbled. Berserkers and Oracles dropped into crouches, covering their heads as the debris cloud rolled and boomed.

In the sky, a mirror-surfaced portal opened.

"Tobek, you've got company," Bix hissed, doing her damnedest not to shout. The Berserkers on her island stepped to the threshold like runners on the starting line. She obliged them by widening the gate. If they got the summons, she sure as shit didn't want a bottleneck to slow them down.

"The blast buried the shard further," Tobek griped. "Priya is refusing to leave it behind and so am I."

Bix watched Devourers descend by the dozens and bit her tongue. Tobek knew she was waiting on his go. She didn't have to nag him, no matter how tempting it was. However, the go call he gave was to his men. Two teams of Berserkers from her island launched through the gate, drawing weapons as battle cries announced their arrival. Oracles, the ones fit and mobile, chased after them, peeling away to grab their sisters while the men engaged the anti-gods.

Ashtad positioned himself with the next batch of eager soldiers.

"Sit your ass down, architect," Uki called to him. "This test isn't for you. You and the Sage are going to have your opportunities soon enough."

Ashtad turned on the old Oracle, prickling with elitist umbrage. Before his ego let him say something he'd regret, he got a tablet in the chest. Cian's half-blurted words made no sense to Bix, but they made Ashtad's brows draw down to his nose.

"Bix, get the Oracles out of there now," her erstwhile boss said in a flat tone that Bix knew from years of being on his team of elite operatives meant ugly was imminent.

Shadows surged from her into Tobek's World like a rising fog of pitch black, hunting the Oracles' unusual resonances of a human's null space laced with a shiver of a Fate's Other World magic. She passed through and around Berserkers, who paid her no mind in their conflict. Devourers, on the other hand, skirted and evaded like prey taken by surprise. The anti-gods' reactions gave the Berserkers an advantage, but only briefly. Once the Devourers understood she wasn't coming for them, they laid into the Berserkers like the pod-raised militaristic species they were.

Darkness snatched Oracles, and gates swallowed them, dumping the women back on the island of safety. The Oracle farthest from exfil was, naturally, the shard keeper digging through the debris at Tobek's feet while he braced for the approaching troops of Devourers. Anti-gods advanced over the ruins with ease, as though wading through Styrofoam, surrounding Tobek and cutting him off from his men.

Tobek had taken his stand directly above the shard. If he'd put more weight on his left foot, he'd sink the two feet needed to leave a print on the shard's surface. Alas, Priya wasn't digging in that spot. About three sword lengths separated Tobek from the closest Devourer. He wanted them closer. They wanted to be closer.

Oh, for fuck's sake.

Bix's darkness fanned around her Berserker. An aura of serpentine black shadows snapped and lunged at the Devourers, creating the distraction needed to dive beneath Tobek's boot and retrieve the shard while more shadows bundled up Priya. Oracle and shard dropped into a gate and onto the last open seat on the log.

"Have fun storming the castle," Bix whispered through her darkness, letting it carry across the battlefield before returning to her corporeal form.

Her damn man laughed. Spun his sword and laughed. The mania in his tone was amplified by his men as the melee began in earnest.

"If the shard's not there anymore, the Devourers can use magic against our guys, right?" Cian asked, staring at the last opened gate as though his life was the one about to be lost. "Our guys just have swords and axes and regular weapons."

Ashtad handed the kid his tablet and pointed to five spots around the edges. "See that? Points of a pentagram, yeah?"

Cian gripped the frame of his tablet with white knuckles. "The foundational elements are weaving new intersections around Chief?"

"I think he's summoning them," Ashtad said, pinning Bix with a trepidatious look.

A smattering of Oracles tittered knowingly.

Bix felt her features puckering to mirror Ashtad's. Had Tobek unconsciously summoned Resen's counterattack at Guild Hall? Had the foundational elements responded not to the shards activating, but to Tobek reacting to the arrows launching? Prior to his recent evolution, Tobek had wielded complex Mids' magic through elaborate spells anchored by pentagrams. As she watched him gleefully hack his way through Devourers, his skin blistering from their toxic blood spatter, she had to wonder. Neither he nor she knew the scope or boundaries of his new and improved self. Whether he'd initiated Resen's attack or not, there was still the probable outcome of him being liquified for calling such potent powers into himself.

"This isn't good," Cian groaned. "That changes load balances. We built the data centers on the assumption the intersections on the existing Mid Worlds were fixed within n parameters. Shit, man.

If Chief can create intersections on demand, then we need to calculate for increased output and random variables. We're going to need more centers, and that's going to take time we don't have."

More Oracles laughed.

"Ah, Sages," Priya hooted, waving her shard like a fan. "Always thinking you're the smartest beings in the room until life shows up."

"Told you your tests were coming, architect." Uki winked at Ashtad. "You want to ascend to a deity greater than a Mid World guardian? You're going to have to get neck-deep in magics that aren't rooted here. That starts with the Fates' contribution to Resen."

Ashtad accepted the guidance with an inclination of his head and leaned over Cian's shoulder, exchanging mutters with the kid as Cian tapped faster and faster on his tablet.

Bix's attention kept returning to the sight of Berserkers versus Devourers. The good news was they were evenly matched when it came to brute strength and skill with weapons. The better news was that the men had evolved into entities who *could* kill Devourers, meaning the gods and Bix were no longer the only ones capable of taking down the enemy permanently. That was huge for the men, Resen, and the Mids.

The bad news remained the multiplying numbers of Devourers.

Despite every Berserker from Bix's island joining the fracas, Devourers kept coming through the portal by the baker's dozen. No matter how many anti-gods they slaughtered, the Berserkers were outmanned five-to-one, and Tobek had yet to call a retreat.

"Bix, might want to change the door to a window," Ashtad said without looking up from Cian's tech.

Bix did as asked without argument. She trusted Ashtad to have a good reason for trapping the Berserkers on the battlefield. Altering the gate didn't change the view from Oracle island, it simply prevented anyone from crossing Worlds. All the boys had to do was make a run toward the window, and she'd flip it to a threshold again.

The Oracles filed out of the longhouses to watch the wide window of battle like some big-screen TV. Younger Oracles sat on the ground in front of the logs, keeping a healthy distance from the fire trough. Others crowded shoulder to shoulder behind the logs. The Oracles seated on the logs shuffled their seating order so the shard keepers flanked Bix, creating quickly filled seats on outer ends.

"Heads up," Cian called as he and Ashtad stared through the window. "Eyes on the skies, everyone."

Sword in his prosthetic hand, Tobek raised his natural hand to the sky. A circle of purple nimbi appeared inside a circle of blue, and within their frame, greens painted a pentagram. Bix bolted up from her seat, heart in her throat, blocking her scream of denial as the foundational elements of Resen shot a stream of unfiltered magics down Tobek's arm and into his body. The comm in Bix's ear keened a toothaching pitch before cutting out. Tobek glowed brighter than a neon sign until he was a big ball of light driving the Devourers to their knees. Tobek aimed his sword at the portal.

Denials screamed through Bix's head as five of the longest heartbeats thundered in her ears before the portal blew. The frame shattered into silver dust. Mirrored droplets fell in a downpour over Berserker and Devourer alike. Bright jewel-toned blast waves rushed over the terrain, lighting up Berserkers like Christmas trees from hair to boots and linking the men together in a net of hunter-green magic. Devourers caught within the net screamed and writhed before exploding in tarry spatters.

A unified groan of disgust came from the Oracles. Cian snickered. Ashtad whispered, "Fuck."

Bix teetered on the tips of her toes, eyes fixed on the waning light that had consumed Tobek. Liquid, gas, or charcoal. In which state would her Berserker be? Godsdamn it all. If he'd done this intentionally… If this was the test he'd wanted… She'd… He'd…

Tobek's light went out, and with it the netting linking his men. Those closest to his position ran toward empty space. She couldn't see her big blond bear of a Berserker. He was down. Down as what, who knew?

"Bix?" Xipil's calm voice came through her comm. "I'd like to send science teams to the battlefield. We need to understand the physical and environmental effects of what just happened."

"Tell me there's something tangible left of him," she managed with minimal quavering as Berserkers chased down the Devourers who'd escaped the net. Her watch chirped with the notification of a new image. A tap projected Tobek's picture down her sleeve. He sprawled like a broken man over the ruins, skin blackened and blistered, long hair burned to smoking roots, uniform incinerated, blue eyes wide but dull, prosthesis and sword reduced to a metallic puddle dripping from irritated amputation scars. Definitely unconscious. "Lightly crispy, then?"

"We've seen him in worse condition," Xipil admitted dryly.

"Gurp's going to read him the riot act." Bix braced her hands on her knees, bending forward and exhaling loudly. Relieved gasping slowly turned into rueful chuckles. She was going to kill Tobek once he healed.

"The goblin is already in peak form at the head of the scientists' queue," Xipil confirmed.

"Opening beer hall gates," she said, flopping down in her seat and acknowledging with a smile the sea of wistful and charmed expressions from the women surrounding her. "Leaving the door open until instructed otherwise."

"He's in good hands. We'll see you back at base, Bix."

At that, her comm went quiet. She kept the viewing gate open, just in case. Who knew what aftershocks Tobek's little stunt would instigate?

"That's what we call real entertainment," Moira crowed and wagged her shard in the air. "Chimera, it's time. I would have you hear our truths."

CHAPTER 19

Bix inhaled a clarifying breath, homing her focus to just this World. She breathed in the floral and spicey fragrances wafting from the garden along with the pure clean of unpolluted sea water. It was time, at last, to hear what the Oracles had to say about the defense of the Mids and the sunsetting of the ether. Bix bid her shadows to withdraw the partial containment pyramid from her body and balanced it above her lap within a frame of protective gates.

"Are we a quorum, then?" Benilda perked up. She flapped a questing hand behind her, in the general vicinity of the longhouse. A younger Oracle stepped from the doorway and placed a shard firmly in the blind Oracle's hand.

"Six of nine," Ezichi confirmed, the trenches of wrinkles around her lips erased by the breadth of her smile. "Six of us made it to the reclamation, sisters. Our predecessors would be proud."

Six Oracles raised their copper-colored, picket-shaped shards to shoulder height and cheered. That cheer echoed across the island from every Fate-tried woman. At last, the end of a trial that had gone on and on for seventeen hundred years.

Talk about endurance and stamina.

"Parrhesia and satyagraha," Bix said, resting her hands in her lap, beneath the partial pyramid pulsing with primordial magics of chaos and order. "I am the power who seeks your truths, Oracles of the Past, Present, and Future. Be bold and unafraid in your declarations."

"A chastisement from the past," Ezichi began, and her shard hummed. "Malice and balance cannot coexist, thus the Mids cannot give you the succor you seek until you finish grieving the loss you refuse to confront."

Before Bix could respond with any of one of the dozen questions rising to her tongue, Priya jumped in.

"A gentle reminder from the past." Priya pressed her shard to her chin and gazed at Bix with sadness. "You made the conscious, deliberate decision to embrace absolute weakness and vulnerability in the time of your greatest anguish. To understand why, you must face the cause and consequences of that pain before you will be able to capture the ether."

Ezichi's and Priya's shards tumbled end over end to affix themselves to the completed angels' panel of chaos, thus beginning the Fates' panel of order. Bix glanced to the window at the Berserkers arriving in hazmat suits and setting up decontamination tents for their gore-covered brothers. Tobek lay at odd angles on a cot carried by his men. Grief, Ezichi had said. Grief would explain why Tobek wouldn't talk about why she'd left him all those years ago. Grief would explain his uncharacteristic response when she'd asked about it at the coal plant.

The cluster of raw pain within Bix's memories strained against the reinforcements of thorny malice, causing her eye to twitch. Yeah, whatever Ezichi and Priya wanted her to deal with had to be inside that blister. She'd promised herself she'd deal with it *after* Resen was up and running. *After* she knew her loved ones were safe. According to Ezichi and Priya, however, she didn't have that luxury anymore. She could question the veracity of the visions from the Oracles of the Past, but there wasn't a point. Their truths were *their* truths, the shards wouldn't have released themselves otherwise.

"An assertion from the present." Moira balanced her shard on her fingertip. "The shards you think you've lost are precisely where they need to be in order for you to hear the truths from parties who matter in *this* moment of change."

Bix wasn't sure how those Devourer confessions were going to be elicited, much less comprehended. She had a lot of her language skills back in her skull, but her Devourer linguistics were rusty. As for the demons, better if Ogun got to them and their shards before she did. Hangry. Happening soon. Killing the shard keepers herself was probably bad what with the rite of transference.

Gin took a deep breath, then pulled aside her mask. "The second assertion of the present: the seventh panel keeper will reveal themselves once the others are complete. That they remain hidden from all hunters, including you, is a feature of the device's design."

Had to mean the seventh piece was different in composition from the sides, which meant a different sibling had been involved. Leave it to the original Chimera to make stuff more complicated than necessary. She bit her tongue as the paired shards of the present joined the paired shards of the past as part of the containment pyramid. This was turning out to be the most concerning case of confessions, but then, dealing with Fate-based stuff was always tricky at best and bite you in the face at second best.

"A caution from the future, Chimera." Benilda paused as her shard brightened and trembled in her hand. "The caretakers of the Mids must face the Devourers without your intervention. However, you must protect us all, even our enemies, from those whose desperation has driven them past the brink of rationality."

Bix cocked her head. Protect the Devourers? Did a mortal of the Mids really just make that demand of her? Of course Bix would protect the anti-gods as a species. They were part of her balanced diet. That was why she had to draw a hard line with Ogun about how involved she would be in the defense of the Mids. However, Benilda was making her question the "from whom" variable.

"An encouragement from the future." Uki tapped her shard against Bix's arm and smiled with soft understanding. "You have to give him back his sword so he can finally serve as the champion you knew he could become for this collective."

Bix's brain blanked as her lips formed the words "his sword." Who what now? Uki poked the pointed end of her shard above Bix's heart, in the spot where Bix used to carry a piece of Tobek within her.

Tobek.

Bix's attention snapped to the window overlooking the Berserkers. Tobek's sword. Not the liquified one. *His sword of light.* Oh wow. She'd forgotten all about it. The damage he'd wrought to the Mids with that sword while he'd been a demigod still pissed off for trading his divinity to the Fates had been epic. As in the stories of his ruthless bloodlust persisted to this day. Naturally, he'd forfeited the sword of light and his original prosthesis when she'd gone all High Executioner on his degenerate demigod ass. It'd only been a few epochs since she'd hidden it…somewhere. Oops.

Bix leaned toward Uki. "Don't suppose you know where I put it?"

Uki tipped her head against Bix's and chuckled as the last pair of shards fit into the incomplete Fates' panel of order. "Oracle of the Future, sorry."

Bix shared Uki's laugh and then stood. "Oracles, keepers, and caretakers alike, thank you. Thank you for protecting these shards through the generations. Thank you for protecting each other and the Mids. Your truths have been heard. Your advice heeded. Your rebukes taken to heart."

Her shadows carried the incomplete containment device through the gathering of Oracles, allowing them to finally see what they'd sacrificed their freedoms for. Thinly layered gates boxed in the partial pyramid to protect everyone from its potency. Since the Oracles were mostly human, their combined presence grounded whatever magics still came through. Didn't stop Cian from backing as far away from the thing as he could when his crystalized shoulders glowed faintly. Ashtad caught the kid by the front of the kid's hoodie before Cian stepped off the edge of a cliff.

"Bix, I hate to interrupt." Xipil's voice whispered in her ear. "I've got Drew on the line. Insistent on getting through to you now."

"Go ahead, and include Cian and Ashtad on the call, please." Bix casually ambled to the last guys on estrogen island as unease prickled over her skin. She'd left Drew at Guild Hall primed to inhabit an archer's body. A lot of hours had passed since Drew had last made contact. Not good.

"Chimera," chirped an unfamiliar masculine voice over the comms. "Look, I've made a bit of a discovery. You need to see it. Now."

Bix, Ashtad, and Cian exchanged bothered scowls. Drew never called Bix by her moniker unless Drew was giving her grief. The cadence of his speech wasn't Drew's cadence, nor was the word choice. When dealing with a draugr, those details mattered.

"Sure, Drew. Not a problem. Just give me the location," Bix responded as if nothing was amiss while her shadows folded the partial pyramid into her corporeal state.

"Swamp Fox Road, Alexandria," the impersonator said with a giggle that ended in a pig snort. "Can't miss me."

"Be there in five," she said, signaling Cian to cut the line.

"Isolated Drew's comm within our network and notified Xipil via text that the line's compromised." Cian flipped his tablet to face Bix, giving her the street-view visual of the area. "That address is a movie theater complex that's closed for remodeling. Smack in the middle of ground-level shopping, multistory condos, and lots of parking garages. The signal from Drew's comm is coming from inside the movie theater. An upstairs theater, based on elevation."

"Massive collateral damage if Bix doesn't play by the rules." Ashtad shoved his damp hair from his face. "Do we think Drew is sending a coded message, or that someone stole the draugr's comm?"

"The latter, which means they have Drew. That's really all I need to know at this point." Bix closed the viewing window to the Berserker battlefield and forced a good-natured grin as the Oracles mockingly objected to their loss of masculine entertainment while bending to the myriad tasks required to house their sisters from the other sites.

"Drew was at Guild Hall keeping tabs on the Chweds' shards," Cian murmured, fighting a yawn. "Did she leave by choice or was she snatched?"

"We don't know. The Berserkers have the hall under surveillance but were ordered to not enter because of the chaos inside." Bix let the shiver of an idea that the archers' attack had been a guise for something else to pass without closer examination. Right now, she had to focus on getting Drew home. "I'm going to send you two back to the coal plant. You need food and sleep. Bunk down with the boys, that way if something comes up, they can call you in. Okay? Gurp's probably already made your beds."

Shockingly, neither argued with her. Cian couldn't because the yawn he'd been fighting overtook his face.

"We'll worry about the humans' segments after you get a solid six hours of sleep. Tobek's going to be offline for at least that long if not days, so take the breather." She looked at both of them pointedly. "I mean it."

Bix couldn't take a break, not with Indraja's shard hunter still amassing pieces. As soon as she secured her bestie, she'd return to Guild Hall and convince the masters to give up their segments. After the shards had attacked their membership, the masters might be feeling the pressure to divest themselves of the protections turned weapons.

"Bix, if someone's holding Drew against the draugr's will, that someone has to be an upper-midlevel god or greater." Ashtad took Bix's hand in his and gently uncurled her nails from the punctures in her skin. "That someone could be Indraja."

"Or her new shard hunter, or an upper-ranking Devourer. I'll take on any of them at this point. There aren't many entities left who are ballsy enough to make demands of me. Most have learned better." Bix stared at the half-moons of exposed mist and midnight in her palm and honed her temper into malice. Malice was useful. It might not be able to coexist with succor like the Oracles had warned, but Bix wasn't after succor right now. Little did Ashtad know that Drew could be *killed* if trapped in the body of a greater god or anti-god and suffocated by their divinity. Bix wasn't going to tell him. Some secrets weren't hers to tell, especially since Ashtad and Drew didn't actually like each other. Respect? Grudgingly. Like? No.

"I'll talk to Xipil about Guild Hall, see if anyone noticed Drew leaving. Go rescue our captured teammate, Bix." Ashtad put on his politician's smile and raised a hand in farewell to the Oracles watching their little confab with intense interest. "I'll make sure the kid gets some sleep."

Bix knew that meant Ashtad wasn't going to sleep. He'd keep overwatch while she ran the retrieval mission. It was what they did. Their team. They looked out for each other. With a nod of understanding the unspoken, she opened gates beneath her guys and dropped them at the back of the beer hall in the coal plant.

Malice primed for conflict, Bix said her goodbyes to the six formerly separated enclaves of senior Oracles coming together as one sisterhood on a tropical paradise. She would've liked to have lingered among them for a little while, but no one harmed her bestie without repercussions.

Drew had better still be alive, or Bix was going to go on a World-ending rampage. Wasn't going to be Mid Worlds that ceased to exist either.

CHAPTER 20

The stink of industrial adhesives, freshly pressed vinyl, and dyed olefin overwhelmed the unlit theater. This was one of the smaller viewing rooms, where films about to leave circulation would be shown. Rows of shrink-wrapped extra-wide red recliners with cupholders and flip-up trays lined one wall, waiting to be bolted into their prenumbered placements. Exposed soundproofing foams were nestled between exposed wall studs. Huge speakers pointed at different segments of the would-be audience for that lauded surround-sound experience. Large and small spools of color-coded cables leaned against the framing of the massive screen, some reels more spent than others. The peculiar view of seatless rows stepping ever upward toward the unfinished back wall revealed no balcony, just the projection window.

Bix had expected a stage. Gods loved to perform in the heated glow of footlights and spotlights. Apparently not true of the deity seated on stacked five-gallon construction buckets smack in the middle of the theater and surrounded by rolls of carpet.

Not Indraja. He didn't emit the resonance of a greater god like Indraja, nor did he ooze the taint of a Devourer. The god on the buckets was an upper-midlevel Mid World guardian radiating with bits of extra magic that didn't belong to him. The first belonged to an Other World entity, specifically Drew. The second belonged to a single shard of chaos. The third belonged to Bix and the fragments of her missing memories.

Fuck.

Every keeper of her memories had proven to be nuts. The fragments of her arcane knowledge, smaller than pixels and not enough to provide any useful information, baited the gods' curiosity to the point it drove the keepers mad. Microfragmentation had been her method of encrypting her knowledge. The madness was an unfortunate side effect, one that never worked in her favor.

"Chimera, the address I gave you was Swamp Fox Road, but it seems this little bit of technology your draugr was keen to keep contains a tracking device too. Clever, for a lesser entity. However, the old Chimera wouldn't have needed it." The memory keeper spoke as though profoundly congested as the floor lights came up.

A snout explained the congestion. A short, round, pale pink snout. A pig's snout. Belonging to a pig-man god. Man-pig god? Not a fearsome tusked wild boar. No, nothing so venerated. His tactical gear embroidered with a flourish of logographs down his right front placket couldn't hide his paunch any more than his modified boots hid his cloven feet.

In the depths of memories Bix did possess, recognition flared. Since memories were relational, his story unfolded rapidly within her mind. It was a first for her, recognizing a memory keeper, but bound to happen now that she'd reclaimed five of seven memory segments. The sixth segment was contained in the deity sitting before her far too smugly.

Once upon a very distant time, this guardian had been an admiral, the chief military officer for his pantheon, with scores of soldiers under his command. His true form was a strong-jawed, sharp-eyed, androgynous beauty, lithe and muscular. Greed, pride, and lust had been his downfall. Since those attributes were common to most gods, the fact he'd earned himself the inalterable visage of a flop-eared, pale pink piggy spoke to the depths of his depravity.

"Can't muster a glamour, can you, Pigsy?" Bix taunted, widening her stance and crossing her arms as her hungry shadows slithered from her spine to form a lattice along the theater walls and ceiling, assessing the situation from multiple angles. "The Jade Emperor cursed you well when he stripped you of all authority and kicked you out of the pantheon."

Three things Bix desperately wanted had been nicely packaged inside a delectably divine meal. If she'd still been a feral amnesiac, she would've instantly husked the pig and sprung the obvious trap. Alas, the Pigsy she'd once known was far too smart to offer himself as bait without there being one hell of a gotcha. So, while she didn't have the time or the desire to entertain a divine ego, he had Drew. Thus, she had to apply a shred of patience to suss out his game.

"Mind yourself, Chimera. You do not have the upper hand here." His poorly stifled porcine squeal ended with a grunt as he unzipped his jacket and retrieved the shard of chaos she'd sensed upon arrival. He swept the pewter fragment through the glow of the floor lights as though it were a small dagger. "This little bauble defends its bearer against greater magics. Extensive testing revealed its response is proportional to the power behind the attack."

Bix had figured as much after contrasting the reactions of the shards at Guild Hall responding to Chwed magic versus the reactions of the shards the Oracles had used to blow up their outposts after goading demons into attacking with divine magic. Theoretically, if she, a cosmic entity, attacked Pigsy with anything more potent than a fist to his face, the shard would incinerate miles more than the few blocks of this theater complex. Possibly hundreds of miles.

Gotcha number one, noted.

"I gather that is why we're sitting in the middle of a shopping center topped by condominiums and apartments." Bix sauntered to a spool at the front of the theater and flipped it with her shadows so it made a proper perch. "How very like you to use innocent lives as shields. If you have that trinket to protect you, why take the draugr?"

She hoped she sounded apathetic, because mentally, she was tearing her hair out wondering how the hell he had gotten his mitts on Drew and a chaos shard. True, the gods' shards were chaos shards. However, she'd recruited *knowledge* gods to keep the gods' segments of the containment device. Pigsy was not a knowledge god nor did he emit the taint of a Devourer's curse that would've marked him as an escaped prisoner of Indraja and the anti-gods. No way would Indraja have just handed it to him, so could he possibly have *stolen* it from the greater goddess? If so, that would make him useful. Hell, it would've made him an ally if he hadn't taken Drew.

"Oh, the shard will protect me from a direct physical assault by you, but the draugr is here to protect me from your other aspects, like that pesky teleporting of which you're so fond." He jabbed the pointed tip of the shard at his chest. "I will smother your dearest friend out of existence before you can dump me in the lap of the Consortium, or anywhere else, for that matter. We both know you can feel the draugr's weak presence inside me, so don't bother asking for proof of life."

Gotcha number two, noted.

"You have my attention, Pigsy. What do you want?" Bix clacked her heels against the wooden spindle as the notion of embedding her stilettos in Pigsy's skull became more and more appealing. He had her over a barrel and knew it. She wouldn't sacrifice Drew any more than she would allow the humans or Chweds in this area to come to harm. Yes, she could discern Drew's resonance wasn't all it ought to be, which made her extra twitchy and extremely anxious. Pigsy was the kind who killed just to prevent someone from having what they needed.

"I want what they failed to get me." Pigsy flicked his wrist, and rolls of carpet unfurled, heavy enough to thump and whump down the stairs, depositing headless corpses at her feet.

The shoes, the pants, the shirts… Bix recognized them.

"These are the archers from Guild Hall. Wait. *You're* behind the attack on the guild masters?" she accused as a second assessment of the bodies located the archer she'd positioned Drew to inhabit. That explained why Drew had jumped from a Chwed into a god strong enough to kill the draugr. Last body that still had a head. Drew would've chanced it with a god rather than suffer the indignities of being noncorporeal. Drew was reckless and prideful like that.

"The draugr thought it could take over me. *Me.* As if I haven't battled armies from Other Worlds countless times during my life." Pigsy squealed with delighted derision. "Cursed or not, I am and have always been a god of *war.*"

"You are and have always been a god of the spoils of war, a god of *greed.* Slaughter is a fringe benefit to you," Bix snapped as her temper wedded with her distress. She had been right there, right in the thick of the attack on Guild Hall, and hadn't sensed any part of this. Worse, she'd practically delivered her best friend to this mad god. "Why, Pigsy? What do you care for unionized Chweds? Surely you're not that desperate for their souls?"

Souls were the food of the gods, which also made souls the currency of the pantheons. Pigsy was a glutton, yes, but his possession of a shard, his abduction of Drew, and the timing of his intrusions was building a dread knot in her gut.

"Corrupting souls before consuming them does add a certain piquant flavor, I shan't argue." He waved a carefree hand. "It was easy enough, of course. Mortal desires never change, despite the passing of time. More food, more money, better shelter, better health, and pretty please will I save the life of a loved one?"

"I don't care *how* you corrupted them, Pigsy, I care *why.*" Bix immediately regretted letting her temper flare as he adopted a mulish moue. She had to be more mindful of his broken mind and violent inclinations, which, pot-kettle.

"The why should be obvious." Pigsy harrumphed with disgust. "The *weapons?* The Chwed guilds are hoarding weapons that could drive the Devourers from the Mids."

Her heart stilled and malice wriggled beneath her skin while her brain scrambled to fit what he'd just said into every assumption on which she'd been operating this entire mission. Small problem. Didn't fit. Surely he couldn't mean… Surely he couldn't be…

"You…" Bix had to pause to keep her corporeal state from exploding into a storm of unbridled wrath. "*You* are the other shard hunter? The demons pursuing the shards, the weapons, as you call them, they're *yours*?"

"Soldiers who never deserted me, cursed by the Jade Emperor to wander as demons for eons until they renounce me. Tell me, how does that compare to the loyalty of the Berserkers, who had no choice in being tethered to a failed demigod by rage?" He sneered and lifted his multiple chins.

"The Berserkers? What do they have to…" Bix stopped speaking as the obvious slapped her and ratcheted her fury higher. "*You* led the attack on Hywl's team. *You* have Sophia. *You* took Drew, on top of all that? Who are you planning to trade them to? Who is giving you your targets? Who is sending you after my friends and my toys? Who is helping you beat me to the shards?"

Bix's darkness could no longer be restrained. It blasted throughout the theater like a thick, thorny foam, writhing with her rage. Pigsy leapt up from his buckets with a squeal.

"Temper, temper, Chimera," he cried. "We don't want anything to happen to your little friends, do we?"

Drew. Drew. Drew. Focus on Drew. Focus on how feebly the resonance of her best friend struggled within the body of the god of greed. Any fast moves and Pigsy would end Drew. Teeth grinding, Bix exerted considerable effort to back her shadows away from the mad god.

"That's better, Chimera. Better," he said patronizingly, waving the pewter shard under his nose as though inhaling the bouquet of a cabernet. He hummed with exaggerated satisfaction. "I've spent years collecting these precious little slivers. Ever since a *human* worshipper left a piece in my holy temple. *Human*. The idiot thought he'd trapped an evil spirit inside. He had no idea it was protecting him from violent magic. A pity he had to die before his blathering made it to the ears of the Jade Emperor."

Bix spared a passing thought for the murdered human shard keepers before returning her focus to the god's words. Her heartbeat slowed to a reasonable pace. "You said you collected the humans' 'slivers'? Plural? The one you're holding isn't the only one you have?"

"Only a fool would keep all his leverage on his person when meeting with a greater power. If I don't depart here hale and in full control of my mental faculties, every sliver I have collected will be used as a weapon to avenge me. My army will carry on this war even if I fall." He slid the shard into his jacket pocket and preened with menacing delight. "Yes, to answer your question. Yes, I got them all. Every last one bestowed upon a human and a few that weren't. It's been a fantastically stimulating hunt, and I'm not done yet."

"How can you be sure you have all the humans' shards? How did you even know there were pieces other than those given to humans for which to search?" she challenged, both pleased that she didn't have to dig through the human diaspora of the last seventeen hundred years to find the shards, yet decidedly furious he'd stolen them. How many wars had he instigated in his quest? His greed had driven all empathy from him, turning Pigsy into a psychopath. That didn't bode well for Drew or the mortals in this mixed-use complex. She had to tread very, very carefully lest she be the only thing still standing for miles.

"*She* told me," Pigsy said, as if Bix was daft.

"She being...Indraja? Are you so clueless you don't know she's in league with the Devourers? Did she play upon your greed to trick you?" Bix bit her lip, again regretting the heavy mockery in her tone as he threw the buckets that had once been his chair at the big screen. They tore through the fabric and echoed off the back wall.

"How *dare* you?" Pigsy poked himself in the chest, skin flushing with outrage. "I am a Mid World guardian. My life, my magic, my power is rooted in these Worlds. I am not some fool to betray the wellspring of what I am. I am no ally to the fatuous

Indraja. I and my army are trying to *defeat* her and those damn anti-gods."

"Then we're on the same side. There's no need for you to attack me and mine. Give me the pieces you've stolen, so I can expose the army of the anti-gods amassing at our borders. Then you and your demon army can vivisect them with all the gleeful hatred fomenting inside you." Bix mentally reached for the oasis of logic, one offering a glimmer of hope in the middle of this disaster. She'd worried from the get-go that the shards would be taken out of the Mids and beyond the ether to lead her on a long hunt across galaxies. But if Pigsy had the shards, they remained within reach. The demons' shards, at least. The Devourers' remained a problem.

He slowly shook his head. "You're too broken, Chimera. I know that because part of you lives inside me. You're far, far too weak to use the weapons I've amassed. I have an army of the divine. We've studied these little weapons. We have an advisor who knows how best to deploy them. You have nothing but some pathetic outraged humans who couldn't even fight off one of my scout teams."

Bix bit back a defense of Hywl and the Berserkers. They weren't the issue. The entity handing out the cheat codes to the containment device? Capturing them, along with rescuing Drew and Sophia, that was what mattered. That and assembling the damn containment device.

"Who is your advisor, Pigsy?" she whispered as menace prodded malice.

"Give me the weapons the dimwitted Oracles were hoarding," Pigsy demanded. "I'm willing to make a trade. Two, in fact. The draugr in exchange for the Oracles' share of the weapons. The goddess for the angels' share."

"Give me the draugr, the goddess, and every shard you and your army have stolen, and I'll tell the Consortium to stand down its pursuit of you and your demons," she countered, wondering if she could husk him faster than he could destroy Drew. The memories of hers that he carried could prove problematic.

Absorbing them would overwhelm her and bench her for untold time, which she couldn't afford right now. Could she avoid them and get Drew before Pigsy retaliated? She wasn't sure. What about the godsdamned shard? Could she neutralize that before it leveled all of Alexandria and then some?

"You...you called in the Consortium?" Pigsy stumbled back as if she'd just stabbed him. "The very organization that got us into this mess? You...you turned them against me? *Me?* A Mid World *guardian?* You are more than broken, Chimera. You are a traitor to these Worlds."

The god vanished. Taking Drew with him.

"Pigsy? Pigsy!" Bix flared her senses, seeking his resonance. Nothing. Frustrated, thwarted, impotent rage escaped from her on high-pitched keens as her darkness ripped apart the interior of the theater. The next time she got within range of that damned god, he would be hollowed out.

Light blasted across the torn movie screen.

Sounds of a traffic jam pouring through the surround-sound speakers now dangling precariously from unsecured wires jerked Bix around to face the screen. She stepped over corpses of the beheaded archers as the perpetual traffic jam idling in front of Guild Hall came into focus on the screen. The video shook with movement, offering a glimpse of the demon wearing the camera as it bounded across parking lots. Other demons came in and out of frame as the demon army established a perimeter behind the Berserkers.

"When my advisor suggested I abduct the Chimera's best friend, I scoffed. When has the Chimera ever cared for someone other than herself? But my soldiers convinced me to believe the rumors of a new Chimera, one who fought the Consortium's corruption. A new Chimera who would finally defend these Worlds." In the video, Pigsy stepped forward with a shard of pewter and a shard of copper in each hand. He looked directly into the camera. The red pupils of his divinity glowed brightly in his pale pink pig face. "But the Chimera has proven she has no care for the lives of lesser entities. She has allied with the Consortium and betrayed us all. This is what such treachery has brought her."

Chills crashed over Bix as two demons stepped forward carrying a big black body bag between them. The body within the bag writhed, very much alive.

"I offered you the goddess, Chimera, and you rejected my generosity. Thus, I will use her to claim the weapons and defend the Mids." Pigsy laughed triumphantly and slammed the shards into the body within the bag, then yanked them free. Ichor spurted through the holes. The demons swung the bag again. Swung. Swung. The bag split. Through the fissures, a telling glow spread.

"Sophia," Bix breathed with rising dread. "No!"

Pigsy's demons flung the body bag over the Berserkers' heads and the high fence surrounding Guild Hall, exposing Pigsy's nefarious plan.

"Xipil, retreat," Bix screamed, praying her comm was live and that the film was in real time. "Xipil, Guild Ha—"

The film captured every horrific moment of a goddess exploding with unfettered Devourer-tainted divinity and waves of copper magic answering from the shards in Guild Hall. Ground broke. Buildings cracked and crumbled. Men, demons, and mortals launched into the air in sprays of viscera. Power lines tangled with phone lines, making sparks rain. Vehicles spun, airborne. The camera melted.

Earthquakes shook the theater with enough force to send Bix to her knees. Ominous creaking walls accompanied crashes and bangs as fixtures dislodged and shattered. The projector tumbled out of the loft. Floor lights flickered. Aftershocks rolled through, bringing the screeching alarms of emergency doors swinging free of their locks.

The tremors stopped. Ten miles from the blast zone.

"The guilds. The Berserkers. Oh no, not the Berserkers," Bix whispered as darkness reached for certain tragedy.

CHAPTER 21

Bix connected to motes of darkness to arrive at the smoldering ruins of Guild Hall. Gates hadn't worked; the destination had changed too much. What had been just another urban armpit of industrialization was now a smoking crater three miles wide and at least fifteen feet deep. She was the first on scene. The wails of sirens placed their significant distance. Cars and buildings that hadn't been incinerated had been blown back, creating a ring of piled-up destruction around flattened terrain that surrounded the pit of rubble. Fires large and small dotted the outer ring. Blown gas lines, spewing water lines, and downed electrical lines would keep mortal rescuers busy and at bay for a considerable time.

Just as well. This wasn't a mess mortals could fix, much less help. Late-morning sun hid behind the blizzard of ash and snow as Bix waited for a Devourer portal to open, summoned by the magics Pigsy had so callously unleashed. Malice teetered on a precipice of despair, part of her hoping for the conflict just so she could feel useful. Yet the sky remained abysmally gray, as if the Devourers knew she was waiting for them.

The anti-gods refused the gauntlet.

"Damn you. Damn you all," she seethed, and her voice broke. There would be no outlet for her fury or her guilt. She cast her tentacles to spider throughout the pit, questing for any life. Not a single flutter of the magics of the shards or the demons came from the area. Pigsy had succeeded. Bix was too late to stop the theft or apprehend the murderers of the guild masters, bystanders, and Berserkers. So many Berserkers.

She thought to rail, to rage, to tear everything—every city, country, continent, and World asunder in the throes of her grief— but that would make her no better than the villain Pigsy and his so-called advisor were convinced she was. Contrary to popular belief, she did care. Immensely. She cared about the lives of lesser beings who didn't even know the dangerous times in which they lived. Remorse added extra weight to her corporeal state as recriminations tempered her malice. A violent wrath was more than she could muster.

"Chimera," someone called from the flat terrain above the ruins as magics native and Other World peppered the safer elevation. "Chimera?"

If they were aboveground, they didn't merit her attention. She owed any potential survivors her entire focus. This disaster was wholly her fault. The slivers belonged to her. She'd put them in the hands of lesser beings who were never meant to discover the shards' destructive abilities. Protective? Yes, certainly so. But this? Eleven shards had concentrated their energy against the might of an upper-midlevel goddess, who—through no intention of her own—had instigated the devastation. The shards' response proved proportionate to the attack, yet again. The only thing that made this disaster worse than what could have happened if she'd instantly ripped Pigsy apart instead of letting him slip through her fingers was that here she knew many of the victims. Here, she'd listened to the guild masters refuse to hand over their shards because they feared for their lives. How right they had been while still being so wrong.

"Chimera," someone else yelled as more magic arrived aboveground.

She kept to her task. She wouldn't fail any potential survivors the way she'd failed Drew. She'd left her terrified best friend in the clutches of a god who was insane enough to kill the draugr. Was there a remote chance Pigsy hadn't quashed Drew in his fit of indignation-driven slaughter? Doubtful. Not with an ego the size of the god of greed's. Pigsy had gleefully racked up a hell of a death toll, and now he had the Chweds' shards along with the humans' shards to do even more damage. What had Bix done to stop him? Nothing. She'd taunted him, but never touched him for fear of exactly this. So much needless death. Of friends, of family, of innocents.

She clawed at the patch of skin above her heart, at the faded Eternal Knot that had once connected her to Tobek and his wellspring of constant comfort. Nothing but cold remorse drifted within the mist and midnight of her corporeal state. Without Tobek's guidance, she wasn't sure how to grieve. She was too powerful to wrap herself in an emotion like that without accruing casualties. How could she mourn the loss of her best friend and so many Berserkers without making things worse for the mortals?

"Bix," a third party shouted. "Bix, can you hear me?"

Denied the catharsis of functional grief, she leaned into the only emotion that seemed appropriate. Anger. Anger was manageable. Anger was a constant companion. Anger allowed her to focus on Pigsy's "advisor." A "she" who had told him about the shards. "She" who had confirmed he'd collected all the humans' allocation. Who was "she"? Not Indraja. Pigsy had been very clear on that. So who was this other player? Who would know about the containment prism? Who would know to whom Bix had given pieces and how many pieces? Fates and Oracles were one possibility, but unlikely. Fates had played no small part in Pigsy's fall from grace, and Oracles were humans whom he would've slaughtered. Who, then, was coaching a Mid World guardian? Why had they chosen him? And did the fact he had Bix's memories factor into it? Whoever it was knew things Bix should but didn't.

Other World magic surged in front of her, and a god took shape. Ogun. In second-skin battle gear.

"Bix," he said with soft concern. "Come away from the blast zone."

"You were supposed to have tracked the demon army and rescued Sophia. I gave you notice. I played the political nicety." She evaded his touch and continued her search, deliberately not naming Pigsy. That Mid World guardian had her memories, her shards, and the deaths of her best friend and Berserkers on his hands. Nobody was going to get to him before she did.

"They kept Sophia out of the Mids until moments before this blast." Ogun walked with Bix, his boots crunching over concrete chunks and asphalt chips. "You understand priorities. Mine must remain centered in this collective. There is too much to be done to be ready for the fight."

"I'm taking that as your blessing to deal with this army of demons as I see fit." Bix drew up as her tentacles shivered from contact with pips of Other World divinity tainted by Devourer magic. Sophia.

In pieces.

Bix fisted her hands over her heart and whimpered as the weight of self-loathing bore down on her. How could she have let this happen? Sophia was a teammate, and Bix had delegated Sophia's rescue to someone who didn't have the bandwidth. Fully her mistake. She should've gone after Sophia herself. She should've prioritized lives over shards, not the other way around. Except shard keepers were dying too, faster than she could get to them. So many deaths. So many she should've been able to stop. If she'd had all her marbles, she could've. She would've known who had the shards, who else wanted them, and how to rise to the level of omniscient cosmic entity.

"Bix?" Ogun whispered. "What is it?"

"It wasn't Sophia they were hiding beyond the Mids." Bix brought the bits and pieces of the knowledge goddess to the surface, cradling them in a basket of midnight and starlight. "Just the shackles you'd made."

Ogun swallowed audibly, staring at the globs of dirt-encrusted, ichor-drenched divinity. A vein throbbed in his temple. "Give her to me. There is a well of souls in the bowels of the Consortium's chambers. It will speed her healing."

"Aren't you too busy?" Bix sniped.

"Bix," Ogun sighed with wounded disappointment. "We are allies. Let me do what you cannot."

"I can't send her back to the Consortium. Surely you understand why," she hissed. Returning Sophia to a place she'd been tortured for years was beyond cruel, no matter the good intention. Bix refused to add to Sophia's trauma any more than she already had.

Ogun grunted with a sagacity that said he truly did understand. He rolled one forearm over the other, again and again. Iron manifested, molten, molding and shaping into a large urn. He pulled his arms free, then smoothed a hand over one end, sealing the bottom. Raking his nails over the sides brought spell sigils to the surface. He snapped his fingers, and a god Bix didn't recognize appeared beside him.

"Fill this with ripened souls and return immediately." The Chairman of the Consortium handed off the urn.

"Demons feasted on the souls of today's victims before they fled," Bix absently noted. "Cleared the entire area. The bulk of the demon army must've been standing by for rapid cleanup."

"They could've staged anywhere, on any World. Part of preparing for the battle against the Devourers involves units of war gods deploying across the Mids. Demons seeking to work off their punishments are among them. Not every demon is part of this other army."

"Which complicates hunting the right demons." Bix was going to have to hunt by shard resonance, shards broken into tiny fragments to evade detection. There had to be another way, a better way. A way that would enable her to hunt the shards here in the Mids and across whatever galaxies the Devourers were stashing them in. With Pigsy having amassed the humans' and Chweds' shards, only the seventh segment was safely with its original keeper. That keeper would remain hidden until the six sides were assembled into the containment pyramid. She needed someone way smarter than she was to teach her how to hunt quickly and efficiently. Fortunately, she knew just the entities.

The unknown god returned with the urn filled with opalescent souls. Ogun took it and dismissed the other god before tilting the mouth of the urn to the basket of darkness holding Sophia's remains.

"Pour Sophia in here. As she heals, she has the choice to reshape herself or the urn to accommodate her growth," he explained. "When it's time to replenish, let me know where to send the refills."

Bix didn't hesitate. Healing wasn't her bailiwick, and Ogun gained nothing by prolonging Sophia's ordeal.

"Now, Chimera, will you allow us, the Consortium, to do our job and manage this crisis? Please?" He gestured to the flattened terrain ringing the pit above them.

Gods, Fates, dragons, and angels, all in humanoid form, watched and waited. Some with curiosity. Some with annoyance. Every one of them openly judged how their new Chairman and the infamous Chimera interacted. She couldn't rally her usual disdain for them; they were here to do as caretakers ought. She had no business standing in their way. Simple surprise made her hesitate, nothing more. She was so accustomed to their indifference that their active involvement was unexpected.

"Yes, of course." Bix nodded, recalling her darkness into herself. "If you find anything left of the Berserkers—"

"I'll have their remains delivered to the coal plant," he interjected. "Now, go get those weapons from the damned who did this. Husk the demons if it pleases you. I have no patience for friendly fire on my doorstep."

"Okay." She closed her hands over the lip of the hip-high urn and opened gates to the two entities who could school her in how to find her lost toys. "Thank you for this."

CHAPTER 22

Red garnet triangles inlaid in corridors wide enough to accommodate whole mansions pivoted in the floor, pointing Bix in the direction of her oldest brother. Thick, glossy black baseboards reflected her shoes, while black ceiling gables disguised the shadows accompanying her past triptychs of long arched windows overlooking nebulas in various stages of birth and decline.

The shadows weren't her shadows, but they were familial.

"Eko?" she called, "Are you home?"

The shadows overhead surged down the hall and took a hard right. A moment later, a joyous roar flooded the space, followed by the thunderous arrival of her ginormous minotauresque eldest brother. Blacker than black, with spiraling horns veined in red glitter that framed his wild mane of cherry-red hair, her eldest brother was Knowledge Innate, also known as Instinct. Aligned to their mother, the Chaos, Eko had been Bix's original tutor, along with his twin. They'd stepped up again to guide her through her broken state, for which she was incredibly grateful.

"Little sister," he cheered with his three cherry-tuft-tipped tails whipping behind him. "This is a prison. I am always home."

Their siblings had locked him up for a reason she didn't

yet know and none of them would say, but she was his ticket to freedom. In exchange, he had to help her punt the Devourers out of the Mids without killing everyone in the process. He didn't seem to begrudge the terms or timing of their deal, or the fact she kept pestering him. His delight each time she showed up here was infectious. Sometimes, she visited just because she liked his company, and right now, she could use a little bit of happiness to take the edge off her misery.

"I've made a mess, and I need to learn how to clean it up." She extended the urn containing Sophia toward him as her bottom lip quivered. "A special toy broke because of it. Can you fix her, please?"

"You are…sad." He tilted his head until his horns brushed his broad shoulder. "This toy must be extremely special for you to share your sorrow with me. I am honored."

"My best friend died, and I don't know how to grieve among mortals," she whispered, her voice hitching. "Everything in me demands a violent release for this pain of loss, but that will cause more harm to those I care about."

"The violent instinct is your chaotic half lashing out. The half of you beholden to order perceives that reaction as disproportionate, thus you struggle to express yourself." He stroked her cheek with the tip of a cherry-tufted tail. "We did you no great service by teaching you to suppress your emotions rather than to cope with them. For that, I apologize."

"You are forgiven, of course." She leaned into the soft fluff of his tail. "Some things I have to learn for myself. However, I *am* hoping you can teach me how to fix the goddess in the urn."

"You are driven to balance out the loss of a close friend by restoring something of equal importance. But the toy in the pot does not compare to the toy you lost, thus you have brought another broken toy with you. Two for one, I believe it is called." He curled his three fingers—he wasn't missing any; three was his sacred number and it manifested in various ways throughout his preferred form—encouraging her to follow him.

"I, uh, yeah, I need help with that too," she admitted, suspecting he sensed the partial containment prism she carried within her. "The goddess first, though, please?"

"Then stop lollygagging," he called, far ahead of her.

Due to their gross size differential, she had to use gates to keep up with him as he led her along winding passages peppered with gods and Devourers trapped in suspended terrariums like action figures in display cases. Eko stepped into a workshop that would've sent most sane beings fleeing for their lives. Parts and pieces of assorted flora and fauna in varying scale sat in jars on coasters of notes or tacked to walls with complex engineering drawings. Gases of multitudinous colors spiraled through multifarious tracks of tubing, while beakers of scented liquids bubbled without the aid of burners. Metals and minerals sprouted from ceiling coves and corner nooks. Clouds filled with tiny planets drifted as uncontained biomes. All her siblings were creationists, and Eko had his unique methods for making new galaxies, Worlds, or species. Bix didn't examine too closely whether he'd built his samples from scratch or had farmed them from existing places. That might ruin the awesomeness. Marveling at creationist magic in action was fast becoming her favorite pastime.

Eko swept his arm in a circle parallel to the floor, and workbenches walked away to clear a space. Three taps of his fingers released red sparks that multiplied and solidified into a new workbench. A large transparent tray with shallow sides appeared atop the bench.

He narrowed his eyes of flames at the urn, which was about the size of a dollhouse thimble compared to him.

"May I adjust scale?" he asked, beaming when she nodded. He gave the urn the hairy eye, and it quadrupled in size. He dumped the contents into the tray, careful not to slosh souls or goddess bits.

"This toy can reassemble itself, which you know. Thus, things are not as they seem. Delightful these games you offer me," he mused, tipping the tray and studying the slurry. He grunted quizzically, and his brow wrinkled. "Ah, I see now. This is no longer a pure creation. There are things here that don't belong, including things from you, but not just you. This is why your toy cannot reassemble as she was designed. I must caution against corrupting Mother's storage containers."

"Mother isn't the only one who makes those storage containers now, is she?" Bix adjusted her corporeal state to be less dust-bunny size and more sister size. The change in perspective required a few moments before feeling natural. "Would I be off base to believe you were the one who not only innovated but also suggested this style of storage to her in the first place?"

Gods were entities of chaos. Her mother, *the* Chaos, the eternal feminine, the womb of all existence, possessed infinite aspects and needed a means by which to store those aspects while simultaneously having them contribute to the greater reality. Those aspects were the seeds of divinity bestowed upon a god at the time of their ascension. In short, gods were glorified Mason jars with power-coded lids.

"They are less disruptive than titans." Eko shrugged, but the fire of his eyes danced merrily. "You have not scaled yourself to fit in here in previous visits. Would I be off base to believe you are gaining comfort with your place in our family?"

His throwing her turn of phrase back at her made her chuckle as she looked around for a safe place to sit. "I'm slowly unpacking my memories and regaining comfort with all I am."

"But you've not yet unpacked the important ones," he admonished, reaching between his shoulder blades and scratching the huge, red star-shaped scar that had formed when he and his twin had separated. "Come for a visit, brother. Interesting things are happening with little sister's toys."

A single speck of a bright yellow star flitted from Eko's scar. One star became two, two became four, four became sixteen, and on and on until Bix's second brother, Knowledge Amassed, aka Experience, took shape. The walls of the prison chamber pushed outward, creating room in an overcrowded workshop for the giant white fox with bright yellow socks and matching tufts on his ears and four tails. Esiw, the first son of order, aligned to their father, the Cosmos, and the second of Bix's original tutors, arrived with all the indulgent reservation of an academic chancellor who'd long ago given up on his students' ability to produce something novel.

"Little sister," Esiw greeted with an inclination of his head. The starlight of his eyes sharpened and his head tipped to the other side as he took in the tray of Sophia bits. "Attempting to infuse order into a chaotic entity? What foolishness is this?"

"She is a knowledge goddess cursed by the Devourers with the taint of their essence to explode if she doesn't retrieve the missing pieces of this." Bix removed the partial containment pyramid from within her and let her shadows carry it to her brothers. "Fully assembled, it should hold the ether I had some titans create. In pieces, however, each fragment is a weapon."

"A weapon your toys are using against each other? This is what prompts your visit today?" Esiw slipped a tail beneath her shadows, relieving her of the containment pyramid. His tails tossed it, stroked it, poked it, and wiggled it before handing it off to Eko. The brothers switched spots, Eko examining the partial pyramid and Esiw inspecting the slurry.

"This is made by the youngers," Eko said, picking at the pyramid. "Curious that you went to them for aid with your ether."

"That might've been a mistake, but I can't recall why I went to them instead of coming to you two."

"Esiw would not have helped me build any kind of container for your ether," Eko laughed. "He is too much like Father and believes when something is no longer useful, it should be unmade."

"Containment implies you intend to use the ether again later, only without incurring the cost of creating it." Esiw arched a brow. "That is not an act of balance."

"And I am the entity of balance," she finished for him. "Speaking of balance and the lack thereof, can you extract the Devourer curse from the goddess, please?"

"Why didn't *you*?" Esiw asked as though she was defending her dissertation.

"I didn't do this before because I don't want to cause her more harm." Bix wrinkled her nose and hovered a fingernail over Sophia in pieces.

"A partial truth. You *think* you didn't want to cause her more pain." Eko cast Bix a sympathetic look. "Your instinct, however, warned you off. All is not as it appears with this, hence why I called Esiw to help you learn."

"The only way *you* learn is by being involved in the discovery and the ensuing disaster. Lectures result in selective hearing. Thus, I will help, yes, but you must participate." Esiw drew a cloud cluster of suns closer to the tray, illuminating the specks of order within the blobs of chaos. "Here is the first of your problems, little sister."

Esiw sat back on his haunches and raised his front paws over the tray. Pips of bright order separated from the darker chaos of Sophia. There were two different hues of order, one more bronze, the other more brass. Esiw pulled one paw higher than the other, and the pips sorted themselves by color.

Bix spun a brassy pip with the tip of her nail. "The brass ones are pieces of me protecting her knowledge to prevent greater powers from husking her."

"Indeed." Esiw twitched one paw, and all the brass bits dropped back into the tray. The bronze bits he kept in the air. "These others? Can you identify their source?"

"Devourers," she scoffed. "I drained their essence from a World, I know it well."

"Do you? Or do you only know what is on the surface?" Esiw tapped a claw against a pip. The dot splintered, exposing a teensy ball of crackling pewter energy. "Look again, not at the dressing, but at the contents. Your presence is hiding her knowledge from outsiders. What is the Devourers' presence hiding?"

"Tempest? That's her magic." Bix didn't have to think too hard about the answer. Chasing the shards made the truth obvious. "Is that how the curse works? It recognizes the containment shards because the curse is constructed around a piece of the pyramid's creator?"

"Magic is nothing more than energy in motion." Eko blew across his fingertip, sending a cluster of bronze pips to drift in front of Bix's nose. "Which way is the energy flowing in these little bits?"

She reached out, not with her usual darkness, but with a filament of light that wrapped around the bronze bits like a shell around a snail. The chaos of Tempest's magic vibrated against Bix's light of order. Pushed. Like it was trying to escape.

"The greater entity controls the flow." She stiffened as rage rose within her. "*Tempest* is controlling Sophia's curse?"

Esiw nodded, and his ears twitched as though capturing the sounds of Bix's internal shrieking.

Tempest was Indraja's ultimate boss.

Tempest was Pigsy's advisor.

Tempest was playing both sides…against Bix.

Pigsy was a tool of distraction, and Indraja was just another step in the enemy's hierarchy of means. They were merely toys of a greater power, like all the other traitors.

Before being tasked with ending the ether, Bix and Phobos had been pressing their combined network of intelligence assets for the Devourer higher-ups, the ones who could permanently end the siege on the Mids. Bix had been hunting Indraja for her crimes against the Mids, the Consortium, and the pantheons, but most importantly because that greater goddess was in contact with the enemy's shot callers. It hadn't occurred to Bix to look way higher. She hadn't fathomed that the leadership of the enemy was her family.

Had Sophia known? The knowledge goddess had been reluctant to confirm Indraja was behind the attack on the angels even though Bix had been convinced. Sophia wouldn't argue with Bix, certainly not in front of others, because the goddess revered the mighty Chimera.

No insistence without proof. Hence Sophia's eagerness to hunt the demons. Hence her choice of being captured by Pigsy. The quest for proof. Proof to give Bix. Acts Bix should've recognized, having spent the last year plus in constant pursuit of irrefutable proof of crimes by greater powers. Who in their right mind would roll up to a temperamental cosmic entity and say, "Yo, your sister's the bad guy"?

Sophia must've suspected, though. A knowledge goddess kept prisoner by the enemy for that long had to have sought the how behind the who. Indraja had led the Devourers to Sophia and the other gods holding containment shards. But how had Indraja known who and where to hunt? Bix had foolishly assumed the greater goddess had mapped the ether, then offered up the other gods as sacrifices to prove fealty. In retrospect, a glaringly stupid assumption. After all, the ether was built by *titans*, who vastly out-everythinged a greater god.

It all made sense now, how Indraja had known. How Pigsy had known. All about the shards. Where they were. How many there were. Who had them. What they could do. Who else but the cocreator of the containment pyramid would know that? Who else *could*?

"Why?" Bix massaged her temples, wondering yet again how she'd gotten everything so wrong. "Why would Tempest care? Why would she bother with anything happening in the Mids? It's all so beneath her."

Eko and Esiw swapped pensive glances.

"What? What am I missing?" she asked.

Esiw tapped a tail tip against her skull. "You already have the answer, but you refuse to examine everything that comes with it."

The festering abscess in her mind quickened its throbbing, and she jerked back from her brother's touch. "I know. I got the message from your Oracles. I also know that without all my memory segments in my head, my brain is going to autofill blank spaces with what it assumes to be logical answers. But logical doesn't mean factual."

Esiw's ears flattened as his gaze bore into her. "That is a fair argument. I accept it. Sadly, that doesn't change the circumstances of Tempest's involvement in your sanctuary."

"It doesn't really explain why Tempest hid her influence either." Bix crossed her arms on the workbench and considered Sophia's slurry. "Why mess with the Devourers and a curse? She can make Sophia explode without embedded bits, a benefit of being Mom's daughter. Unless…"

Bix reconsidered the incomplete containment pyramid. Its assembly was very elaborate. Complicated, even. Why? A single panel in one piece was too puissant for anyone other than a First Child to touch. And the transference rite? Who had created that?

"Unless?" Esiw prompted.

"These pieces can only reassemble through a rite of truth telling." Bix reclaimed the partial pyramid. "Am I capable of that? Of placing such a spell on the broken parts?"

Eko chuckled and Esiw beamed as if she'd unlocked a new level of the game. The fox's chest swelled, his mouth opened, and…

"The short answer is yes, if you were the one who broke it," Eko answered, cutting off his twin. "It's all rooted in how you, as the two-in-one, unmake things."

Esiw snapped his jaw shut and glowered at his gabby twin.

"Even though the youngest twins created this, my breaking it would prevent them from putting it back together themselves?" Bix asked as the reasons for her leaving weapons of mass destruction among the fragile Mids started to make sense.

"Yes, absolutely. To end what we have made is part and parcel of your role as High Executioner," Esiw rushed to say before Eko could.

"That's why I did it, then, shattered it into tiny pieces and scattered them across the Mids. I did it to prevent Tempest from getting her hands on it, to prevent her from capturing the ether and using the ether as a cosmic weapon." Bix smiled at the broken pyramid. She hadn't been stupid in her dispersal. She'd buried the shards in the safest place she'd known. She'd weighed the risk of the lesser races versus her sister wielding the shards, and the denizens of the Mids had won. "Tempest wants her toy back.

Tempest is the one dispatching Devourers and demons after the shards. That…that…*Gah!*"

"What are you going to do about it?" Esiw challenged, curling a lip and exposing one sparkling white canine.

Bix cast her darkness and light around all the bronze pips holding Sophia's curse. Bix was the two-in-one, equal parts Chaos and Cosmos, the High Executioner for All Worlds. With no effort, she drained the order from the shell and the chaos from the seed, consuming both energies until nothing was left of Tempest's little cheat.

"Be careful," Esiw chided. "The potency of the disputed toy, broken or not, can still raze your sanctuary."

The smoldering pit of what had been Guild Hall was very fresh in Bix's mind. Knowing that her sister was behind it? Knowing that her sister was playing with lives Bix valued? Bix shouldn't be surprised, not after what Tempest had inflicted on her while she'd been a total amnesiac adrift in the ether. All it did was hone her malice and focus it on its proper target. Tempest.

"For all you are currently struggling with the rediscovery of your emotions, do not forget that Tempest is Mother's daughter and aptly named," Eko cautioned, pouring a mostly purified Sophia back into Ogun's urn, then returning both to a Mids-appropriate size. "Whatever rules of engagement you conceive or imagine to be in play are restrictions placed upon you, not her."

The dragon keepers Svante and Malthe had warned her someone was using the Devourers to lay siege against the Mids as a way to force Bix's hand. An old trick from the dragon enforcer's war book, they'd said. Their truths had been spot-on. Thanks to her brothers' help dismantling Sophia's curse, Bix now knew who was behind the siege. Next step? Figure out what else Tempest wanted from her, beyond the containment pyramid, and why it required an attack on her sanctuary.

"Tempest thinks she's going to sink my battleship?" Bix folded the containment pyramid into her corporeal state. "Psht, please. By consolidating who has the remaining shards, she's given away her position, and the next move is mine."

Flipping her hair over her shoulder, Bix grabbed the urn and leveled a confident smile on her brothers...praying they bought her false bravado. Tempest's game didn't change the facts that Drew and a platoon of Berserkers had died on Bix's watch. Yes, the safety of the Mids was at risk, but her relationships mattered more. She might not be able to grieve properly, but she damn sure owed the dead a show of respect.

"Thank you for your help, brothers. It's been enlightening." She opened gates to the Primary Mid World. She had a battalion in mourning to face and dreaded it.

CHAPTER 23

Fairly certain the clinic-morgue and the beer hall were overflowing with grieving soldiers, Bix opted to arrive in the parking lot in front of the main building of the coal plant. The blizzard that had struck during the demise of Guild Hall had dumped a heaping two feet of snow before glazing over, then adding a dense crunchy topper of frozen rain. Whether due to Gurp's installation of modern in-ground heating or Tobek's application of comfort spells, the sidewalk in front of Dysmorphic, the body modification shop, was clear. The parking lot had been plowed, creating Berserker-height snowbanks. Alas, the snow continued to fall, erasing their efforts. Low clouds, plump and gray, made the middle of the day feel more like early night.

The silence was eerie. The roads were abandoned. Not so much as a bright-orange salt truck braved the weather. Not a gull or a squirrel in sight, not even a footprint marred the sea of fresh white. Either the weather guild was having a fit of pique over what had transpired at Guild Hall or the Consortium was deliberately keeping the DC metro area under lockdown. Both, perhaps.

Time flowed differently in Eko's prison, so while Bix felt as if she'd been gone mere hours, days had in fact passed in the Mids. Eventful days, no doubt.

A knock on the tempered-glass door of Dysmorphic called Bix's attention to the squat goblin motioning her inside. She hadn't noticed the Closed sign shining in the shop window, but it made sense. No customers were likely to roll up in this winter wonderland. Girding her loins for the disappointment, betrayal, and straight-up dislike the Berserkers were sure to have for her, Bix used gates to enter the shop, carrying Sophia in the urn.

The din of a well-oiled military in action washed over her. Berserkers in dress-white uniforms with vibrant blue embroidery down the chest and back panels of their fitted coats hustled along the passage from the beer hall to the clinic with purpose. Tromps and stomps of boots thundering up the stairs to the apartments carried through the mail-room walls that separated Dysmorphic from the beer hall. The programmable gate hidden on the backside of the stairwell hummed with activity and tickled Bix's gatekeeper aspect.

"How bad were the losses?" she asked Gurp as she set the urn of Sophia beside an empty waiting-area couch.

"Too many." Gurp cast a mournful look at the activity in the hall. "Three days funerals. Men returning now."

"Should I go away, Gurp?" she whispered, silently cursing her quavering voice. "You'd tell me, right? If I should go away and leave them to their rites? I should. I definitely should. I didn't stop the deaths, and they don't need me standing here as a painful reminder. I'm sorry. I'll go."

She opened a gate and hefted the urn, but Gurp laid his hands atop hers and lightly squeezed.

"Is good you here," the goblin assured. "Respect. Yes?"

"A very deep respect." She sniffled and wiped a tear in her shoulder. "I want to honor them, but I don't want to inflict myself on them."

"Come, come." Gurp set off through the body modification shop, the hem of his fancy embroidered white tunic swishing around his squat legs as he seamlessly wove through the traffic of Berserkers. Bix waited to see which way he went before shortcutting through gates to meet him beside the beer hall doorway.

Half the hall had been converted into triage and the other half into a science lab. The gate to the Mid World that had hosted the skirmish between Devourers and Berserkers remained open, offering a glimpse of white-and-yellow decontamination tents. The evaluation of aftereffects was still underway, but the steady traffic between Worlds was over. Of greater concern was the cleanup of the triage area. The smell of disinfectants overpowered everything else.

Bix braced herself as Berserkers took notice of her presence. She adored these guys and valued them beyond measure. Losing even one hurt, and losing their respect hurt even more. Hiding from them, though, avoiding the consequences of her inaction, that benefitted no one. Her grip on the urn tightened, but she lifted her chin and forced a sympathetic smile that probably looked more pained than uneasy.

Weary smiles answered. A few breathless murmurs of "my lady" came from passing men. The fleeting gazes were fewer than those who avoided looking her way altogether. They blamed her. Fair. She owned that blame.

"Come," Gurp called to her as he entered the beer hall, then pushed through a door beside the stage. He led her across the spotlessly clean commercial kitchen where men donned hairnets and aprons, while others started prep for the next meal. The goblin opened the door to a huge walk-in freezer and motioned her inside. "Go, go. Take urn too."

Bix had a lot of questions but didn't ask any. One simply did not interrogate the goblin. She carried Sophia's urn past the rows of skinned animals swaying on meat hooks, deliberately not thinking about those animals having been alive. The men needed to eat. A lot of men. A lot of meat. Not thinking any…

She shouldered through the heavy plastic curtain separating the butcher section from the other frozen goods and halted.

"Sweetheart," Tobek breathed on an icy sigh, taking the urn and setting it aside before sweeping her up with one arm and holding her close to his frost-covered chest. Chunks of ice clung to his hair, face, and the scars of his amputated arm. His white pants were stiff, not in the fun way, but from the frozen fabric.

"Tobek, I've missed you." She wrapped her arms around his neck and snuggled against him. Cold didn't bother her, and she really, really wanted the hug from her big blond bear. He was—and had long been—her emotional rock, and she sorely needed his steadying influence, especially now.

It took a few beats to realize they weren't alone. Three parka-clad men sat in folding chairs to one side of a wide bench that still had the imprint of Tobek's bulk within a frame of solid ice. A white-and-blue uniform coat and button-down shirt lay across the ice. Thick fractals glistened over the embroidery, insignia, and buttons. Obviously Tobek's discarded clothes.

Over the course of his latest evolution, Tobek's native state had become that of a block of ice to which he reverted when egregiously injured. The damage Tobek had incurred against the Devourers must've qualified, and Gurp must've taken to storing Tobek in the freezer to speed along the healing. That, at least, explained why they were in a freezer and why Tobek looked like the abominable snowman.

"Days have passed, yet your scream continues to echo in my bones," Tobek rasped into her hair. "Give me another moment or two to be selfish."

"My…? Okay." She'd happily give him all the time he needed, but she wondered how he'd heard whichever scream. She'd been doing a lot of yelling lately. Meanwhile, she reveled in the fact he had zero reluctance to show affection or offer comfort, particularly in front of whoever else was in the freezer.

Taking a deep breath while tightening his hold, Tobek squeezed her until she squeaked and then set her on her feet. "You have questions. Probably need a sitrep too."

"Let me first offer my sincerest condolences for the men you lost." She set Sophia beside a rack of ice creams and finally got a good look at who else was there. Xipil, Runjit, and Ashtad. Two wore their dress whites under their parkas, while Ashtad was in all black. Funeral attire. The battalion really had just returned from paying final respects. "Guys, I'm so sorry. I wish I could've saved them."

"They died in the line of duty, shoulder to shoulder with their brothers," Xipil said softly. "A noble end to an otherwise interminable service. May we all be so fortunate."

"Hear, hear." Runjit raised a fist in solidarity.

"That Sophia in the urn, Bix?" Ashtad asked, pointing with his thermos.

"Yes, she's been cured of her curse now. She needs time to heal." She waved off Tobek's offer to perch on his knee as he took a seat on his ice slab. "How did you know?"

"Your comm was live at the theater." Ashtad tapped his ear. "We were upstairs in ops listening to the whole confrontation with Pigsy and Ogun afterward."

The battalion had heard their men die. They too had been unable to save those soldiers. What a nightmare for the brotherhood.

"The guys pushed your comm feed to the freezer here, allowing me to listen while I recovered." Tobek jerked his chin in the direction of a speaker grill high up in the stainless-steel wall.

"I'm sorry any of you had to hear that ending," she murmured as more regret and sorrow added to the slump of her shoulders.

"Even when I'm in my native state, I am always attuned to you, but hearing the details allowed me to call on the foundational elements to contain the blast zone." Tobek took her hand and bounced his thumb along her knuckles in time with his heartbeat, reminding hers to slow down and echo his. "Without us working together, the casualties would have been much worse."

"Pigsy is a foe not unknown to us," Xipil explained. "We have faced his army many times over the centuries. Once he confirmed he had Sophia and the humans' shards, his next steps were sadly predictable. You are not alone with your survivor's guilt, Bix."

"Though I think I speak for the entire battalion when I say none of us ever want to hear you scream Xipil's name like that again," Runjit noted dryly.

"Seconded," Xipil concurred.

Runjit was such a stick in the mud that it took Bix a minute to realize he'd cracked a joke. She plopped down on Tobek's lap with a small smile as the tiny moment of levity made failure slightly more tolerable.

"What about the Chweds of Guild Hall and the humans in the area? Did any of the innocents survive?"

The question came from the urn on a hoarse rasp as fingers, still reconstructing, curled over the lip.

"I'm afraid Guild Hall was a total loss, Sophia. The foundational elements lessened the damage, but they couldn't arrest it completely." Tobek hung his head. "The death toll is in the thousands. There are some mortals still in intensive care who were on the perimeter of the blast."

Bix recognized his posture of defeat and shared it. The most vulnerable races had always been fodder in the machinations of greater entities, but it didn't make it right. She too wished she had done more to stop the needless casualties, but she couldn't let Tobek shoulder the blame for the actions of a mad god set in motion by Bix's sister. That was her burden to bear.

"None of you should beat yourselves up for what happened. The collision of powers was exacerbated by additives in Sophia's curse. The enemy remains the Devourers and those who sent them here." Bix lightly tapped Tobek's Eternal Knot buried beneath layers of ink. The knot had once bound them together, but now it bound him to her siblings...including Tempest.

Tobek's vibrant blue gaze dropped to her hand upon his chest, then lifted to meet hers, his unspoken question plain. There were parts of her life she didn't share with the team, and her family was one of those things. She could count on one hand the exceptions who knew of her siblings, and two of them were in the freezer. She'd fill in Tobek on the sibling problem later.

"While you were gone, we've been tossing around ideas about how to get the shards and Drew away from Pigsy," Ashtad said, drawing Bix back to the pressing issues.

"I, uh, Drew's, uhm…" Bix couldn't finish the statement. A fat tear plopped onto her skirt, followed by three more.

"Are you sure?" Ashtad gently tapped his thermos on Bix's knee. "Are you positive? Because I've lost count of the times I believed the draugr dead only to be greeted by a snarky 'Sparky' coming out of a stranger's body."

Bix huffed a wet chuckle but shook her head. "There's no way Pigsy let her live."

"Forgive me, Chimera, but I must beg to differ." Sophia raised her head from the urn, skin mostly mended and hair regrowing rapidly. "Pigsy held two points of leverage over you: me and the draugr. He sacrificed me to demonstrate his resolve. He wants the shards you have, thus he still needs Drew alive to force you to hand them over. You should expect him to contact you for a second meeting very soon."

Bix looked to Tobek as a single speck of hope dared to shine within her. When it came to strategy, there was no one better than her Berserker. If there was any chance Pigsy, a god Tobek had faced many times, would've kept Drew alive, hostage or not…

Tobek brought their clasped hands to his chest and nodded. "I think Sophia's—"

The freezer groaned a low eerie warning as its walls bowed. The wail of a siren slicked through the speakers, and red lights flashed behind thermal glass tubes.

"Guys?" Cian's voice crackled over the line. "Guys, a Devourer portal just opened over the Washington Monument."

CHAPTER 24

They weren't ready. The Devourers shouldn't have been able to get this far inside the collective. The Primary Mid World was supposed to be safe. Resen wasn't ready. The Consortium wasn't ready. The Berserkers weren't ready.

No one was ready for this.

That thought kept churning through Bix's mind as Berserkers hale and hampered deployed across the snow-blanketed DC metro area through gates she provided. Bix, Tobek, and Ashtad stood beneath the rippling mirror portal at the base of the Washington Monument, listening to the ominous cracks spidering down through the marble and granite tribute to human history. The fifty flagpoles surrounding the monument had bent in half, pinning the American flags to the ground. Any vehicle, be they parked or struggling through the blizzard, had been flattened as if whales had landed on them. Along the National Mall, centuries-old construction endured while newer buildings twisted and collapsed into each other. Humans and Chweds alike fled into the streets only to flee again as rubble rained faster than the snow. Asphalt buckled, and sections gave way to sinkholes that exposed the curved tops of underground Metro tunnels. The city had been built to withstand ground tremors and the gusts of seasonal storms; no one had expected a direct down blast ripping through the atmosphere.

"If this is the damage to an industrialized city caused by a portal opening, how much worse is it going to be when they attack?" Tobek called above the pandemonium.

"Why aren't they coming through?" Ashtad asked, eyes wide within the frame of his furry hood as he took in the disarray around them. "Why aren't the Devourers attacking?"

"They've gathered their shards," Bix said, absurdly relieved. They were here, the shards the Devourers had stolen from the gods and the dragons. They were on the other side of the portal and not strewn across multiple galaxies. She didn't have to hunt them. The unmasked and unbalanced resonances of chaos and order throbbed with each ripple of the portal's surface.

That the shards were *aimed* at the Mids and DC in particular, well, no part of that was good. Powered by an army of deities, the shards' blast would make the tragedy at Guild Hall look like a spilled can of SpaghettiOs.

"The soldiers are the second wave," Tobek said. "The better strategy is to use the shards to knock out any defense we have before they send the troops."

The only defense they had were boots on the ground, troops that shouldn't include Bix. A fight against the Devourers had to be fought by the Consortium. A fight against the shards and Tempest, however, was on Bix. If only she had the Chweds' and humans' shards to combine with those she possessed to overpower the Devourers' shards…which she should. Pigsy had said he wanted them to defend the Mids. No way had he missed the portal opening.

Bix fanned her senses across the District and out to the surrounding counties, searching. The Consortium was rallying below them, powers native and Other World amassing, but that wasn't what she sought. There. Coming from the south and east, from the suburbs and riverbanks of Maryland like the cavalry on horseback. Shards. Chaos and order. Faint. Ever so faint, but their magical resonance, oh, so much purer than the demons carrying them.

She laid her hand against Tobek's prosthesis, a monstrosity of mixed metals, all spikes and hooks. "Pigsy's coming."

"Son of a sorner," Tobek snarled, spinning his sword in his natural hand. "He picks now to attack the Consortium?"

"No. He's a Mid World guardian. His methods may be unconscionable and his mind corrupted, but he's still driven to defend the Mids." Bix pivoted slowly, tracking the positions of Pigsy's shards as the approaching demon army circled the District, establishing a perimeter beneath the portal. "He's bringing the shards to defeat the Devourers."

"Which is exactly what they want." Sophia, whole and restored to her glorious divine self in a white pantsuit that blended with the snow, appeared beside Bix. "This is about the shards. All the pieces the Devourers are missing are in one place now, hence the opening of the portal."

"The pieces both Bix and Pigsy have collected. How'd they know Bix had returned to the Mids? How have they known where all the other pieces are?" Ashtad summoned a ball of electricity to hand, testing the way the energy reacted to the presence of the portal.

"Does it matter?" Sophia leveled a too-knowing look at Bix. "They want the shards badly enough they're willing to engage the Chimera to get them."

Tobek's rage-bright blue gaze swiveled up, snowflakes reflecting the glow. "How many pieces do the Devourers have?"

"The full gods' collection and two-fifths of the dragons' segment." Sophia answered, her voice a sultry rasp hinting at her past trauma. "Plus three bits from the Oracles. Pigsy's demons lost to the Devourers at the Oracle outposts, hence his particular aggression in claiming the Chweds' parts."

"Pigsy has all the pieces belonging to the Chweds and the humans. I have the completed angel panel, three-fifths of those given to the dragons, and two-thirds of the allocation bestowed upon the Oracles." Bix did the math and didn't like the answer.

"That puts Pigsy in a better position?" Tobek widened his

stance as the comm in his ear chirped and chattered with his men confirming location readiness.

"To do what?" Sophia challenged. "He thinks he's going to blast a hole in the portal, but he's more likely to level anything in a twenty-mile radius. The only thing he's certain to do is antagonize the Devourers into burying this region in a seabed."

"So how do we protect the mortals from this clash of cosmic weaponry?" The snowfall around them rippled, and Ogun with his faithful hound joined them. Displeasure etched his every feature and oozed from his rigid posture.

"We close the Devourer portal." Tobek sniffed and shrugged, causing another chunk of restorative ice to tumble from his arm.

"Our old foes will open another portal, or two, or three," Sophia chimed in. "How many consecutive times can you close a portal?"

"What are our other options?" Ogun stared pointedly at Bix.

Bix wished she could see the future as possibilities and outcomes churned through her mind. Bix could rupture the portal and blow up the eastern seaboard in the process. Similarly, she could move the portal as she'd done during the dragons' conflict, but Sophia had a point. There was nothing to stop the Devourers from opening more. Not with Tempest calling their shots. Not when her sister had the shards within reach.

Tempest wanted the containment pyramid. Why? Now was not the time to ponder that. Eko had warned Bix that any preconceived rules of engagement hampered Bix not their sister. So Bix had to be more unpredictable than another daughter of the Chaos. How? What would Tempest least expect her to do? What would stymie her sister and still protect the Mids?

A low thrum built overhead.

The portal yawned its maw, disgorging torrents of pewter spliced with copper. Alternating rays of pewter and copper answered from the high ground in the District. The shards' magics aimed by the Devourers and the demons clashed in the air, igniting more than atmospheric gasses in unnatural flames of glittering bronze over the snowbound city. Cosmic pressures pushed upward and downward, neither gaining ground.

Bix stumbled and staggered as the imbalance of shards contained within her juddered with enough force to erupt from her spine amid spears of darkness. The panels glowed copper and pewter, vibrating wildly. Bix grabbed her segments and stared at them, baffled. They wanted to do…something. What?

Eerie crackling multiplied as the sky fires expanded and pressures seeped outward, inflicting damage across the greater metro area.

Magic is energy in motion, Sophia shouted into Bix's mind. *The greater entity controls the flow. Activate your pieces, then control the resulting flow of magics. That is what your sister will not expect.*

Easier said than done, but good to know Sophia had been eavesdropping on Bix's conversation with her brothers. Not that the knowledge goddess was wrong, of course. How to do it, though? If Bix aimed her shards from the ground, she'd blow the portal. The resulting backlash would bury the greater metro area. If she came at it from the portal's mouth and pointed at the Mids, that'd be stupidly destructive too. That left the most effective spot as squarely in the thick of it, so gates delivered her and the incomplete pyramid into the heart of unnatural fire.

Diluted familial magics battered her, a painful reminder that she was not fully up to snuff. It'd be so much easier if she could just swallow the conflagration with a gate, but it wouldn't stop the shards from being activated again and again. She wasn't keen to use the Primary Mid World as the board for cosmic Whack-a-Mole. All the shards were in the same general location right now. If Tempest thought she could get them, then Bix ought to be able to do it too. Hell, she ought to be able to do what Tempest *couldn't* do. The containment pyramid was equal parts chaos and order. Tempest was mostly chaos. Bix, however, was the two-in-one, equal parts.

This was a trial of balance.

"Balance," Bix whispered to herself, centering the completed panel over her sternum. "Equal parts darkness and light, chaos and order. To balance the energies around me, I must first harness them."

Her innate starlight brightened into fine streams, flowing from her into the clash of chaos and order. Filaments of natural darkness followed suit. Starlight sheathed the shards' chaotic magics while darkness coated the orderly, extinguishing the cosmic fire.

"Opposing magics once harnessed must be aligned, from conflicting to complementary." Bix focused on the completed panel, using it as the first building block. It was the angels' piece, formed from chaotic magic, thus, to balance it, she pushed her starlight against it. The pewter triangle brightened, humming.

It lurched in her grip, as if a greater magic was yanking it. Chaotic magic. Tempest.

"Oh, no, you don't, sister." Bix held fast and poured more light into it. The hum strengthened to a sonic wave. Sound took on texture, texture became tangible as it traveled up through the Devourers' portal and down to the District. Tugs of resistance. Frantic but strong. Bix reached deep within herself and called up more starlight, bolstering the connection of magic, of energies in motion, of being the dominant power.

At the edges of her vision, swirling blue nimbi built around plum. Resen's foundational elements. Responding to the greater magics. Not good. Not now.

She…she couldn't do a damn thing about it. Not and hold on to the shards. Yet if Resen interfered in this cosmic squabble, the explosion would sink more than the District. It'd blow the World out of existence.

Tempest's magic pulled on the triangle harder, the creator trying to reclaim her creation. Bix couldn't let that happen, but her grip was faltering. And the foundational elements' movements skirted the edges of the highly pressurized field, causing fluctuations. Not good. Not good at all.

Five bursts of hunter green within the auroras of the foundational elements ignited multiple circles of green at the perimeter, pushing the swirls of plum and blue away from the pressurized field.

Tobek.

Bix never had to ask; he just *knew* exactly how to support her. She was going to kiss the daylights out of her Berserker, as soon as she got her toys back. Steeling her resolve, she tapped reserves long disused and surrendered the last confines of her corporeal state. Midnight and starlight dominated everything.

The pull on the completed panel abruptly ceased. Devourers screeching and bleeding tarry goo tumbled through the portal, bodies sacrificed to the shards ripping free of their flesh prisons to respond to Bix's summons. Up from the District, demons surged, shards in monstrous hands and claws like offerings. Each cursed god stared boldly into her expansive night, allowing her to see their desperation breaking through their masks of determination. To a one, they raised their shards and bowed their heads. The instant they breached her midnight perimeter, the demons released their shards and fell away.

Gifts. They'd wanted her to know their pieces were gifts. To her great shock and curiosity, the demons so loyal to Pigsy were more determined than their leader to save the Mids. They were *giving* her their shards. Did they finally believe she was no longer the enemy? Did they finally trust her to save them and these Worlds? Proof through action. Perhaps it went both ways. Regardless, she was grateful.

"You may seize my weapons, Chimera, but I still have your precious draugr. This isn't over, not until every last Devourer is dead." Pigsy flew toward her, hands bleeding as he tried to cling to the shards answering her summons. Unlike his army, the god of greed refused to see the truth in the actions unfolding before his eyes. Perhaps it was his madness, but it was more likely plain old pride.

Though Pigsy meant his words as a threat, what Bix heard was confirmation that Drew was alive. That emboldened the starlight within her. A chuckle built and spread throughout her expansive state. Drew was alive! As soon as Bix wrangled these shards into compliance, she was going to rip her best friend out of the god of greed then drain Pigsy of everything but the seed of his divinity.

But first, she had to defuse the threat to the Mids and secure the shards.

Slivers of chaos and order danced through her on textured waves, unwilling to fit into their final positions to build the containment pyramid. Damn. The rites of transference. Every shard bobbing around her had been stolen. Unable to bond with their thieves, they'd come to her, but they wouldn't comply with her. Fine. She had them. Tempest didn't. That was enough to call a win for now.

Bix folded the loose shards of the six panels within her native state, ending the standoff. The movement changed the pressure within the field. She heard the unnerving pop before she felt the recoil. The Devourer portal imploded.

Oh shit.

Bix spun with a scream to glimpse the blast hitting the District. Instinct called forth starlight to illuminate the timeline of the Mids. Bix yanked herself out of the moment.

CHAPTER 25

A rich royal-blue bubble domed over the greater DC area, from West Virginia to the Atlantic coast, a result of archangels in full feathered form calling forth their innate magics to manipulate all things related to air and atmosphere. The waves from the pressurized blast rippled over the dome like warm glaze on cake. Beyond the dome, gods of wind, massive and glorious against the backdrop of rolling gray nimbostratus clouds, pushed back concussive waves and neutered tornados spawning from the collision. The swirling purple and blue nimbi of the foundational elements filled in the hole left by the Devourer portal, mending the protective layers around the Primary Mid World.

Bix bit her lip as emotions welled, happy ones. Relieved ones. Collaboration. Among the Consortium. It was finally happening. It'd only taken them seventeen hundred years. Drifting between shock and glee, she descended under the dome, where the landscape was not at all the traditional overbuilt, overpopulated flatland.

The dragons had called up the bodies of water and banks of land to wrap the District in barriers. Aided by gods of terrain and water, the metro area resembled a rabbit warren, highways having been replaced by flat-topped mountains that would absorb any shock waves that made it past the angels' barrier. Within the looming shadows, thin threads of Fate shimmered, weaving circumstances to drive mortals to shelters created by Chwed guilds and protected by deities. Berserkers labored beside animal shifters and ogres to rescue and transport trapped and wounded mortals.

A giggled gasp escaped Bix as she took in the many races of the Mids working together to save one another. It was admittedly less awesome for her that they had to save themselves because of her screwups, but they'd done it. They'd rallied. They'd come together. Yes, this was just one tiny spot in the greater collective, but it could catch on. After all, if the Consortium led, truly led as their positions demanded, the outcome of this clash with the Devourers would be better societies. An evolution of community and cohesion.

Until greed ruined it all again. That was inevitable. Speaking of greed and ruining things, where was Pigsy?

Winding through the maze of debris and defenses, she came upon demons aiding the mortal races. Some she'd caught hefting entire buildings off blocked roadways or scooping vehicles out of bodies of water. Others were helping fortify protections. Without them holding a shard, she had no idea which were Pigsy's demons. Not that it mattered, not to her. They were saving this city. When the call for aid had come, they'd answered. Those who had followed a despot for a leader to get to this point had been loyal to him in their own despicable ways. Loyalty wasn't a common trait of gods, cursed or not. That loyalty was a redemptive quality, particularly when paired with showing up for the greater good, so Bix didn't husk the demons. Instead, she cast threads of darkness to pierce each demon as she found them and took only their curses, leaving the deities in their natural form. Let them continue to fight beside their kith and kin for the better of the Mids. This was the dawn of a new era of rapid change and fluid alliances. Maybe after millennia of damnation, a little grace would go a long way toward setting the condemned on a course of noble acts.

If they really messed up, she'd come back and drain them later.

Bix found a curse-free Sophia in cahoots with the dragons to protect the Library of Congress. Ashtad and a team of demigods minded a power station with the aid of Chweds and humans.

Proceeding closer to the crumbled chunks of what had once been the Washington Monument, Bix froze. Her emotions short-circuited. Tobek. Smoldering. Not in a good way. A puddle of molten metals and bubbling magics pooled around his legs. Ashes of charred flesh hovered in the air around him. His once-broad shoulders were burning back to his clavicle. His arms and weapons were gone. No trace of his glorious mane and beard lingered in the green flames consuming his skull. His heavily inked torso was naught but blackened flesh peeling away from his rib cage save for his Eternal Knot. That hand-sized patch of skin remained unmarred and glowed with the six sacred colors of Bix's siblings. What should've been bones in the exposed skeleton of his lower body were instead complex weaves making intricate patterns of purple, blue, green, and red.

Horror. Bafflement. Elation. All of them skittered through Bix at the proof of Tobek's continued evolution toward something akin to a First Child. He was calling on more than the foundational elements from the ground. He'd figured out how to tap into the divinity that had created the core of this World. She'd never doubted he was brilliant, but it would be nice if his remarkable genius didn't encourage his fetish for immolation.

Poor Gurp. The things that goblin dealt with for love of Tobek. While the goblin should've been safely ensconced at the coal plant, he and Runjit stood at the ready to scoop whatever remained of Tobek into a cooler for transport. All hail the brotherhood of Berserkers.

Assuming Xipil had kept Cian at the coal plant, there was one team member waiting on her. One who'd been a hostage of a mad god for far too long.

Spotting the enlarged pig god atop the Capitol building wasn't hard. A simple gate allowed Bix to join the keeper of her memories, misguided misanthrope, and pawn of Tempest. She did a double take at the pure hate and awe contorting his rounded features as he stared up at what would've been the shard struggle.

"Oh, Pigsy, you're so accustomed to taking that giving offends you to your very core, doesn't it? Did you know that the moment you stole your first human shard, you alerted my sister to your existence? Once she discerned you held *her* shard and *my* memories, well, there was no escaping her influence, was there? She told you to take Drew, to what? Hurt the heartless Chimera? Yet when your men told you I'd changed and become a better, caring entity, your pride didn't let you believe them. You should've listened to your army. Trusted them instead of my sister. It's time your soldiers had new leadership." Bix jabbed a tentacle through the god of greed's porcine outer shell, plunging deep into the chaos of his natural state. The starlight of her forsaken memories shimmered, forming a barrier around a tiny ball of pale glacial blue trembling with Other World energy.

Drew.

Drew was not doing well at all, but Pigsy hadn't killed the draugr. He *couldn't*. His threats had all been bravado. Bix's memories were shielding her best friend from Pigsy's overwhelming divinity. Here lay proof of the impossible, proof that Bix's displaced parts of self recognized the draugr. If Pigsy hadn't been a memory keeper, Drew would've been smote.

Could Tempest have known Drew would be safeish? Or was her sister testing her? Testing Bix's capacity to care? At the moment, it didn't matter.

Alas, Bix couldn't reach her bestie without absorbing the shield of memories. Her missing parts wanted to come home. Even now, auroras built among them, prepping for her summons. The assimilation would take Bix out of the game for an indeterminate period while the displaced linked with the replaced. She was older than the concept of time. She had a lot, a lot, a lot of memories that were missing pieces. In many ways, her mind was like the containment pyramid: broken, weaponized, and meant for a greater purpose.

Sadly, when she took on her lost bits, she blacked out. Went places. Did things. Took things, sometimes people. Sometimes, she even ruined stuff, like faithful legions or entire Worlds. Her conscious mind had no clue once her subconscious assumed dominance. Eko, Esiw, and Phobos had seen her through previous mind repairs. If she was smart, she'd return to Eko's prison and let her brothers protect galaxies from her unsupervised id.

If she didn't have such sticky fingers or volatile magics, she could linger here, outside of time, and take as long as she needed to put her marbles back together. Tempest wouldn't be able to do a damn thing about it. But then, Bix and her explosive rehabilitation would be the danger from whom no one could escape. After all, time in the Mids still flowed forward for everyone but her.

When it came to her memories, damage control had to be the priority. Unlike her initial confrontation with Pigsy, she now had all the shards of the containment pyramid. She wasn't worried about the demons or the Devourers pursuing them anymore. Tempest couldn't get them, so her sister had no reason to continue to exacerbate the situation in the Mids. The collective was as safe as it could be, for the time being, and so were her loved ones. Except Drew. She owed her bestie freedom and an apology toot sweet.

Taking a deep breath for lungs that didn't exist, she spared one last look at the glorious cooperative disaster of the District. The Consortium would have their hands full spinning this to the magic-ignorant human population while simultaneously soothing the magic-aware Chweds. Assuming, of course, the Consortium still thought they could keep everyone oblivious to the invading army. Hopefully, Ogun would convince the Consortium to overturn those foolish policies.

She wouldn't be around to see the cleanup. Neither would Pigsy.

"Ah, Pigsy, got yourself caught between squabbling siblings, and sisters to boot." She patted his pale pink head. "But your biggest mistake was absorbing Drew. You see, little piggy, relationships are what matter to entities far, far older than you. Everything else can be replaced. *Is* replaced, in fact. Best friends, however, are hard to come by, so this is the end of the line for you. It's important you're fully aware of it."

Starlight brightened as Bix returned to the timeline. Pigsy inhaled sharply and flinched away from her, but her darkness was faster and engulfed him whole. He fought her, of course, but she drained him of everything save the seed of his divinity, her memories, and her best friend. Her displaced memories prevented him from reducing to a translucent husk. They would keep him functional, but they would also make him believe he was she, operating on fragments and pixels of encrypted history. Letting him linger in that state would be disastrous, and Drew was in no condition to take control of the god.

Even now, Drew remained small and cowering, nary a spark of mischief or rebellion. It made Bix nauseous with worry. If her native state had had a heart, it would've shattered again. Instead, guilt was a tang that infused her night. She didn't know how much longer Drew could hold on to life trapped within the cage of Bix's displaced bits. The memory assimilation had to happen. Now.

Bix reached through darkness for the familiar hallways of Eko's prison.

The moment she materialized on the triangular garnet floors, chaos tangled around her and yanked her out of the prison.

CHAPTER 26

Struggling against darkness that didn't belong to her, Bix ruthlessly forced panic and confusion beneath the rise of malice. She knew these entanglements. She knew the battery and bludgeoning attempting to harm her native state as it had her corporeal once upon a time when she'd been a total amnesiac adrift in the ether. She wasn't that girl anymore. She wasn't lost and confused. She wasn't afraid of her corporeal need to breathe, to eat, or to survive. She knew her ass from her elbow now. She knew her darkness from her light. She was the godsdamned two-in-one.

Starlight brightened within her, shoving past the thickets of dark malice to flare with the might of the morning sun.

The assailing darkness recoiled with a shriek that twisted into a humorless chuckle. "Oh ho-ho, lookie what the bratling finally remembers how to do."

"Back the fuck off me, Tempest," Bix snarled, dimming her light to take in the familiar nothingness of the ether. She hated and loved this place. Knowing she had to end its existence was bittersweet. Dealing with the youngest of her sisters, however, was straight-up infuriating. "You're not getting the shards."

"Your confidence has always been so vexing, and this time, unearned." Tempest solidified her state into the torso, arms, and face of a woman with a lower body and headdress of five dozen tentacles emblazoned with muted pewter logographs of her chaotic attributes in languages from galaxies far, far beyond this one.

"Really? You think you can take them from me? Try it." Bix held to her form of feminine midnight and starlight. She wouldn't give her sister the opportunity to abuse her corporeal state, not again. Not ever again. Besides, she was packing a rousing god, a sickly best friend, some misplaced memories, and a broken containment pyramid inside this state.

Tempest darted forward until her nose touched Bix's and stared into her eyes. "I don't have to. All I have to do is wait for you to grieve the loss of your precious friend. You've never been able to keep it together when you're in mourning."

Wariness rippled through Bix. The Oracles had also mentioned dealing with grief before she could finish this mission. That Tempest thought she had the upper hand because of it... The roiling tangled clump of dangerous memories hammered within Bix's skull, bulging, threatening to burst. The thorns of malice reinforcing the barrier strained. Nope. Nope. Not the time to deal with it. Later. After Drew was safe.

"You told Pigsy to absorb my friend. What a petty move for a cosmic entity." Bix didn't give ground, not even to Tempest's tentacles trying to coax Bix's into being. Her sister was trying to get a rise out of her. Why? What advantage did Tempest gain if Bix lost her temper? This wasn't just another god she was dealing with—it was another First Child. That more than upped the stakes. It changed them completely.

"You needed motivation." Tempest jabbed a fingernail squarely in the center of Bix's midnight brow and mewled with frustration. "You have the pig. He has your friend and your memories. Why haven't you reclaimed them yet?"

"I was on my way to do that when you interrupted me," Bix noted dryly as a stray thought slapped her. "Wait, you *wanted* me to find Pigsy? That's why you upped the bait with Drew? You want me whole again. Am I taking too long for you? For something you need from me? That you need me to be fully powered to deliver. Is *that* what this is all about?"

"Do it now," Tempest demanded, introducing a fraction of space between them. "I've watched you reclaim the other parts of your mind from the serpent, the hunter, the coyote, the mercenary, and the bat. So delicious your self-inflicted torments. So precious, your simpering and whimpering. Ricocheting off planets you destroyed. Beating down titans from whom you stole. Husking gods who worshipped you. All your dizzying trips. All your disastrous agitations."

"That's why I do it under the supervision of our brothers. I am too dangerous otherwise." Bix couldn't get a read on her sister. Tempest was…tempestuous by nature. However, Bix was fairly sure Tempest was also impatient, which was downright odd for any entity as old as they were.

"You don't need our big brothers to shield the galaxies from you. We're in the ether. You can't destroy anything here. Well, nothing worthwhile, at least."

"Except for the Devourer army you built to invade my sanctuary," Bix countered.

Tempest circled Bix, hissing. "They're entities of order, you nitwit. I didn't create them, but like all toys, they're fun to play with. Manipulate. The toy Indraja. She's been very helpful. Your toy Phobos? Less so. But, I'm sure he'll come around soon."

Phobos. Shit. Bix had sent him to find the gods the Devourers had captured. He hadn't checked in. Then again, he would've chafed at the notion he needed to. Didn't mean Bix shouldn't have followed up. But like Sophia and Drew, Bix hadn't. Her own team. She'd been so focused on gathering the shards, she'd assumed the others would've called out if they'd needed her.

Assumed. Again. That thing about assumptions really biting her in the ass, hard and repeatedly.

"Tempest, my process of healing is not yours to dictate. I will do this where I feel safest, and that's with Eko." Bix snapped her teeth at her sister as Tempest invaded her personal space, again.

"You either do it here, now, with *me* as your guide, or that life you so cherish inside the pig is gone." Tempest bared her teeth in response, exposing the sharklike multiple rows.

Revulsion and dread shivered through Bix. No way, no how did she feel remotely comfortable being completely vulnerable in her sister's presence. Not when Tempest had repeatedly demonstrated what a detriment to Bix's well-being that was. Hell, Bix still woke up some nights covered in cold sweat from the nightmares of Tempest assailing her in the ether.

Bix reached for Eko's prison again. Again, Tempest hauled her back.

"We can keep this up for eons, bratling," Tempest jeered and coiled around Bix. "As long as you're broken, you're no match for me. Eko isn't coming to your rescue. He's imprisoned. Esiw? He wants you to take back your memories almost as much as I do, so he sees no point in interfering. As for our eldest sisters, Movement and Music? They're too busy watching the disaster unfolding in your precious sanctuary to care about our tiff."

"Tempest…" Bix snarled even as her darkness warned that Drew was perilously close to dying.

"Better hurry, there's more than one life you care about in jeopardy." Tempest stuck out the tip of her tongue and bit it until it bled the darkest silver. Each droplet contained an anguished wail louder than that of a banshee or rudaali with enough sonic pressure to deafen a titan. It was a torture Tempest had used often enough on Bix while Bix had been feral and clueless. "Don't think time is on your side just because you can access it. Going back in time doesn't guarantee you get what you want, so I advise against trying to change the present."

Damn her sister. She was right. The past couldn't be recreated in perfection, and the odds were high that circumstances would get worse instead of better if Bix erased the present.

Tempest was the last entity with whom Bix wanted to go through the assimilation that rendered her completely vulnerable…but this was the ether. This moat had been designed to be destructive, its barriers designed to contain that destruction. If Bix had to do this without her brothers' aid, then she only had the matter of time away from her team to worry about. Then again, the ether had multiple time zones, some that flowed faster than the timeline of the Mids and some that flowed excruciatingly slower. All she had to do was find the right pocket of slo-mo and pray she didn't travel out of it too often. There was a slim chance she might be able to get through her crazy with mere moments having passed in the Mids.

Worst case, Tempest stole the shards from her while she was unconscious. Her sister still had to reassemble the six panels before the seventh would reveal itself, and, according to their brothers, Tempest couldn't repair what Bix had broken, even though Tempest had made half the panels. It was risky. Tempest could unleash the combined power of the shards on the Mids, but why would she? Tempest could cause greater havoc without the help of a trinket. No, whatever nefarious reason for which Tempest wanted the containment pyramid, she needed it whole and operational. There were a lot of possibilities for what Tempest could do with or without the shards, but there was a certainty Drew no longer had time for Bix to dither.

"You're going to regret this, Tempest," Bix vowed. "Because I'm going to remember why I instinctively hate you so much."

Tempest laughed hysterically. "That's the whole point, you idiot."

Muttering nothing kind, Bix brightened her starlight, revealing the multiple time zones within the ether. The slowest flow was easy to spot, and so Bix moved—via gates—into that pocket. It might take Tempest a beat or twelve to catch up, but by then, Bix would be well on her way to reclaiming what was hers.

Confirming she was alone for the moment in the slo-mo zone, Bix withdrew Pigsy from her darkness and jabbed one thorny vine inside him.

"All right, missing bits of me, let's get this over with," she muttered.

The lights of her displaced memories flashed, and the auroras shone as they snaked their way to the thorns welcoming them home. Flickers of images. Fleeting scents. Pokes of sensations. Tickles of tastes. Bursts of emotions. Rattling. Smashing. Stirring. Seeking. Seeking. Seeking until they overwhelmed Bix's lucidity.

In the final brief moment of conscious control, Bix delivered Drew to the safest place she knew, a place where her bestie could be independently corporeal and regain much-needed strength. Gates transported Drew to the peace of a different timeline in an Under World with a mutual friend who might welcome the familiar face.

As the ginormous knot of worry finally loosened itself, Bix surrendered to memories, gorging on missing details.

CHAPTER 27

The pustule of festering memories popped, the sixth infusion of forsaken history too much for the barriers of Bix's mind and malice to hold back. The deluge of her familial saga drowned her repeatedly. Surfacing in lucidity for the briefest moment, she could swear Esiw was with her, cradling her in the plush nest of his four tails. Yet before she could latch on to that anchor, she plunged deeper into the morass of truths she did not want to know. The pain, oh gods, the pain. All those emotions she'd felt and buried, ill-equipped to cope with them, they demanded their due and her introspection. She screamed her agonies. Refought battles she'd never win. Loved deeply. Lost egregiously. Suffered betrayal repeatedly.

A song called to her amid her tragedies, luring her, giving her a path back to sanity. Bix grabbed hold, trying desperately to focus on the notes and the rhythm. The violet eyes of her sister Music widened with joy, and the song built around her, drawing Bix closer, closer… Bix couldn't hold on. Her wrath was too mighty, her fury unbound and hungry for vengeance. Back into the psychosis she tumbled. Over and over, the struggle repeated. A glimpse of Esiw. Then falling back. Hearing Music's song. Then spiraling lower beyond reach.

Until finally, the cruelest of miseries laid itself out in unflinching detail with gaps too eager to be filled by logical suppositions instead of grim facts. She rejected the patchwork offered by her wounded mind. The missing details were too pertinent and too critical as to why she'd kept only the seed of malice when she'd broken herself into pieces. The frames around the missing truths were ledes to the story of her family's involvement in her greatest heartbreak. Whatever they'd done to push her past anger, hate, and revenge was still out there in the final memories waiting to be claimed. They'd done something, though, something in which they were *all* complicit.

Damn it, as much as she wanted to explore the truths and gaps to ferret out the complete story, she really couldn't dwell on the worst of the abridged tales trying to be retold. The potential for pure fiction was too high. She'd have to let it go until she had the final segment of her memories. She'd have to keep playing the grateful fool with her siblings until she was whole again. Most of her siblings, that is. Tempest and Tempest's twin were not going to be spared Bix's immediate wrath. Bix was crystal clear on the cruelties they'd committed in the moments before and immediately after she'd given away her mind and magics.

At last, she now knew why she'd forsaken her all and her everything. At last, she remembered the who and the what that had led to that moment and that decision. At last, she understood the emotions paired with the events that had broken her mind, body, and spirit.

She was going to torture the unmerciful hell out of Tempest and Tempest's twin…then she was going to throw herself at Tobek's feet and beg forgiveness.

This time when she returned to reality, Bix didn't build mental dams as she had after prior assimilations that had allowed her to postpone confronting truths. This time, she was fully aware. No more hiding.

"Here she comes," Music trilled. "She's locking into her human form. Seems to be holding this time."

"Toy, are you capable of caring for her now?" Esiw asked.

"Through your intervention and generosity, I am. Thank you." Phobos's conciliatory tone came a heartbeat before the brush of Other Worldly silks fitted around Bix's body, clothing her in familiar comforts.

Bix stretched and flexed, testing her corporeal state. Plush fur tickled her cheeks and calves. She opened her eyes to find herself in a white-and-yellow nest. She hadn't hallucinated that part. Or the part about Music being with her, for that matter. Initially, she was happy Esiw and Music had been with her during her rehabilitation and total vulnerability, but her latest acquired memories quickly soured that feeling.

Still, until she knew the reasons behind her resentment, she had a part to play of the bumbling youngest child, ever so thankful for the insights of her elders.

A firm hand, tawny and of flesh, clasped hers and helped her from the cradle of Esiw's tails. The sardonic smile, the hint of a fang, the choppy layers of glossy dark hair, and the amber eyes with red pupils that warmed with relief as she allowed him to pull her to her feet all belonged to Phobos. The Greek god of fear, whom Tempest had said was a prisoner of the Devourers, stood hale and impeccably attired before her. True, he was tethered to her, unable to resist her unconscious summons when her pain exceeded her tolerance. But his state of well-being could only be attributed to Esiw's understanding of their bond.

"Phobos, as always, thank you," she said as genuine gratefulness nudged its way to the surface. She grabbed his shoulder, using the contact to reestablish her perspective and sense of corporeal self.

"As your caretaker, I am honored to be at your beck and call," Phobos intoned with an obsequious bow. The tilt of his head exposed the half-moon shaped metallic implant behind his ear. It was a gift from Esiw that allowed Phobos to reach Bix regardless of timeline disparities. Handy, that.

Despite her simmering tumult toward her siblings, Bix harbored no ill will for Phobos and didn't want to make him a victim of her temper. So, she packed away the hiss and seethe ready to explode at her siblings. She wasn't ignoring or denying those feelings, she simply would deal with them later. She was an expert at compartmentalizing, which was not the same as being emotionally stunted. She'd spent way too long being the latter. Fortunately, Tobek and her friends had taught her how to excel at the former. For now, she embraced the joy of seeing Phobos unfettered and at his usual equanimity.

"The speed and skill with which you respond is appreciated." Bix couldn't resist needling him just a little bit, knowing full well how much feigning deference irked the god of fear. Phobos was smart enough to play dutiful minion when among First Children. There was a reason her siblings let him thrive.

Taking in their surrounds, Bix tapped her feet against the… the unmoving golden gasses of a nebula? That shouldn't be… Oh.

"We're outside time?" she asked.

"A necessity." Esiw grunted disapprovingly. "Your tantrums reverberated along multiple timelines. Those, combined with your persistent traveling, have caused havoc across universes. Music and I brought you here to mitigate the damage you were wreaking."

Music was the eldest child aligned to their father, Esiw the second. They could access time, and, as creationists, they could access the many futures too. Bix must've really, really borked up the greater existence if they'd intervened.

"Sorry about that. I'd hoped I'd spend most of my time in the ether," she admitted with a lick of actual remorse. She hated that lesser entities got hurt whenever she couldn't control herself. "Tempest insisted on being with me through the process."

"Tempest is still in the ether, waiting impatiently for your return." Music helplessly fluttered her hands. "Little sister, she did not escape your struggles. I believe she enjoyed what you wrought upon her. I worry for both of you."

"That worry is not unfounded." Bix extended a sheen of starlight toward Music, letting it glide along the rippling lines of purples curved into a feminine form. It was the best she could offer in terms of assurances under the circumstances. "Tempest and I have unresolved issues. Violent issues rooted in cruelty, perceived and actual."

"Faced them, then, have you?" Esiw let a hint of wariness tint his tone. "The things you've been avoiding?"

"Six out of seven memory segments all snug as a bug, no dirty truths left unexplored." Bix tapped her temple as her emotions took a sip from the well of bitchiness. "I anticipate the seventh will supply the finer details. I'm very interested in why I was overcome with hostility and a chilling sense of betrayal toward every member of this family, to the point that I chose to break myself into pieces rather than seek your assistance. You've been so helpful in the aftermath, perhaps you could fill in the blanks for me?"

Esiw and Music had the grace to appear concerned if not contrite.

"When you remember, you will know," Esiw evaded with his favorite patronizing phrase.

"Of course," Bix accepted with false sincerity. "Plus, it gives you time to warn the others that a reckoning is coming."

"Oh, little sister…" Music warbled, sounding almost tearful had crying been possible in her sister's preferred state.

"I don't suppose either of you know what happened to the partial containment pyramid I was carrying or to the loose shards?" Bix forced an amiable smile. Now was not the time and here was not the place to hold her siblings to account. They were immortal. They could wait until Bix possessed the unabridged story.

"Tempest," her siblings said together. Esiw gestured for Music to continue.

"Tempest has them." Music sighed. "You let go of your prizes when fluctuating between states."

Had Bix not just incorporated the memories of the damn pyramid into one fluid story, she would've freaked out at the news. Luckily, however, all the tricksy details trembled at the ready, eager to be called up and put to use. That tale was complete and included a surprising throughline.

"Well then, Tempest and I have an appointment that I really must keep." Bix examined the gunmetal-gray octopods painted atop her crimson lacquered fingernails, appreciating how Phobos paid attention to the tiniest details of her appearance. "Best to return to the flow of time."

"Little sister?" Esiw beckoned softly. "You deserve a full accounting of our actions and inaction that led to your gross self-mutilation. We are not hiding from that difficult conversation. We are merely waiting for you to be fully ready to hear it. When the time comes, we will accept our share of the consequences."

"I'm going to assemble the containment pyramid, take down the ether, and watch Resen finally launch. After that, as the appointed champions and guardians rout the Devourers from my sanctuary, I will give great thought to that reckoning. Until then, thank you for your continued support." Bix slid her arm around Phobos's, ignoring his slight jolt, and opened gates to the ether.

CHAPTER 28

The song of nothingness in motion welcomed Bix back to the ether. The only illumination came from her starlight and Phobos's aura of divinity. She let go of her caretaker and shoved her hand through her hair, biting back a sigh of self-recrimination.

"I'm sorry, Phobos. I'm sorry you were captured by the Devourers. I'm sorry I left you to languish with them. I'm sorry I didn't contact you immediately once I learned my sister was puppeteering Indraja, who's been puppeteering the Devourers."

Phobos smoothed the lapels of his burgundy suit and arched a disdainful brow. "Who said I wanted to be rescued? Remember, prisoners learn a fair amount about their wardens, particularly once the wardens relax their guard."

"You're saying that to make me feel less guilty, which is uncharacteristically kind of you. But I know if you got caught, then your twin came rushing to your rescue and has been captured too." She wagged a finger at him. "So, how many of your spies did you leave in the Devourer camp after our bond freed you from them?"

"Enough to create a beacon," he said through a deliciously malevolent laugh.

"What about them being husked? That's a huge risk you're taking."

"Indraja is a greater goddess known to husk lesser gods, yes, and Devourer generals are notably voracious. However, the pantheons are not without their own tricks." Phobos cut her a sly grin. "As the only twinless member of your generation, you might be unaware of how difficult it is to break the connection between birth mates. That includes mental connections."

She was not unaware. Not anymore.

"How quickly after your capture did my sister make herself known to you?"

"Your sister is the one who caught me. Indirectly. Indraja is her interface with us puny gods and anti-gods." Phobos pursed his lips and lifted his chin. "Everything Indraja has done since you disappeared in the ether centuries ago has been dictated by your sister. While I do not know the reason, I am confident in the assertion that your sister is obsessed with you to an unhealthy degree. I say that as a god with many siblings whom I adore yet whose passions are often detrimental."

His siblings were emotion gods who ran the gamut from unrequited love to terror. His mother was a goddess of sexual lust and his father a god of battle lust. When it came to the crazy of family, he was acquainted, to put it mildly.

"That is the nature of Tempest's primary aspect." Bix offered an apologetic smile. "She and her twin are the embodiments of motivation. She motivates outward as the whip, the lash, the external push one feels to gain, accomplish, and achieve. She is social pressure, familial obligation, corporate demand. Everything that bears down on us originates with her."

Phobos's nostrils flared, and he recoiled. "She is the root of countless fears."

"She's not all bad. Because of her we have friends who don't let us quit and mentors who encourage us to achieve our potential, like a certain god of fear I happen to know."

"Yes, well." Phobos sniffed and tugged his cuffs. "Why don't you go deal with *your* sibling while *I* complete the task you laid out for me which involves rescuing *mine*?"

"Phobos, you can't do it alone. That's suicide." She sighed. "I've overtasked too many teammates, which led to their capture and near deaths. I'm supposed to be wiser now, so I can't add you and your brother to my list of screwups."

"Is that external or internal motivation?" he quipped, arching a brow.

"As vicious as she seems, she and her twin helped raise me." Bix looked askance as fond memories of Tempest flitted through her bruised mind, only to be chased by the overwhelming sadistic ones. "Whether you want to see it or not, her influence is enmeshed in our existence. Admittedly, it's more potent when she applies it directly to you, as she doubtlessly has with Indraja."

"This whole disaster has gone on far too long because the pantheons, along with the rest of the Consortium, did not rise to the challenge of foreign invasion when it was just an annoyance. It is a fair expectation that we do so now. That expectation may have been placed upon us by you, and our desire to meet it delayed until your sister got involved, but ours is not to ponder the why and wherefore of First Children. It is simply to protect what is ours if we want to keep it. We very much want to keep the Mids." With every word he spoke, his tailored suit fell away and was replaced by fitted undergarments that covered him from wrists to ankles. "When I say 'we,' 'us,' and 'ours,' Chimera, I mean the gods. Ogun has forced us into line, finally. I'm not going back to the Devourer camp alone. There's a well-experienced mobile guerilla force of hunter gods ready to strike on my go."

"Not planning to annihilate the camp, then?" She watched in fascination as his armor—usually laced and buckled into place by his minions—manifested where it ought. From gauntlets to greaves, his magic secured them in place. The show ended with his xiphoi strapped across his back and his Corinthian helmet tucked under his arm. With most of her marbles back in her head, she realized his armor was an amalgam of best concepts across multiple eras, a benefit of his doting stepfather being the pantheon's blacksmith, no doubt.

"That was the idea until I got there. Their numbers are extensive, their resources nigh-on limitless. What we've managed to do is gather valuable intel that confirms what you have long espoused." He held up a mail-clad hand to stop her snark. "We need Resen operational if the Mids are to stand a prayer of rebuffing their forces. So, go, get the damned containment device from your sister, then remove the ether and expose the enemy forces for all to see. We cannot let them hide anymore."

"You do know if you pull hard enough on our bond, I will feel it, right?" she asked as a cloud of navy and mulberry gathered around him. "Don't make me come looking for you, young man."

"Go, Chimera. Whatever your issues with your sister, it is your battle to fight. We can't stop Indraja while she's protected by a First Child." He slapped his helmet over his head, and the last swirl of clouds took him away.

Alone in this segment of the ether, Bix let malice rise and began to revert to her native state. Stopped. No. She was eighty-eight percent back to her old self. She needed the physical reminder of what she was fighting for and all she'd truly lost. This humanoid form was fragile and vulnerable. It would serve to keep her from crossing that thin line when it came to her sister.

As for finding Tempest, Bix was the architect of the ether. She'd lived inside this contained explosion far longer than anyone realized. She knew all its secrets, including its patterns and tempos. Locating Tempest wasn't hard. Her sister was a fount of chaotic power.

CHAPTER 29

The screech of absolute fury and frustration brought a contemptuous smile to Bix's lips as she appeared behind her sister. Shards of the containment pyramid floated around Tempest, shooting farther away whenever Tempest tried to force the pieces together.

"You can't mend what I've intentionally broken, Tempest," Bix reminded. "It's my cosmic duty to unmake what you have made, to maintain balance in the greater existence."

Tempest stiffened and glanced over her dark shoulder. A sneer exposed her shark teeth as she waved the one completed panel of chaos with the partial panels of order affixed to it. "If you're so confident now, unmake this."

"Nice try." Bix held out her hand and the completed panel flew to her. "You were so anxious for me to hurry up and remember All the Things, sister. Guess what? You got what you wanted. I'd commend you on your patience, but that's not a word with which you are familiar. 'Suicidal nag' are words you probably know."

Chuckling cruelly, Tempest slowly turned to face Bix. Pewter-encrusted tentacles floated around her. Sharp, jagged hooks lined the edges and undersides. "Do you remember, finally? Is it there in your coward's brain? The reason you shattered yourself?"

"Everything," Bix lied, somewhat, closing the distance to her sister and never looking away. "Everything that led up to it. Everything that happened after it. The sound of your keening disbelief as I gave away my memories to ensure you and your twin could not use *me* as a weapon of mutual destruction is a sweet, sweet memory."

The slap stung hard enough to bring tears to Bix's eyes and set off a ringing in her ear. A trickle of mist bled over her lip. Bix studied her sister from under the fall of her bangs. Without thought, Bix did what she'd failed to do centuries ago when she and Tempest had danced this same dance. Starlight speared Tempest through the throat. Inside Bix, malice rejoiced. Her sister stared at her with eyes wide and mouth moving soundlessly. Tempest's tentacles tried to free her from the spear. Failed. Light was order. Tempest was chaos. Not that the blow would kill Tempest. It just demanded Tempest exert effort to extract herself.

Tempest gave up her corporeal form and slid free of the spear, slinking away from Bix before re-forming. "Well, it seems you *have* healed yourself with the pig's secret prize."

"The last time you tried to bully me, I was drowning in anger, wrath, and rage, seeking an outlet for my violence." Bix drifted through the ether, collecting the loose shards and stowing them within her. "You and your twin knew I was deep in the throes of the third stage of grief, and you foolishly sought to exploit it to get what you wanted. But, you pushed me too far. You pushed me, and I didn't fight. I shut down. I denied you what you two craved by taking myself out of the game. By giving away my abilities, the High Executioner was no longer in the business."

"We thought you'd understand," Tempest rasped, restoring her voice box. "We were in the same kind of pa—"

"Bullshit," Bix bellowed, and the continuous explosion that was the ether carried her venom. "You cannot fathom the pain I was in. You are a creationist. You can make anything on a whim. I had just lost—"

"Something you should *never* have had in the first place.

Something you knew you'd never be allowed to keep," Tempest screeched, causing the explosive waves to ripple faster, wider, stronger.

"Who are *you* to decide that? Who are *you* to have any say in *my* life?" Bix snarled, advancing on her sister.

"I ask you the same question," Tempest countered, meeting her halfway, sharklike teeth on display. "Who are *you* to decide my twin and I cannot end our existence?"

"I am the godsdamned *means*," Bix shouted. "Without me, you cannot die."

"You have no idea what it's like, the relentlessly unending frustration with *everyone and everything*," Tempest seethed. "No matter how much I motivate them, guide them, lead them by the bloody nose, they still flail about, simpering, whimpering, and *whining* over and over and on and on. The billions and trillions of entities out there too incompetent to succeed."

"Bitching about your purpose? How very like those lesser beings," Bix jeered. "We all have parts of our jobs we don't like. Grow up."

"It's inescapable, their constant clamoring for help." Tempest caterwauled and pulled at her tentacles. "They broke me, bratling, they broke *us*, my twin and me. When Desire and I could not abide another moment of their clamoring, we came to you for help."

"And I said no," Bix reminded flatly.

"Which is why we asked again. Again, you refused. We then demanded. You refused. This has gone on for far too long. You haven't left us any choice," Tempest argued.

"Your choice was to accept my answer." Bix forced her hands to hang loosely at her sides, even though she wanted to claw out her sister's eyes. "Instead, in an unsurprising demonstration of supreme selfishness, you deemed your needs more important than those of every other member of our family. *Every.* That includes Mother and Father, in case you've forgotten who they are and how quickly they can end everything, including us."

"See, that's where you're mistaken." Tempest shook her head

and wagged a finger as a manic smile dawned. "They are the origins of existence, but they are separate entities. Only you are equal parts. There is nothing you cannot unmake. *Nothing and no one.*"

"You are so eager to end your own existence," Bix scoffed as nausea rose and her head swam. Having a heated debate over murdering her own family was as revolting as it was incredible. "You don't care who or what you harm. You no longer feel anything when others hurt. Empathy is lost to you, by your own doing."

"I've been demonstrating that fact for ages," Tempest derided, dancing the dance of opponents with Bix. "Misery. Company. All that."

"No real company. Just you and your twin, eternally linked, feeding on each other's wretchedness." Bix gestured around them, continuing the waltz in the key of torment. "Where is Desire, by the way? Why isn't he helping you steal the broken containment device from me? Better yet, why isn't he helping you make a new one? Hmm?"

"He is busy hunting other means of forcing your hand," Tempest sniped, jabbing a razor-edged tentacle at Bix.

Bix knocked the offending appendage away with an arm glowing with starlight. "Doesn't it piss you off, just a little, that he's not here for you? Without him, you *can't* make another containment device. We both know the reason you want the volatile ether is to blow every sanctuary of our siblings out of existence until they join you in pressuring me to give you what you want. You *need* him here with you right now, and he *refuses*. I'd be livid."

"Desire and I are working toward the same objective. We simply have different methods. A twinless bratling like you can't fathom the bond we have." Tempest flared her tentacles, aiming her hooks at Bix. "Just look at the Devourers as proof of our cohesion. They are *his* creations, but they follow *my* command."

Bix sucked air through her teeth and grimaced. "Yeah, I mean, I get that he made them as a tribute to you. Their coloring and all makes that pretty obvious. But Desire is, at his core, all about the numbers and always needing more, more, more. This is why I'm a little less clear on whether he *gave* the Devourers to you, or if you *commandeered* them. To me, it looks like you stole his toys. What's it going to look like to him?"

"They're militaristic by design. They follow orders, not free will," Tempest said with disdain. "Desire understands that."

"Does he even know they're inside my sanctuary? That they've become *your* toys? If he were here, would he wrest command away from you? Would he sound the retreat? Send them away?" Bix studied her nails while she struggled with her temper. She desperately wanted to rip Tempest to shreds. No. Smaller than shreds. Motes. Atoms. But the physical attack wouldn't convince Tempest to call off the Devourer army, and Bix couldn't lose sight of the greater mission to save the Mids.

Tempest chuckled darkly. "Oh no, bratling, your precious Worlds aren't going to be rid of the Devourers so easily, not until Desire and I have what we want. What we *need*."

Her sister was wholly focused on making Bix suffer until Bix killed Tempest and Desire. No way in any hell was Bix going to do that. Sororicide and fratricide were big nopety nopes. Letting Tempest live was the perfect punishment. However, letting Tempest live in this highly dysfunctional state was bad for every other living thing everywhere. Bix had no idea what the right solution was. The last time this issue had come to a head, she hadn't gone to their older siblings for help resolving it. Her reasons were linked to the hostility she held for them, but she didn't know the details of why.

She needed more time. Time to complete the containment pyramid. Time to bring down the ether. Time to ensure Resen's successful launch. Time, when all that was done, to gather the final segment of her lost mind. The last segment held the answers about her family, including any efforts Bix had previously made to help Tempest and Desire. Tempest wouldn't wait patiently for her to be ready, not without a high body count, so Tempest had to be neutralized in the meantime.

Boy, it was a good thing Ashtad had taught her how to lie like a sunken freighter during their tenure as spies.

"Okay, Tempest," Bix said at last. "Summon your twin, and we'll do this."

Tempest narrowed her eyes and tilted her head. "Do what, exactly?"

"Give you what you need." Bix crossed her arms, being deliberately vague and hoping this most recent memory assimilation had unlocked enough of her powers to allow the illusion of unmaking her sister. In truth, she was banking on Desire being seriously displeased once he saw what Tempest had done with his toys. After all, he was personal motivation, which, at its worst, was rapacious greed. History was full of the very bad consequences for those who had stolen from the powerful and avaricious.

"Just like that?" Tempest challenged. "I'm not buying it."

"I'm not emotionally crippled anymore. I get it, what you want and why you want it." Bix shrugged, putting her years of spy training on display. The best lies were ninety percent true. "Empathy is something I embraced while living the life of an amnesiac. Once I set upon the path of rediscovery, I didn't let go of it. I fostered it. It's been rough, not going to lie, but it's a good thing to have, particularly when one is the High Executioner."

"So you'll do it," Tempest pressed. "Right now?"

"In exchange for the Devourers departing this galaxy, never to return." Bix clung to her unsteady courage and waited for Tempest to nod. Worst case, Desire showed and wasn't pissed at Tempest but at Bix. She had a loose Plan B that involved Eko and his prison, but that didn't guarantee the safety of the Mids. "Go ahead, summon your twin. It's a both or none-at-all deal. You are opposite sides of the same coin. Can't smelt the coin if the whole coin isn't here."

"Desire," Tempest whispered, her voice breaking as the tentacles of her headdress pushed apart the tentacles along her back and raked their hooks over the copper star hidden beneath all the black and pewter. "Brother mine, it is time. Finally. The bratling has agreed. Come to me."

They waited in the silent nothingness of the continuous explosion. Bix's heart thundered and her stomach flip-flopped, doubling down on the nausea inherent to fear. So much was riding on this bluff.

Longer they waited…waited.

Tempest cursed in some very old languages and tried summoning her twin again. Still nothing. Bix did her damnedest to keep a placid expression, oh heck, she even infused a bit of concern into her furrowed brow as Tempest practically shredded her own spine desperately beckoning her twin.

Could it be? Could Bix be that lucky?

"Tempest—" Bix began as hope calmed the riot in her guts.

"No. He'll come. He will. He *will*," Tempest shrieked, continuing to maul herself and cry out her twin's name.

"Tempest, stop," Bix soothed as a shred of actual compassion managed to surface. It fast became clear Desire had no interest in answering his twin. Blessings be, Bix and the Mids might've caught a break. "Go get him. The offer remains on the table."

"What is your trick, bratling?" Tempest ceased the self-mutilation and zipped into Bix's personal space. "Don't try to sell me a fable of forgiveness."

"This isn't an act of forgiveness, Tempest." Bix cupped her sister's cheek and stroked it with her thumb. "It's a means of getting you the fuck away from my toys."

Tempest snorted and jerked her face out of Bix's hand. "I have to hunt him. He's likely traveling timelines to foresee that which will force your hand."

"Oh, what is one possibility but the doorway to a thousand outcomes?" Bix gestured broadly to the ether and tried not to panic about Desire monkeying around in the future. "I'll be home, whenever you two are ready."

"The Devourers remain, bratling, and so does my command to them to destroy your *home*." Tempest snickered as she tapped a mote of darkness. "That order doesn't end until Desire and I do."

The moment her sister's resonance cleared the ether, Bix let her knees buckle and the façade of bravado fade to slack-jawed relief. She'd bought herself and the Mids a little bit of time, but only a little. At least she had the shards that refused to assemble into a containment pyramid that was needed to bring down the ether so Resen could go live and protect this collective from the Devourers. What would protect the Mids from her siblings if she couldn't figure out how to help Tempest and Desire without killing them? Nothing, probably.

Bix cradled her face in her hands and groaned. What a mess. What a disastrophy.

A sharp twang in her side doubled her over with a gasp. Twice more the twinge twanged, making her whimper through the discomfort inflicted upon her corporeal body by...

Shit. Phobos. That was his tether to her.

Curiosity was swift to rise as Bix reached through her bond with her divine caretaker to locate him. Oh please, oh please, oh please let Indraja be the reason he was summoning her because good godsdamn, Bix was *famished*.

CHAPTER 30

The District. Phobos was in the dystopian District of Columbia, Primary Mid World, aka Washington, DC, aka, the headquarters of the Consortium, aka the hot mess of hope and multiracial cooperation. Greater gods towered above the area in their truest forms, forms that made the entire planet seem small like a hacky sack. Divine torsos loomed over the horizons while shouting heads bickered across the moon in tones of rolling and clapping thunder. Wild gesticulations knocked aside wisps of ether trying to reclaim its place between Worlds. Gone were the heavy clouds of winter storms, leaving clear skies at dusk to uplight the pissed-off highest echelon of divinity.

All collaborative rescue and reconstruction in the demolished District had paused as the population stared skyward, dragons beside angels beside Fates beside humans beside mid and lesser gods beside glamourless Chweds. Everyone gaped at the half dozen greater gods having it out. Four against one in shackles, with the sixth playing moderator. No, not moderator. Judge. It was a trial. Four greater gods were making their cases to Ogun against a goddess with unmistakable coral hair and defiant posture.

Indraja.

Bix covered her open mouth. "What in the...?"

"I do not require your assistance. However, I believed this was a moment you did not want to miss." Phobos adjusted his helmet under his arm, grunting with a wince. His skin was blistered and raw in the gaps where his armor had failed to protect him from the blood of Devourers, blood that was designed to inflict maximum pain upon the divine.

"You're not mistaken." Bix glanced to her other side, where Phobos's twin stood in human street clothes. His spine was as rigid as his brother's, but his skin was in far worse condition. His scar-enforced sneer didn't hide his smirk of satisfaction, though. Boredom was the bane of gods, so Bix had no doubt all the spies Phobos had recruited to suck up some novel torture at the hands of Indraja and the Devourers were similarly wounded and as profoundly smug. "I take it everybody got home okay?"

"The Chairman requested we deliver all gods captured and covert to the Consortium to be fed and debriefed." Phobos tipped his chin in the direction of the Capitol ruins. "The gods to whom you entrusted shards are there, with Sophia."

The knowledge goddess caught Bix's eye and beamed, holding up the clasped hands of two of the six other gods whom Bix could now instantly identify as the watchers she'd tasked to monitor the ether and protect their segment of shards. It was nice to have those memories again. To recognize the lives she'd directly changed. For better and worse.

Within her, loose shards trembled. Agitated. Bix bid fine threads of darkness to extract those vibrating shards and place them in her cupped hands. Shards of chaos. Seven of them. The moment Bix uncurled her fingers, the shards zipped across the distance to the watchers with whom they'd bonded. Haunted eyes lifted and surprised smiles dawned as the watchers clasped their shards to their chests and bowed.

Bix's need to assemble the containment pyramid didn't outweigh the former captives' need for closure with Indraja, so she let them be for the moment. She wasn't worried she would lose the shards or the gods again. Now that she'd leveled up, she knew how to find them. Better still, she knew how to summon them.

"And Indraja?" Bix asked, eying the greater goddess swinging her shackled wrists as she argued with the prosecution. "How'd that happen?"

"Did you really believe I had the *only* Consortium-sanctioned mission regarding the Devourer camp in the ether?" Phobos chuckled malevolently. "For all Indraja meddled with and corrupted the Consortium, she was unaware of recent policy changes that permit greater gods to exist in the Mids on the condition of fealty to the Chairman. Without your sister to protect her from her peers, the enemy of the Mids is finally standing before all to account for her sins."

"Emphasis on *all*," Bix noted with awe. No secret tribunals here. Ogun hadn't been kidding when he'd committed to changing the way the Mids were run and making an irrefutable show of it in the process. Putting a greater goddess on trial in front of Chweds and *humans*? Bix's head would've exploded at the mere thought, but fortunately, she'd put herself back together bigger, better, stronger, faster.

Speaking of greater powers flexing their might, the foundational elements were notably quiet for all the god woo on display. Was that because Tobek was down for the count or because something was wrong with Resen? Bix scanned the massive audience, searching for the unique resonances of Ashtad, Gurp, or even Tobek.

Young Ba'al and the child Sage are safe with the Berserkers across the river. Sophia's light touch on Bix's mind was welcome. *They are more determined than ever to have Resen ready to launch as soon as you bring down the ether.*

"And Tobek?" Bix asked quietly. Yes, she remembered she could, in fact, invade a god's mind, but the power influx tended to melt their brains, so she saved that feature for titans and greater entities. Besides, Sophia was already in her head.

Sophia's bright expression fell, and her shoulders slumped.

The core of who he is exists, but he has yet to re-form in any manner. Perhaps he needs more time?

Bix considered it, then recalled the truths of the Oracles. It wasn't time Tobek needed. He needed to be made whole so he'd stop short-circuiting and finally become the champion she'd long known he could be. The Oracles had also said she'd have to finish grieving before she could contain the ether, and she couldn't do that without Tobek.

Not the part to which she was looking forward, but she'd run away from it for far too long. Time for big girl panties and whatnot.

She laid her hand upon Phobos's arm. "Thank you for rescuing my watchers. I have to go now."

Phobos arched an inquisitive and passably concerned brow.

"Chimera," the sky boomed. Okay, not the sky, Ogun, actually, but his voice traveled through the atmosphere and brushed the World before it vibrated against her ears.

"I am here, Chairman of the Consortium," Bix whispered to her midnight and let it carry to the night sky settling like cloaks around the greater gods. She really needed to get to getting because she still had a mission to complete, but Ogun's use of her moniker let her know a formal request was about to be made. Cue the pomp and circumstance of politics and her duty to the greater existence.

"The Consortium calls upon the High Executioner for All Worlds to deliver judgment upon the goddess known to all as Indraja." Ogun peered down upon the District as did the other greater gods seated with him.

Venomous loathing, pure and deep, twisted Indraja's haggard features.

"You and I ruled out ego or greed being Indraja's motives since she played the puppeteer instead of the showman," Phobos reminded under his breath. "I believe you are about to discover if it was love or revenge that motivated her."

"The painful side of love," Bix said, knowing he'd understand better than most. "It is what drew my sister to her, for she too has lost herself in it."

He looked at her fully and inclined his head as Bix gave up her corporeal form to become the cosmic embodiment of balance, equal parts starlight and midnight, the High Executioner feared by all. The necessary evil.

Bix expanded her form around the greater gods, encompassing the entire Primary Mid World. "Chairman of the Consortium, are there facets of this case of which I am not aware?"

"No," Ogun said succinctly.

Considering Bix was the one who'd built the case against Indraja, Bix would've been surprised if Ogun had said anything else.

"Indraja, I know your means, your methods, and your mentor," Bix intoned, ignoring the surprise on the faces of the prosecutors when she said the last. "However, the worst behaviors often sprout from a seed deprived of nurturing and fed only shame. There are many paths to redemption. Which will you choose?"

"I will always choose the one that left *you* gutted, weeping, and feeble. My only regret is that this collective didn't burn to less than ashes," Indraja spat, much to the horror of her peers. "You husked my betrothed on our wedding day, right before the ceremony. Because of you, I was a jilted bride, complex contracts between my pantheon and his destroyed. Shame poured down upon my pantheon as other pantheons broke their contracts with us. My family and my pantheon were *forced* to reject me, to banish me. Left with nothing but loathing for you, I have shed the limitations of a mere planetary goddess and built myself into a greater goddess, amassing more power and influence than the vaunted Consortium. I don't want your mercy, Chimera. I only want your misery."

A prosecutor opened his mouth, but Ogun silenced him with a look. This whole production was a formality and a charade, but optics mattered, particularly at the dawn of a new era. So Bix, no longer emotionally repressed, decided to make a point for all to see.

Indraja may have been Tempest's tool, but Indraja had orchestrated the maiming and deaths of Bix's spy team, friends, lovers, and allies. For Indraja, every decision had been a personal attack intended to inflict maximum lasting damage to Bix and her fragile psyche. There was a price to pay for coming after the High Executioner. It was twice as costly for coming after her loved ones.

Starlight and darkness pierced Indraja. First Bix fed, because she was hungry. When there was nothing left of Indraja to feed on, Bix gathered the goddess's seed of divinity, the gift from the Chaos at the time of Indraja's ascension to a planetary goddess. As long as Indraja had this seed, the goddess would regrow. Blank mind. Blank body. Full magics. Nothing but the seed, its magic, and the immortal shell that protected it would carry over to the new Indraja. Folks would tell her stories of the goddess she'd been. She'd hear them, but never connect to them. They would always be stories, just stories. Until Tempest got her hands on Indraja again.

There is nothing you cannot unmake. Nothing and no one, her sister had exclaimed. Tempest wasn't wrong. Hell, Bix had even unmade the glue that had kept her own mind whole.

Right now, she had centuries of abuse to end, for both the victims and the victimized. There were other planetary gods out there. What would one less matter? The Chaos was infinite, her aspects boundless. If Bix's mother missed this particular aspect, the Chaos would simply grow a new seed and plant it in a different vessel. Gods had long overestimated their value. Perhaps they'd overestimated their resilience too. Perhaps Bix had once had a reason for stopping at husking them and perpetuating the immortality myth. If so, it was in the final segment of memories she didn't have. Based on what she knew in this moment, she had a cycle to break and a point to make. A point that needed to be openly demonstrated and clearly understood by the full Consortium.

Do not fuck with me or mine.

A god was a casing for chaotic magic. A seed was pure chaotic magic. Magic was nothing more than energy in motion, so Bix's lights of order cracked open the seed and stopped the chaotic energy. Seven sacred beats passed. What had once been a seed of divinity went up in a poof of darkness and dissipated. Indraja's husk faded out of existence. The goddess was well and truly gone. For good.

Malice writhed within Bix, a joyous dance of rediscovery and victory.

"Judgement has been rendered." Bix held Ogun's calculating regard, then reached out to a mote of darkness within a freezer within a nearby coal plant that had not been spared damage from the conflicts centered in the District.

CHAPTER 31

A lump of colorful wool blankets paced the back of the walk-in freezer in the main building of the coal plant. The sounds of Berserkers investigating and clearing damage from around the compound wafted through the freezer door. Mutters froze on crystalline breaths, tumbling to clink off the open lid of a large aluminum cooler. Purples, blues, greens, and reds shimmered along the interior walls of the cooler and freezer.

Bix lingered quietly by the racks of ice creams in her state of feminine starry night, wondering if her heart would've ruptured had she been corporeal. This was her nuclear family, not the one into which she'd been born, but the one she had built. She'd bonded with Gurp and his pure, bold, huge heart immediately. Tobek, on the other hand, had taken time. Frankly, love had been the last emotion on his or her mind for centuries. Their gross power differences combined with how much he'd despised her and how annoying she'd found him had kept even the vaguest affection away. Until it hadn't. Enemies to lovers, a trope and a truth in their case. She was eager to see how it developed and changed as both of them continued to develop and change. But first, they had some fugly baggage to unpack together.

"Ever wonder if he's trying to answer when he's in that state?" Bix quietly asked.

Gurp stopped his pacing and rolled back the edge of a blanket to expose his bulging eyes and frostbitten nose. "Something not right."

"He can't heal until he's whole." She sank into her night, coming down to eye level with the goblin. "I need to take him home, back to our first home. The one the three of us shared all those epochs ago. Would you like to come along? Visit the old homestead? Whatever may be left of it?"

Gurp waddled to her, worry drawing down his features and making the wart at the end of his nose bob. "You know now?"

"I know why you're afraid of my unbalanced darkness, my dearest Gurp." She extended a finger of mostly starlight and drew it along his cold cheek. "I am so sorry you experienced any part of that tragedy. To give you reason to fear me was thoughtless and cruel. You've *never* warranted anything less than my unfaltering affection and respect. I am also aware that words, no matter how heartfelt, cannot repair the damage I did to our relationship. For what it is worth, I apologize for my actions and for subsequently abandoning you when you too were grieving."

He stared at her, lips pursing, then trembling before launching himself into her arms, a tangle of pudge and blankets. She held him close and allowed herself to feel the tumult of emotions. She didn't ignore them or suppress them. She let them happen.

At length, he pushed away from her, and she set him on his feet. Snuffling and dabbing his nose with a blanket, he gestured to the cooler. "You take. You fix you two. There. Then we three, here. Family. Again. All three."

"Always family." She gathered her form and kissed the top of his blanketed head. She eyed the contents of the cooler. Looked like someone had taken a color-changing LED and stuffed it under a solid block of ice. Leave it to Tobek to be full of surprises. She flipped the lid on the cooler. Wards upon the outside flashed dark green and sealed the box. She'd worry about him suffocating if he were mortal or if the wards hadn't been his obvious doomsday prep.

"Uh, Bix?" a cracking hesitant voice called near the heavy plastic curtain separating the meats from the dairy.

She turned, and gentle joy pushed sadness to the periphery for the moment. "Cian, hey. How are you? Really?"

"I, uh…" He scratched his head and shrugged. "I haven't given that much thought. I've been thinking about those stolen shard bits, right? Like, how we could get them to work if their original owners are dead? And I think I have an answer, but, uhm, I need the broken pieces."

He seemed so earnestly optimistic, if not bleary-eyed, that she didn't have the heart to tell him she could unmake the requirement of the rites. Instead, she gathered the shards from within her. The completed angels' panel and the affixed Oracles' and dragons' partial sides, she kept due to their potency. Cian hadn't reacted well the last time she'd waved the completed triangle under his nose without the protection of gates.

"Wait, wait." Gurp bustled to a crate of ice creams and emptied it out before handing it to the kid. "Now good."

"You're not going to blow a hole in the atmosphere, are you?" she teased as she placed the pieces in the box. She wasn't worried about the shards being stolen again. Her sister wasn't around to divulge the location, and being in the heart of a heavily warded military compound surrounded by Berserkers was probably as safe as third-party storage could get.

"Not a chance, swearzies." Cian audibly gulped as the shards glowed for the briefest moment causing his crystalized shoulders to illuminate before both went inert. "Hey, uhm, did you find Drew?"

"Yeah, kiddo, your roommate is going to be fine." Bix tugged a piece of cheese puff from his unkempt hair. "She's taking a little R&R in the Under Worlds, but she'll be back before you know it."

"Good." He sighed loudly and stood a little straighter. "Thank you, you know, for saving Drew and for trusting me with these."

"Of course." She smiled and tapped a finger on the edge of the box. "Just warn the foundational elements of Resen that you're playing with the shards, oh architect of the system."

"Yes. Yes, that is a good point. Yes. I'm going upstairs to Mister Ba'al, and we're going to code some safeguards. Yes. Right now." Cian held up the box and stumbled backward into the curtain before outright bolting from the freezer.

"Gurp, would you…"

"I got. I got," the goblin assured with a chuckle. "You go. Yes? Come home soon."

"I promise to bring back Tobek in one less frosty piece." With a wink and a wave, she opened gates to a World she'd forgotten for far too long.

CHAPTER 32

A small wooded island waited, undisturbed, in the middle of a clear lake surrounded by lush forests whose colors changed with the movement of three crescent suns and three full moons. Marine life abounded in the freshwater lake, and an impressive variety of animals occupied the outer forests. The species on this World existed nowhere else for they had not been made by dragons or angels. No, this World was one of the original three Mid Worlds created by Bix's eldest sisters Movement and Music expressly to provide sanctuary for Bix. Every detail had been selected to offer serenity and welcome. This was a hospitality World that learned and responded to basic needs. Any resource used in the course of comfort would be replaced.

Two connected wattle-and-daub yurts with thatched roofs opened to the northern and the western sides of the island. Three tree stumps served as seats beside a large firepit on the southern side. A driftwood kayak rested upside down on a hewn stone rack at the base of the grassy slope buffering the blush-pink sand beach. The soft gentle scent of clean water and tall trees in perpetual bloom blended on a playful breeze that kept the island on the cool side of comfortable.

This was where Bix had begun Tobek's rehabilitation from

reprehensible demigod to champion of the Mids. The island had been his prison for centuries while he'd seethed and rebelled against his choice of lifetime incarceration over death. She'd taught him how to temper his rage into something meaningful, and he'd taught her how to permit her emotions to enrich her life. Gurp had taught the two of them how to coexist while minimizing collateral damage.

Laughing at those memories of her earliest years with Tobek, Bix added structure and skin to starlight and midnight, locking into her corporeal state. Naked. There was no one here to see her other than Tobek, and he'd schooled her in the finer details of a corporeal form. All the finer details. Wow. Rawr. Talk about memories worth revisiting. Yeah. Whooo. Her cheeks and more burned at the recollection.

Her toes curled on the warm uneven surface of a large boulder, one of a cluster on the western shore of the island. The drying rock, Tobek had called it as he'd arranged herbs for flavoring future meals or vines for weaving ropes. It was as good a place as any to park his cooler.

"Knock, knock," she said to the cooler, laying her hand upon the wards. She didn't want to unmake them if he'd written them to unlock at her request. Trying a key before the blowtorch seemed wise. The wards shimmered under her palm. The hiss and snick preceded the pop and flip of the lid.

"Hammock, four post, light swing, oversized for Tobek, unobstructed view of the lake, in the path of the breeze, please," she asked of the environment.

The island quaked, causing ripples in the lake as trees obligingly rearranged themselves. Vines grew and coiled around trunks to form the swaying frame of the hammock while silkworms wove the inner blanket. As nature labored, Bix lifted her chin and breathed in the calm of the World. She loved being surrounded by people and crowds and noise and frenzied life. But sometimes, escaping it all to reestablish a balance of mind and body, of desires and demands, to reprioritize, to reflect, to simply reconnect to one's self was as much a necessity as a luxury.

The water stilled, as did the island. Atop the grassy slope on the northern face, a large hammock gently swayed with the breeze, strung amid four stout trees. Bix bid her darkness to heft the big block of frozen Tobek from the cooler and place him squarely in the center of the hammock. Gates relocated the cooler to the doorway of the yurt.

Exhaling, Bix spread her arms and faced the lake. The Oracle of the Future had said Tobek needed his sword to become the champion she'd chosen for the Mids. His sword was no common tempered metal. It hadn't been forged by mortals or gods. It couldn't be wielded by mortal hands, yet he'd acquired it as a mortal demigod after he'd traded his divinity to the Fates. Long before Bix had met him, he'd found the loophole in the rules of that sword that had allowed him to win it in a game of wits against a titan. He'd wrought such epic damage with that damn thing, but the fact he'd won it and wielded it with notable skill had been one of the reasons she'd given him a choice between imprisonment and death. There'd been a keen mind beneath all the rage, one that would've been a great force for balance if—and only if—he could apply his mind before his emotions. Her specialty, albeit in an unhealthy extreme.

Naturally, as his warden, she'd had to take away his supremely destructive toy and the artificial arm that had enabled him to wield it. He'd always been a determined man, particularly as a wrathful prisoner who'd blamed her for the results of his bad decisions. She'd had to break the sword and the arm into pieces, not unlike the containment pyramid. She'd done it knowing he'd eventually find the fragments and not be able to do a thing with them. Oh, man, remembering his feral bellows and rantings as he'd watched her shatter his toys. He'd stewed in his Berserker rage for weeks.

Ah. The blessedly bygone days. She was so proud of the leader and protector he'd become. He was fallible, but no longer hated himself or others when he made mistakes. The well-being of others came before concerns for himself, which was a huge pivot for the demigod whose entire focus had been his personal glory. Mind, he kept throwing himself under the bus with great regularity, but that came from confidence in his immortality and his endless curiosity…okay, and his pain fetish. He wasn't perfect, but he welcomed responsibility and accountability, and encouraged others to do the same. His greatest satisfaction came from lifting others up and helping them succeed. That made him a worthy champion for the holistic welfare of a World collective.

He'd more than earned the right to be made whole again. She'd already released him from his tether to her, so he was no longer her prisoner. He'd had the opportunity to walk away from everything related to the Mids, including her. Instead, he'd held her tightly and demanded the job for which he'd been training for ages.

At last, she'd undone enough of her own mess to be able to give it to him.

With a smile and a happy sigh, she cast rays of starlight and threads of midnight around and into the lake to forage deep beneath the muddy basin and bring back the broken pieces of his prosthesis. Moonlight bounced off retrieved snapped rivets of brass and sheared bands of engraved silver. Farther still, in the thick of the woods beyond the lake, her elements dug up fragments of his sword. She pulled them around her like abundant petals of a peony.

Unmaking the breaking required concentration. She was out of practice, but she knew the basics and the theories. Everything in existence was energy. Magic was energy in motion. Creations were energies in defined and confined spaces. Breaking a creation involved changing the confinement. Unbreaking a creation required her to read the definitions in the fragments and to remove the barriers that interrupted them. She wasn't actually repairing anything; that would require an introduction of replacement energies. That she couldn't do.

She closed her eyes and gave her attention to reading the scripts of creation and removing the extraneous boundaries. Starlight and midnight worked together to reverse the changes she'd done to Tobek's silver arm and sword of light, smiling as she recalled the time in the basement of the coal plant where their shared desires had manifested, for the briefest moments, a replica of this prosthesis. He'd fainted immediately after due to numerous injuries, poor guy.

Having the real McCoy this time around should close the circuit of his internal rewiring. His skeleton was being replaced by higher magics, as she'd glimpsed in DC during his literal meltdown. Those magics were seeking his missing parts to rebuild him, thus his prolonged stay as a chunk of ice. Logic would dictate the magics regrow an arm of flesh instead of seeking out the prosthesis, but Tobek had worn the silver arm longer than he'd had the arm with which he'd been born. In his mind, in his internal coding, the silver arm *was* his arm. As for the sword, he needed that to direct the magics he called into himself to their utmost devastation, particularly against the upper echelon of Devourers staging in the ether. Instead of a wizard's wand, it was a warrior's weapon.

After the crescent suns had set and the three moons had taken their places as a rotating triskelion in the sky, she finally finished restoring Tobek's god-forged arm and the titan-forged sword. If she hadn't been a First Child, the damn things would've crushed her beneath their weight. The wards and spells in the engravings of each ensured no one but Tobek could wear the prosthesis and wield the sword. Very bad circumstances would befall those who tried. Her darkness carried his trophies up to the hammock. The closer the arm got to the ice, the louder it hummed and the brighter the ice glowed. She draped the prosthesis over the ice and set the sword beside it, feeling a bit like a set designer for a Viking ice mead commercial. Song and sound synced. She clenched her fists in front of her chest and eagerly waited for the super woo transformation.

Drip… Drip… Drip.

Rolling her eyes, she yawned. "Fine, take your time pulling yourself together. No, really. I insist. The wet spot's all yours. The island can build me my own hammock."

The moment the words were out of her mouth, the island trembled and trees sidled to the western slope to assemble her hammock. Aww. The World remembered her favorite spot. Since she wasn't a fan of nature tickling her butt when she slept, she headed into the yurt to see if they'd left anything that could be used as a nightshirt. What was a few hundred thousand plus years to good textiles? Snorting at her own joke, she crossed the cool earthen threshold of the large doorless shelter Tobek had built by hand during his incarceration.

Things had…changed since she'd last lived here. Taking a beat to search for gaps in her memories relating to this World, she came up with a smattering. Curious. She wasn't worried about strangers crashing the place. The World wouldn't allow it. That meant Tobek had come back here. To his prison. By choice.

Hunh.

The décor had been updated sometime during the last millennium. Unpretentious, rustic, basic living with nature welcomed her. A long hammock of woven seaweed swayed on a cross breeze in front of one window. A tall table curved under the window on the opposite wall. A wooden backless stool sat at a distance, as if someone had been interrupted whilst working. Neatly folded clothes in drab colors of beige, tan, or brown waited on open shelves to the left of a desk. To the side nearest the door hung a greatcoat of navy wool circa the early eighteenth century. A pair of oiled knee boots waited on the floor under the coat. Drawn into the dried mud walls and floor of the yurt were hearth and home spells.

She fetched one of the shirts from the pristine pile and shook it out. Not a T-shirt. Not even a button-down. More like a pirate's, say of the early eighteenth century. Shimmying into it, she laughed as it dusted her feet. Taking a minute to roll up the overly long sleeves, she then tugged a pair of pants from the stack of dark brown and held them up to her waist. The legs came down past her ankles, which would only reach his knees.

"Breeches and a linen pirate shirt?" She grabbed from the pile of tan and was rewarded with a waistcoat. A pang of realization twisted her heart. Early eighteenth century was a bit over three hundred years ago.

When she'd left him.

Tears stinging her eyes, she carefully refolded the breeches and waistcoat and put them away. The World had kept everything as new, ready for Tobek's return. This island was a perfectly preserved time capsule of his place of mourning.

There was no evidence of Gurp having accompanied him, which meant he'd grieved alone. He hadn't gone to the bosom of the Berserker brotherhood right away. She'd assumed he had. He'd mentioned tearing up the Mids looking for her with their help, skirting direct orders intended to keep the guys from finding her. He'd never mentioned this part, though.

Entering the second yurt, she gasped in wonder. It was a wood-carver's workshop. Two workbenches hugged the walls, tall and worn. Awls and chisels of various sizes and styles were neatly racked in rows along the back of one bench. Pots and jars of assorted shades of browns that probably contained varnish and oils waited patiently on shelves above the benches. None of that was what owned her attention. No, the carvings themselves drew her like nothing else. They were statues of people, young, old, infant, human, Chwed, nattily attired, not at all attired, and every one of them incredibly lifelike. Then there were seven statues of her: corporeal, incorporeal, blended. Each one depicted a stage of grief.

She took her time inspecting the craftsmanship in each piece. Sure, she knew Tobek was an artist of uncommon skill, but she never ceased to be amazed by the emotion he managed to capture in everything he did, be it in a tattoo, an abstract metal sculpture, or a carving emerging from driftwood.

One statue stood separate from the others on a crate in front of the east-facing window. A little girl, maybe four years old. Long hair billowing behind her, nightgown rippling over her little paunch and tickling her knees. Her face was uplifted, and her arms raised as if waiting for the dawn to sweep her up in a hug. Tobek had masterfully captured the expression of innocent, joyful adoration in the tilt of the eyes and the dimples framing an openmouthed smile. The girl appeared caught mid giggle. One of the plump cheeks was worn with a finer sheen than the other, as if Tobek had held it often.

There was love in this piece.

Bix slid her fingers around the girl's. Tears fell unchecked. A sob broke as she admired every tiny detail, from the small braids peeking between the waves of her hair, to the eyelet trim on the short sleeves. She didn't have to ask who this was.

This was their daughter. The one they couldn't have. The one they shouldn't have been able to conceive. Demigods were sterile, and so was she. And yet, as old as she and he had been, she'd gotten pregnant. Denial had become disbelief that had escalated into epic anxiety and abundant elation. She'd locked into her corporeal form, terrified that her natural state would unmake the fetus. Tobek had been the epitome of a doting father-to-be and rational consort, encouraging her to pick and choose from every culture which of the maternity traditions she wanted to indulge. He'd read to her growing belly, sang songs to it, and explained science and magic with enthusiasm.

Then there'd been Gurp, who'd been impossibly more excited than she and Tobek about the pending addition. Tobek and Gurp had delivered lots of babies from all races, but none had been the offspring of a First Child. Gurp had devoted himself as her doula and had grand plans for being the child's uncle and manny. Their little family had never been happier or more scared.

Until she'd miscarried.

They'd all thought the cramping was the onset of labor. Bright anticipation had been tangible. Then had come her third push. With it, the undeniable sensation of a life being unmade. Bix had tried to stop her own body from murdering their child, ripping herself to pieces to carve the baby from her womb before it was too late. That wild, feral desperation, that vicious personal dismemberment—that was the reason Gurp feared her darkness.

Bix wrapped her arms around the statue of the daughter who almost was and wept. It didn't matter how much time had passed or how patchworked her brain. The loss still hurt like hell.

Arms, large and strong, one of flesh and one of metal, closed around her. Tobek drew her against his warm body as he sat on the floor and cried with her. She nestled her face against his skin and beard, clinging to him. He buried his face in her hair and held her tightly. There had been times along her road to recovery that he'd shared his bottomless grief with her and his profound isolation despite being constantly surrounded by those who loved him. She hadn't understood his why or wherefore. She did now. He still mourned the loss of his family. Yes, he'd learned how to move forward, but it didn't mean he'd stopped hurting. Losing a child? That pain was permanent.

It was a long while before her emotions were exhausted enough to let coherent thoughts come into being.

"I'm so sorry, Tobek," she whispered, loosening her grip on him.

"No, sweetheart, don't ever be sorry for that. Never," he rasped vehemently, his voice breaking.

"It wasn't my intention to abandon you." She shook her head and stared at his bountiful ink. "I was going to be back before you woke. I just had so much anger, so much pent-up violence that I needed to unleash. I couldn't do that at home. I couldn't do that anywhere in the Mids, not without destroying the collective. So I went to a place I knew could handle my tantrum."

"The ether," he guessed accurately.

"I chose a pocket there where one hour in the Mids was a thousand years in the ether. And I raged. Oh gods, I raged. I nearly burst its boundaries with my wrath." She huffed a snot-laden groan. "That's when Tempest and Desire showed up."

"To comfort you?"

"No. That would've been the kind and supportive thing. They're too broken for that." She skimmed her hand over the transition of flesh to silver where his restored prosthesis melded with his arm. Eager magics thrummed within it. "No, they wanted something from me, and they'd hoped to exploit my suffering to get it. I was hurting and in a mental tailspin, but I wasn't *that* far gone."

"What could they possibly have wanted that justified hurting you even more?" His growl was fierce and protective, and she loved being allowed to be fragile in his presence.

"To unmake them." She sighed. "They want me to erase them from existence."

He tilted her back and stared into her eyes. "How could they ask that of you? Your own siblings?"

"They're in pain. It's an endless and festering sort of pain that refuses to numb because it feeds off their primary aspects. Death is the one thing they've encountered that they cannot achieve. Therefore, it is the one thing they want most." She skimmed her hand down his silver arm, where his amputation scars used to be. "Every time they witness the death of something, they envy its finality. That envy adds to their desperation, which adds to their frustration, which adds to the hate they've developed for me."

"If they cease to exist, what happens to the greater experience?" He tapped his metal fingers against her skin as if relearning the firmness of her flesh.

"They are motivation, wanting, craving, and passion. All the things that push us to be more, to evolve, to create and innovate, to love, to own, to possess. Without Tempest and Desire, all those feelings, and the products born of them, would be gone. Curiosity would be the only driver left."

"Curiosity without motivation is lethargic at best," he harrumphed. "I take it you've considered what they're asking, though? Not out of petty spite, mind, but practicality."

"More than I care to admit. It's a request you've heard countless times before from others, I'm sure." She gathered his beard and played with it, a favorite distraction. "A mercy killing? Putting someone out of their misery? And when you oblige, you do it because you know with great certainty they will never recover from what ails them. Even if their body mends, their minds are too far gone."

"Or vice versa," he conceded with a grunt.

"Tempest and Desire had dispatched the Devourers to the Mids as a threat years before we lost our child. Desire was willing to call them off if I gave them what they wanted. I refused. He asked repeatedly. I refused repeatedly. So that night, my siblings announced their intent to destroy the Mids right there and then if I didn't unmake the pair of them." Bix blotted her nose and eyes with the fat cuff of her sleeve. "On the off chance you survived their attacks, they were coming for you next."

"You unmade yourself instead." He nodded sagely and leaned back against a carved wooden beam. "I'd watched you shred your body repeatedly in those days immediately following the death of our daughter. It never occurred to me you would try to shred your mind."

"It doesn't excuse me leaving you alone to manage your grief. I regret that immensely." Bix sniffed. "You deserve so much better from me."

"Ah, sweetheart." He cupped her cheek with his fleshy hand. "I wish you had found a way to tell me before you did it, but I do understand why you did it. That was an impossible situation and a rather ingenious delaying tactic. But it was just a delay, wasn't it? They still want to die?"

She nodded. "Tempest has grown more impatient waiting for me to regain my ability to deliver what they want. She is behind everything having to do with the Devourers of late. I've bought us a bit more time while she fetches her twin, but I'm going to have to come up with a real solution to their problem. No is the answer they refuse to accept."

He placed his hands upon her thighs. "How can I help?"

"By being you." She stared at him as love, truly potent love, filled her energies. The stars within her glowed through her skin. He guffawed with delight as he traced her myriad freckles of order through her nightshirt.

"You've no idea how I've longed to see these again." He leaned in for a kiss.

She looped her arms behind his neck and kissed him with the tumult of all she felt. Yet, as the kiss turned more passionate, he pulled back. Love and adoration in his gaze.

"When you are whole again, we will continue this all the way through to its mutually satisfying conclusion. But only then."

The cutoff surprised her. And confused her. There was no doubt he wanted her, sexually among many other ways. There'd never been a doubt about that. So why the cold water?

"I'm running at nearly ninety percent capacity," she argued. "I just unpacked the baggage you'd been bearing all alone for centuries. Is that it? Is it the baggage? This wouldn't be a sympathy screw, would it? Or is there something else I should be remembering?"

There were still gaps in her memories, and a few in the story of their failed pregnancy. Like, how the hell had they even gotten pregnant? There were no such things as miracles when dealing with the first and second generation of sentient energies. Stuff happened because somebody in her family did something to make it happen. She was willing to bet the seed of malice to which she'd clung after giving everything else away was due to her family and her dead infant. She was equally certain she'd never told Tobek about her family's involvement for fear he'd unleash his rage on them and be quashed. Once she had the missing pieces of the story, she was going to call a family meeting.

"I am wildly and unendingly in love with every iota of you, every tendril of chaos, every shine of order. It is *my* desire to demonstrate that to the whole of you. Anything less makes me feel as if I am taking advantage." He ran his hands along her arms, shrinking the tangle of linen so its excess didn't overwhelm her body as badly. His gentle touch turned away her darkening thoughts and brought her back into the warmth of his presence. "Can you respect that without it wounding?"

"Yeah. Sure. We've waited this long." She shrugged, casting off the initial sting and any second guesses. She wasn't a hormonal teenager. She could keep her cooch under control. "I much prefer unbridled enthusiasm in my lovers anyway."

He barked a note of merriment and flung her over his shoulder as he stood. "I too will accept nothing less than your very vocal consent and fervent participation."

"That doesn't mean I have to give you up as my emotional support bankie in the meantime, does it?" she teased from her inverted position as he carried her out of the yurt.

"Even operating at a hundred percent, you wouldn't know how." He tossed her in her hammock and crawled up beside her with a wicked grin.

"Oh, *now* you want to share my bed?" She curled into him, wiggling her butt against his groin. He said she had to wait. He didn't say she couldn't play.

"No one wants to sleep in the wet spot," he purred in her ear, reminding her that he was always attuned to her, regardless of whether he was in his preferred or native state. He stilled her hips with a firm silver hand and slid his knee between her calves. "Now, get some rest. You have a containment pyramid to assemble and the ether to take down."

"Yeah, yeah. And you have a defense system to launch." She rapped her knuckles against his metal arm. "At least you'll be able to keep it together this time."

"I've spent so long without it, yet it feels like it's never been separated from me." He kissed her shoulder. "Thank you for returning it and my sword."

"It was long past time for you to be whole again."

"You're next." Chuckling, he manifested a light blanket and quickly succumbed to snoring.

Bix stared at the moons turning in the sky and listened to the steady beat of Tobek's heart. That heartbeat, the one that had trained hers to mimic his, it didn't echo within her anymore, not since she'd fully restored his freedom. The pieces of themselves they'd once exchanged as prisoner and warden, the piece of him that used to beat within her, that was the reason she'd remained corporeal after she'd given away her mind and her magics. A body of flesh and a second heartbeat were the only clues she'd left herself to find her way back to him.

Best decision ever.

CHAPTER 33

Bix returned to the coal plant with Tobek hale and exuding magics that no longer pushed and clutched at hers so much as they swirled around and through hers as if enticing hers to dance. Oh, or maybe he was weaving something that would eventually reveal itself. That could prove intriguing. The movement wasn't as reassuring as constantly feeling his heartbeat, but it could definitely grow on her.

The Berserkers gathered in the beer hall and greeted their chief with enthusiasm. A few of the upper ranks who'd served with him the longest gave him untold grief over the appearance of his silver arm and swanky sword without a proper scabbard. The banter of swords and scabbards quickly devolved into the tawdry, which…boys. Conspicuously absent were Hywl, Runjit, and Xipil. Gurp too.

Concern flickered within Bix, and she reached out to touch the shards. Not in the main building. Not anywhere in the compound, for that matter. No trace of the null spot caused by Cian's humanity either. As concern adopted a predatory edge, Ashtad ambled up to her with a tablet in hand, a knowing gleam in his eye, and a reassuring grin on his face.

"Team still has a mission, right?" he asked insouciantly.

"Launch Resen," she answered, wondering what this had to do with where Cian had gone with the shards.

"Which can only happen once...?" he prompted.

"I take down the ether, which I need the shards to do." She gave him a quizzical glance as he handed her his tablet. On the screen was the image of a familiar fetish club. Interior. Daytime. Mostly empty. Suspiciously unaffected by all the pandemonium that had been unleashed on the District.

"I don't think you and I give our young probationary agent enough credit for the network of assets he has built." Ashtad crossed his arms and leaned his shoulder against hers. "Our attendance is requested. Chief's too."

Since Ashtad was clearly not concerned and obviously up to something, Bix chilled her protective streak and sent a ray of light to tap Tobek on the shoulder. He turned to her with a playful smile and an understanding nod as she held up the tablet. The change in boyish banter confirmed the battalion was in on whatever mischief was afoot.

Ashtad offered her an arm, as did Tobek. Why choose? She made the gate wide enough for all three of them to cross to Hella Fella's chancel where the DJ spun in the evenings.

The renovated church was not empty like the image Ashtad had shown her. Oh, it was in perfect condition, and judging by the supremely satisfied smirk on the bullnecked archangel leaning against the bar, she had a fairly solid guess as to how. Archangel Samael raised a pint and laughed heartily at something said or done by the cluster of Chweds taking up all the bar seats. Cian manned the bar like the old pro he was.

"That's how I met the kid, did you know that?" Bix asked Ashtad, handing him back his tablet before sidling around the altar. "He was behind that bar, black uniform shirt, cleaning glasses when I rolled in for my first hot date with Samael."

"Probably why he picked here to host your little shard shindig and roped the archangel into helping with transportation." Ashtad chuckled quietly. "The District is still a complete disaster beyond these walls, which affords a certain level of privacy that may come in handy."

The club pulsed with the presence of the shards and a collection of folks spanning the magic gamut. Sophia and the six other gods Bix had tapped to keep shards and watch over the ether were trying on the fetish gear from the velvet-lined nooks and laughing like a gaggle of bridesmaids at a bachelorette party. Hywl prowled the nave with his battle buddy Runjit. The former never took his eyes off his divine love, for which he was receiving sufficient flak from Xipil and a handful of other Berserkers standing casual guard at the double-wide doors beneath the choir loft at the back of the church. They took note of their fearless leader and raised their glasses in salutations. Some waggled their arms and hooted. Tobek was quick to join them, manifesting his own drink as he walked and pausing only long enough to give Gurp a metallic low five as the two crossed paths. Gurp headed away from the kitchen, gnawing what might've been a rusted cast-iron pipe.

Up in the choir loft, far from prying eyes and their natural nemesis the archangel, stood a contingent of dragons in humanoid form. Raspoine and Rummir bookended two women. One was a spy Bix and her team had rescued from a supermax prison. The other, a scientist Bix had rescued after the Consortium had ordered the dragon's execution. Seeing the women in the open and in the company of the royal dragon twins was unexpected. Doubly so what with the new Chair of the Consortium and his hound seated down on the main floor at a pub table chatting up Gurp in the unique language of goblins. Ogun had deigned to learn the language of the least respected race in all the Mids and to be seen actively engaged with one? How delightful.

How Drew would've loved to have been in the middle of all this, party hound that her bestie was. Bix's heart panged, missing her best friend, but knowing that Drew's recovery was in good hands. The moment Drew returned to the Mids all hale and high-strung, Bix would throw her one hell of a party.

Ashtad called a ball of electricity to hand and tossed it in the air. It exploded with a pop, crackle, and an array of tumbling sparks. The tiny firework drew everyone's attention.

"Esteemed guests, thank you for coming, and on such short notice." Ashtad bowed from the shoulders. "Recent events have made it clear to one and all, regardless of caste, faith, location, or education, the dangers we are facing from a foreign enemy. Everyone in this club has answered the Chimera's call to rise to the challenge to defend the Mids. For some, answering that call came at a great cost. For others, a great awakening."

A rumble of agreements, commiserations, and a few rueful titters skittered up the walls.

"Now that she is the one in need, it is our honor and privilege to step forward again." Ashtad gestured for Cian to join him in front of the altar.

"Yeah, thanks everyone for coming, like Mister Ba'al said." The kid hustled from behind the bar and took his place beside Bix so he and Ashtad flanked her. Cian tugged a shard from his back pocket and held it flat on his palm like an altar boy with a holy book. "Those of you who have a piece of the Chimera's artifact, if you could present it like so? Please? And get in your groups?"

"Already sorted ourselves, kiddo," a knowledge god called with a chuckle, holding up his shard. "We're not normally this classist."

"Don't lie," Sophia laughed, whacking her peer in the shoulder with her shard. "We totally are."

"Oracles, why don't you two come sit with me?" Ogun practically purred, gesturing to the chairs to either side of him.

Two young women separated from the gaggle around the bar. Bix recognized Cian's upstairs neighbor, a charming girl just two years younger than he. The other one she'd never met, but she was of an age to possibly have interned with Cian at the spy guild. Bix had had no clue the upstairs neighbor was a dawning Oracle, but the way the girl blushed whenever she looked at Cian made Bix's heart sing.

Bix took a second look at the Chweds gathered around the

bar with Samael. Three she recognized as the drag queens—albeit out of their stage makeup—who'd offered her a seat the last time she was here. The others were probably patrons of the club too. Eleven of them. Eleven to replace the guild masters. She recounted the Berserkers at the back, not including Tobek. Thirteen. For the humans' shards. They'd been human until Tobek had dragged them through an evolution of magics into a new and undefined class of Other. Would the humans' shards respond to them? Bond to them? She didn't actually know. The two rescued female dragons filled in for the two Seventh Sons who'd died guarding their shards. Raspoine and Rummir were there to protect their own and the World if needed. The two young Oracles plus Cian in his role as a Sage accounted for the three elder Oracles who'd died before the handoff.

The kid had done it, assembled the originals and recruited new shard keepers. All in one place. He'd made it as easy as he could've for her. If it wouldn't have embarrassed him horribly, she would've hugged him.

"Uh, Bix?" Cian whispered. "This part's you."

Smiling, she uncurled three tentacles of darkness and three rays of light, arranging them in front of her like a wheel with alternating spokes. A single tentacle and a ray of light wove together to hold the partial pyramid comprised of the completed angels' panel and the two partial dragon and Oracle panels within a transparent box of gates.

Awe rippled through the gathering.

"To echo Cian and Ashtad, thank you, one and all, for coming together in the midst of change and tragedy. Thank you for being willing and hopefully able," she paused for the chuckles, "to speak your truths about the readiness of the Mid Worlds to move forward as a collective not only of places, but also of races, species, and communities."

"Hear, hear," Ogun grunted approvingly and double thumped his fist on the table. The Chair of the Consortium didn't have a shard, but attending as an ally, a witness, and possibly to protect the area from the magics spawned from the rite was politically advantageous. After all, he'd control the narrative that came out of this.

"The shards you hold have bonded to your truth. It is understandable that some of you may not feel comfortable making your private revelation public, particularly in front of a crowd, much less strangers." Bix deliberately avoided looking at anyone other than Tobek as she spoke. She didn't want to put anyone on the spot. "Thus, your confessions will be heard by me and me alone. I ask that you do not fear what you are about to experience. If you have ever lain beneath the stars and shared your hearts' burdens with the night, possibly wondering if anything out there was listening, I assure you, the answer is sometimes."

Bix unraveled her corporeal form, filling the church-cum-club with the starlit midnight of her native state and gently cradling every attendee while simultaneously isolating them. Gasps of wonder rose from the Chweds and the Oracles as they hesitantly reached out to run their fingers through her ethereal state. Those attendees who were familiar with her native state murmured a greeting or a wry comment.

"Parrhesia, my witnesses," Bix gently urged. Shards one and all awoke and spun. The partial pyramid hummed. "Speak your truth to power without fear of reprisal. Know that your view of circumstances—no matter how grand or small you may feel— holds value. Speak, for I am listening."

Speak they did. Freely. The watchers from the ether had quite a bit to say. As gods, the speeds at which they spoke likely would've sounded like a singular drawn-out note to a mortal ear, but to the almost-whole Chimera, their complex briefings were very elucidating. The young Oracles were shy and uncertain, but gained confidence as they shared their perspectives with a little bit of encouragement from Cian, who held nothing back. The Chweds had many opinions, views, and fierce beliefs that required no coaxing. Neither of the dragons bothered to soften their frank truths either, to Bix's true delight. The Berserkers were every bit the well-trained soldiers accustomed to briefing higher-ups. Bix could almost see the bullet points in their concise analyses of the situation, yet when she prodded them for an opinion to go with their report, they hesitated. It was very unsoldier-like to offer an opinion. It wasn't that they didn't have them, it was more that they didn't share them beyond their rank. Still, she managed to extract how they really felt.

When all that needed to be said had been said, Bix restored everyone to the shared experience. Shards glowed brightly, spinning and singing on the palms of their bearers. At last, the broken pieces were released to join the others suspended like a chandelier in the middle of the club. Fitting together with bursts of copper or pewter light, the shards built to fragments that finalized as whole triangular panels, audibly throbbing with power and chiming with discordant songs.

Nimbi of blues, purples, and greens coasted along the rafters. The foundational elements of the Mids. Responding.

"They merely wish to make their presence known," Ashtad hurried to assure.

"They too are the creations of higher powers," Tobek rasped, exuding his own colorful aura. "It is like calling to like."

Bix wasn't particularly concerned about that call. Her interest was drawn to the goblin standing apart from the others, rubbing one foot atop the other. What she'd initially thought was a rusty iron pipe on which he was snacking now fluttered like a butterfly with one purple trapezoidal wing and one blue. The final segment of the containment pyramid. The base. Built by her eldest sisters. Blue for Movement's contribution. Purple for Music's.

Of course she'd given it to Gurp. The one being, across all galaxies, who would tell her the truth with an insight few possessed. The goblin whose big heart found the good in the worst situations and the most horrible individuals. The companion who identified needs before they became desires. The most unassuming and unpretentious confidant to the broken, the overlooked, and the unloved. Who else but Gurp would be the keeper of the seventh segment?

Gurp toddled beneath the floating six-sided pyramid and held up his piece.

"Truth," he said, making the wings beat faster. "We family. We all family. Not always good family. Still family. This our home. We fight for our home to be good home."

And with that, the butterfly flew to the pyramid and affixed its outer seams to the base of the triangles, its center unlatched. Flaps waiting to be closed. The different songs of the different panels became one song, crescendoing. The colorful undulations swirled together across panels until they assumed a uniform shade of teal. A single bold chime caused a sonic wave.

Silence. Stillness. Breathlessness.

Bix condensed her state into a less intimidating form of feminine night. The containment pyramid dropped into her outstretched facsimile of a hand.

"And so the time has come to end the era of dark illusions and false securities." Bix inverted the pyramid, carrying it like an empty bouquet as she made eye contact with the royal dragon twins. "Thank you again, everyone, for your help."

Raspoine bestowed a beatific smile upon her, and Rummir managed a half grin. The other dragons gave her two thumbs-up. The soft whisper of wind chimes drifted from the choir loft, and a moment later, the dragon contingent was gone.

Bix turned to her teammates and let out a long breath of relief. "You two, thank you, so, so very much."

"The team has a mission," Ashtad reminded with a smile. "We all play our parts, which includes backing each other up."

"Yep, and that's looking like it's ready to be used." Cian retreated from the pyramid as his crystals hummed. "So, Mister Ba'al and I should get to our launch stations, right?"

"Is Resen ready? Really, really ready?" she prompted.

"Chief remains the biggest variable." Cian rubbed the back of his neck and shrugged. "We ought to study his effect on the foundational elements for at least a hundred years to have enough useable probability data, but, short of that, we're as ready as we're ever going to be."

"I assume he knows he's a launch risk?" Bix failed to stifle an empathetic giggle as the guys swapped resigned glances and nodded. "Okay, then, show me where you need to go."

Ashtad grabbed his tablet from the altar and showed her two pictures. "The moment we see the ether gone, we'll hit the Start button. Give us ten minutes from the time you close the gates behind us. Okay?"

"Got it. You'll probably feel it coming down, so no drinks on the console," Bix teased as she opened gates. Ashtad saluted, then he and Cian bolted through their respective gates. For security's sake, it made sense they wouldn't launch it from a single locale.

Bix turned to Ogun, who watched her with keen interest. "Chairman, if you still desire to call the Consortium into session to bear witness as a unified body, now would be the time."

"This is a historic moment, Chimera." He pushed up from the table and bowed over steepled hands. "I am glad to begin the new era allied with you."

Before she could respond, he and his hound vanished.

"I need to stand with him before the Consortium," Tobek murmured from behind her. "My men will watch over the mortals here, just in case. However, if you could send Gurp and Xipil back to base to prepare for fallout, I would appreciate it."

"Probably wise on all counts," she conceded, opening a gate to the ops room at the coal plant and another in the heart of the Consortium's headquarters. "Good luck today."

"Thanks, I'll need it. Launches never go smoothly." He winked and stepped backward through the gate to Consortium HQ.

"Home soon, pretty lady," Gurp called as he and Xipil crossed to the coal plant.

"The rest of you," Bix said, closing gates. "There's going to be a doozy of a show in the skies here shortly, but please don't risk your safety for a glimpse of history."

"Oy, I've got the watch party covered." Samael dismissed her concern with a flick of his wrist as angels from his choir arrived, setting up the club for said event. "There are cameras outside with clear views. We'll be streaming it live, so make the spectacle worthwhile for us, will you?"

"Chimera, if we may be bold?" Sophia blurted before the snarky quip on Bix's lips escaped. The knowledge goddess drew close, the other watchers in lockstep. "We would very much like to join you to observe the end of the ether."

"To write *The End* in our tomes of knowledge," another god added eagerly.

"I expected nothing less. You are my resident experts on the Devourers, and it is time they are fully exposed." Bix waved goodbye to the mortals still watching her.

Red pupils glowed and divine power surged among the seven gods. A chuckle, not remotely kind, emanated from Bix's entire being as she enveloped the gods and reached out through darkness to the boundaries holding back the continuous explosion that was the ether.

CHAPTER 34

S even knowledge gods glowed with the red auras of their divinity like the red stars of astronomy, beacons marking the outer perimeter of the cosmic defensive moat infested with enemy forces. At much farther distances, gods from the Upper and Under Worlds gathered, shining like a festival's red lanterns.

Beyond the wide swath of Worlds destroyed by Devourers leading to the ether, cherry-red glitter sparkled against a blacker shade of galactic midnight. Her brother Eko observing from afar. In a quadrant on the opposite side of the ether, golden stars gleamed. Esiw wouldn't miss the opportunity to learn something new. Both brothers were doubtlessly there to lend their support and to see if she had recovered enough of herself that she *could* contain the infamous ether.

Less surprising, however, were the undulations of blue and plum auroras belonging to her eldest sisters shimmering in the quadrants between her brothers. Music and Movement were the cocreators of the Mids, so it did make sense they'd attend. The youngest twins were the only siblings missing, and Bix was frankly grateful for that.

Taking a moment to appreciate the feat of creation she had masterminded seventeen hundred years ago, Bix then crossed into the ether itself.

Within the frame built by titans, the ether seemed limitless. No noises. No landscapes. No markers of time. No way of knowing one was being pulled by vortexes across time zones to then be cast like bird shot into another sector of the ether. It should've been a haven, but the pantheons had been the first to use it as a trash can for their husked criminals and defeated political foes. Bix had met a few during her amnesic tenure, some had been going through their own reawakening while others had remained hollow. Then Tempest had used Indraja to usher the Devourers inside and to teach them how to survive as an army.

Some siblings had a knack for ruining a perfectly suitable playground.

Bix remembered now. The conclave of titans constructing this moat and the initial explosions that had dissolved Worlds of midlevel gods situated too close to the Mids. The early attacks by Tempest and Desire. Giving away her mind and magics. More attacks by Tempest. The watchers coming to check on her. The Devourers trying to husk her. She'd been a battered, bruised, and often bleeding flesh bag adrift in a place where only divine or greater powers could survive.

She remembered now. That first terrified moment of reawakening. The endless cycles of agony and abuse. Finally having enough wherewithal to drag her feral self to the convergence of the Under Worlds. The long journey to rediscovery.

She remembered now. Those who'd helped her and those who'd taken advantage of her. Because of and despite them, she'd found her way home to the ones who loved her and whom she loved. What an experience it had all been. What a novel adventure for a First Child older than universes.

Ending the ether felt akin to ending a second innocence. Bittersweet.

With a huff, a chuckle, and a sigh, Bix held the containment pyramid before her and aligned her darkness with the panels of order and her light with the panels of chaos. She pushed her magics with equal measure, and the pyramid pushed back. Slowly, she amped up the pressure, ensuring the creation of her siblings maintained balance as it grew its power. More. More. More.

Rays of blinding light and ribbons of total darkness shot from the pyramid, up and over the boundaries of the ether, down and around from the center outward, binding the ether in tighter and tighter coils of chaos and order, absorbing that which had been created by titans while pressing out all that had come after with booms that shook the neighboring Worlds and caused onlookers to retreat. The fine wisps of ether once stuffed between the gaps of Mid Worlds were sucked into the braid of rapacious cosmic powers that allowed no part of destructive creation to escape, not even the tendrils that had made it inside the protective barriers of some Mid Worlds.

Smaller and smaller the ether shrank, from moat to lasso to crown as the pyramid recalled its chaos and order, winding its bounty into tiny swirling buds of dark pewter and aged copper that threatened to overflow the containment pyramid. It was pretty in this state, the once-sprawling bastion of succor and horror. It had served its purpose to give the Mids more time to prepare a defense against foreign invaders. That it had hosted so much more was part of the beauty of the unexpected, of life.

Smiling softly, she shut the flaps of the lid and removed the break she had inserted ages ago, thus sealing the containment pyramid. There were those who wondered why she wanted to keep the ether when she could've unmade it much more easily. They didn't know how many times the Mids had been destroyed by the Devourers.

They didn't know how many times she'd erased history and reset the present in hopes of saving her sanctuary.

She hadn't sacrificed her mind or magics in any prior timeline, nor had she suffered the heartbreak of a miscarriage. She didn't have friends like Ashtad and Cian, or even Drew in those earlier editions. She'd had Tobek, Gurp, and a different version of the Berserkers. Since her mother never allowed the present to be recreated in perfection—something always changed each time

Bix erased history—Bix had kept erasing time until salvation was possible.

There had been dozens of iterations of ether before this one, some too effective, others not enough. Keeping this ether in this artifact had nothing to do with its future use. It was a trophy, a testament to all that had come before *this* moment in *this* timeline.

She enfolded the pyramid within her and took in the view of a galaxy restored. Dread, anticipation, and hope all bubbled within her. This was it. The moment of truth. Could the Mids stage a defense? Would Resen launch? Would it work? Would she have to erase this timeline and try yet again? None of the previous timelines had brought the Mids this close to actually protecting themselves from her siblings' toys.

Without the ether to hide them, the vast army of Devourers lay exposed. Their thousands of linked tents, their buoyant tethers, their chains of supplies, their cages of prisoners, all hovered as an ominous band about the collective. The enemy had successfully encircled the Mids.

It would be so easy to engulf them all and erase the Devourers from existence. She'd done it before, more than once, in fact, in other timelines. Genocide hadn't worked out the way she'd anticipated, though. No, Tempest and Desire had made even worse horrors to assail the Mids. Horrors that had subjected every living thing, from amoebas to redwoods to humans to the superpowers themselves, to such staggering trauma and tragedy that Bix had ended those timelines very quickly.

Like most turf wars among siblings, if Bix mucked with Tempest's and Desire's toys, they'd muck with hers. Thus, out of all the options the various timelines had presented, the timelines in which Bix had let the Devourers be, the Mids had had a fighting chance. Not that the Mids had ever won, which was why she kept resetting the timeline. However, this timeline was different. This was the first timeline in which the Fates, gods, angels, and dragons had actually collaborated to save themselves. They had no idea just how impressive a feat like Resen really was. Assuming it launched. Like soon. Like now, even.

An abysmal bleat carried along the Devourers' camp. Their answering battle cries sent a shiver through Bix.

Where was Resen?

"Come on, Cian. Come on, Ashtad. Now would be good," she whispered.

Rumbling flowed from the Uppers and the Unders. Pantheons. Rallying. Charging. To fight for the Mids. Forcing the Devourers to defend their flanks.

Bix pulled herself out of the path of conflict.

A deep bong reverberated through the galaxy, chased by an abrupt fluctuation in pressure and a bestial roar, like a muscle car slamming into gear on a cosmic scale. Plums, blues, and greens flooded the sky, knocking back the Devourer camp as the undulating lattice of Resen burst from the Mids.

Bix let loose a whooping cheer. Her starlight brightened. From four quadrants beyond the galaxy, red glitter flickered and yellow stars shone brighter, blue nimbi swirled and purple rays danced. Her beloved siblings. Sharing her moment of joy, which made it all even better.

One by one, the red stars of the seven watchers dimmed, the final chapter of the ether having been written. Sophia and the others gathered around Bix as Resen stabilized. Devourers charged its barriers, only to be rebuffed. Most of them, at least.

"So it begins," Sophia murmured, crossing her once-shackled wrists in front of her. "The delayed war. The fight for their lives. Let us hope the protectors of the Mids have learned as much as we have."

"They're ready," Bix assured. "As long as the caretakers, the guardians, the champion, and the general population work together, the Mids will win."

Character Glossary

THE CONSORTIUM

The governing body comprised of representatives from the four superpower races charged with populating and protecting the collective of Mid Worlds.

THE DRAGON HORDE

Led by: The Dragon Queens
Mid World Entities
Provide bodies for lifeforms native to the Mids
Feed on positive emotions
Named Characters: Raspoine, Rummir, Yashanee

THE ANGELIC HOST

Led by: Archangels
Mid World Entities
Provide bodies for lifeforms native to the Mids
Feed on negative emotions
Named Characters: Samael, Michael, Ariel

THE HOUSES OF FATE

Led by: Heads of House
Other World Entities
Sages & Oracles strive to ascend to Fatehood
Provide threads of Fate that secure a soul to a body
Feed on magic expelled by a soul-tethered lifeform
Named Characters: Skuld, Sunan

THE PANTHEONS

Led by: Greater gods who fought their way to the top
Other World Entities
Demigods strive to ascend to godhood
Provide souls for lifeforms native to the Mids

Feed on enriched souls
Named Characters: Phobos, Hel, Jörmungand, Ereshkigal, Nergal, Deimos, and many more.

CHWEDLONOL (AKA "CHWEDS"): Catch-all term for the myriad magical races native to the Mid Worlds. Created by the Consortium in terms defined by individual Cycle of Soul contracts.

HUMANS: Do not possess magic, they ground magic; unconsciously drawn to magical hotspots. Created by the Consortium in terms defined by individual Cycle of Soul contracts.

Other Books
by K.A. Krantz

Urban Fantasy
The Immortal Spy Series:
THE BURNED SPY
THE PLAGUED SPY
THE CAPTURED SPY
THE HANGED SPY
THE EXPOSED SPY
THE SHACKLED SPY

High Fantasy
Fire Born, Blood Blessed Series:
LARCOUT

THE HERALDED SPY
The Final Book in the Immortal Spy Series
Available Autumn 2021

Want to be notified when a new book is released?
Subscribe to K.A. Krantz's email newsletter at
kakrantz.com

If you enjoyed this book, please spread the word and
leave a review with the retailer of your choice.

Acknowledgments

To my family: I really was working during the plague! To Jenn Stark, the best of CPs, for not letting my characters lob blame bombs then act like nothing happened. To Linda Ingmanson, my development editor, for reminding me to not sacrifice relatability for invincibility. To Toni Lee, my copy editor and fact checker, for correcting me when I use words that do not mean what I think they mean. To the team at Gene Mollica Studios, when I asked for "ominous," you delivered with an added layer of awesomeness.

About the Author

KAK splits her time between Cincinnati and the DC 'burbs with her faithful hairy beast. When not writing, she indulges in a shoe obsession, conducts a love/hate affair with paint, and makes epic messes in the kitchen.

Visit her website at kakrantz.com for free flash fiction, blog posts about her latest fancies, and more. If you're on Twitter, she'd love to hear from you. Tweet @KAKrantz.